Resuscitation of
a Hanged Man

DENIS
JOHNSON

Perennial

An Imprint of HarperCollinsPublishers

It is a pleasure to thank the John Simon Guggenheim Foundation and the Mrs. Giles R. Whiting Foundation for support that made this writing possible.

This first U.S. edition of this book was published in 1991 by Farrar, Straus and Giroux.

The first paperback edition of this book was published in 1992 by Penguin Books. It is here reprinted by arrangement with Penguin Books, Inc.

HarperCollins books may be purchased for educational, business, or sales promotional use. For information please write: Special Markets Department, HarperCollins Publishers Inc., 10 East 53rd Street, New York, NY 10022.

First Perennial edition published 2001.

The Library of Congress has catalogued the hardcover edition as follows:

Johnson, Denis.
Resuscitation of a hanged man: a novel / Denis Johnson.—1st ed.
I. Title.
ISBN 0-374-24949-0
PS3560.O3745R47 1990
813'.54—dc20   90–46283

ISBN 0-06-093466-2 (pbk.)

01 02 03 04 05 RRD 10 9 8 7 6 5 4 3 2 1

For Louie

Life goes into new forms.

—NEAL CASSADY

*Resuscitation of
a Hanged Man*

1980

He came there in the off-season. So much was off. All bets were off. The last deal was off. His timing was off, or he wouldn't have come here at this moment, and also every second arc lamp along the peninsular highway was switched off. He'd been through several states along the turnpikes, through weary tollgates and stained mechanical restaurants, and by now he felt as if he'd crossed a hostile foreign land to reach this fog with nobody in it, only yellow lights blinking and yellow signs wandering past the car's windows silently. There was a single fair-sized town on the peninsula, a place with more than one shopping center in it and boarded-up seafood stands strung along the roadside, and the traveller, whose name was Leonard English, thought he'd stop there for a drink, just one drink, before going on. But he was drawn into a very interesting conversation with a man whose face got to look more and more like a dead pig's face in the dim red light. What they were talking about really wasn't all that memorable—it was more the man's face—but the drinks got slippery and English's money was all wet by the time he got out of there, and as he made a U-turn through an intersection the world seemed to buckle beneath him and the car's hood flew up before the window. English held the wheel and jammed the brake, waiting for the rest of this earthquake, or this bombing or God's wrath, to destroy the town. A shriek, like the tearing of metal train wheels along metal rails, died away. Somebody was opening the door for him . . . but he was opening the door for himself, and now he was getting out of the car. There wasn't any cataclysm. It was just a town at night, quiet and useless, with buildings that looked like big toys or false fronts lit by arc lamps and backed by a tremendous bleakness. Somehow his Volkswagen had climbed up onto a traffic island. The whole thing would have been embarrassing, but he couldn't seem to form any clear picture of what had happened. Blood ran down his forehead and blinded half his sight. The air reeked: the tank was ripped and twenty dollars' worth of gasoline covered the asphalt. In his imagination it burst into flames. A cabdriver stopped and came to stand beside him and said, "You made a wrong turn." English did not dispute this.

To reach his destination at the end of the Cape, English engaged the cabdriver's services, services he couldn't afford any more than he was going to be able to afford this accident.

"He gonna chadge you exry," the cabdriver said.

Chadge? English guessed the driver was talking about the old man who'd towed his car away, but what was he trying to say? "Right," English said.

"You from Bwostin?" the cabbie asked him.

This was just what the policeman had asked him amid the wreckage, saying *Boston* like *Bwostin*. "Mr. Leonard English," the officer had said. Looking right at English's Midwestern driver's license, he had inquired after his origins: "You from Bwostin?" "I just got here from Lawrence, Kansas," English told the officer. *"Kansas?"* the officer said. "Lawrence, Kansas?"—and English said yes. A little later the officer said, "You're drunk. But I'm gonna let you off."

"Drunk? I'm not drunk," English said.

"Yes you are, you most definitely are," the officer said, "or you wou'nt be arguing with me." With a certain vague tenderness, he was applying a Band-Aid to English's forehead.

English said, "I'm a little tipsy. I don't understand what you're saying."

"That's better," the officer said.

English was glad when the policeman left him in the cabdriver's custody, because he felt cut off from the world here, and to be scrutinized by a powerful figure in a place he hadn't even seen in the daylight yet left him shaken. Properly speaking, this wasn't even a peninsula. He'd had to cross a large bridge to get here. It was an island. A place apart.

And now, as they rattled toward this phony peninsula's other end, English was sitting up front with the cabdriver. English was dizzy, and on top of that there seemed to be an exhaust leak, but the driver kept saying, "You're A-OK now, brother." "No, I'm not," English said. They weren't in a taxicab. It was almost six in the morning and the driver was going in his station wagon to his home a couple of towns down the road, taking English dozens of miles out of his way for twenty dollars. "I like to drive," the cabbie said. He puffed on a joint wrapped in yellow paper.

English turned it down. "Grass makes me feel kind of paranoid."

"I don't get paranoid," the driver said. But he was a paranoid personality if English had ever seen one. "This beyond here, this is absolutely black," the driver said, pointing with the glowing end of his reefer ahead, to where the four-lane highway turned two-way. "No more lights, no more houses"—he drew a chestful of smoke—"nuthin, nuthin, nuthin. We won't see no traffic. Not car one." Immediately the red taillights of another car shone ahead. "I think I know this guy." He stomped the gas. "I think this is Danny Moss"—pronounced Dyany Mwas—"is that a Toyota? Cheez, looka how fast this guy's running." They were doing eighty. "*We're* gonna catch you, Danny. *We're* gaining on this sucker." But they were falling behind. "Ain't that a Toyota?" he said. The red taillights ahead went right, and the cabdriver's gaze followed their course as he and his passenger sailed past the turn they'd taken. "Yeah, that's a Toyota! Yeah, that's him! Yeah, that's Danny Moss!"

Actually, they hadn't come to any place of absolute blackness. In a little while the sun was up, burning without heat above the road, and before they reached Provincetown they sped through three or four more little villages, in one of which they stopped and had breakfast. It turned out that Phil, the driver, subscribed to the branch of historical thought characterized by a belief in extraterrestrial interference, previous highly advanced civilizations, and future global cataclysms, both human-made and geological. English now learned something about these things. "All the elemental phosphorus is gonna be like zero, completely gone. We'll be strangling each other in the streets for a little phosphorus," Phil said, "elemental phosphorus. The roads are gonna run with blood. Nobody even knows about it. Nobody's even surprised. Five thousand years ago on the earth they had a big cataclysm and a huge, what is it, whatyoucallit, *megadeath*. Partly because of running out of some of these elements you need in your body, like phosphorus." He got into a philosophical talk with their waitress and told her, "I think our world could really be some form of Hell, you know what I'm saying?" The waitress saw his point. "There's so much suffering here on earth," she said. Phil knew all the waitresses, and it was after nine when they got back on the road.

English fell asleep. When he woke up, the route had gone strange. White dunes made walls on either side of them. European music came out of the radio. They drove through a drift of sand.

In a few minutes his head was clear again, and he was looking at the sandy outskirts of the last town in America. The sun was shining above it now. A tower made of stone rose up in the distance. The seaside curved north, to their left, and the wooden buildings were laid out solid, bright and still as a painting, against the beach.

They followed the road into town and lost sight of the harbor as they came down the main street of shops. Now there were pedestrians moving alongside them in the chilly sunshine. The traffic crawled. "This crowd is nothing compared to summer," Phil told him. Half the shops appeared closed, and English had a sense of people walking around here where they didn't belong, in an area that might have been abandoned after a panic. Three ungainly women—were they men, in bright skirts?—danced a parody of a chorus line by a tavern's door, arms around one another's shoulders. Passing along the walks and ambling down the middle of the street were people in Bermuda shorts and children eating ice-cream cones as if it weren't under 60 Fahrenheit today. On the lawn of the town hall, surrounded by grey pigeons and scattering crusts of bread out of a white paper bag, stood a woman who was very clearly not a woman but a man: as if a woman wore football shoulder pads and other bulky protection beneath her very modestly tailored dress. Another man in a dress was mailing a letter at the blue mailbox just six feet away. And a cross-dresser on roller skates loomed above two others sitting on a bench, patting his brittle wig lightly with one hand, the other hand on his hip, while laughter that couldn't be heard passed among them. A very tall woman, who might have been a man, talked with a bunch of grade-school children out in front of a bakery. English cleared his throat. He had a chance to look at everyone until he was sick of their faces, because the car wasn't getting anywhere.

Phil smacked the horn, but nothing happened. "Horn don't work. This is making me apeshit. I'm gonna run some bastards over."

They found the source of the traffic jam four blocks down, where a huge-bottomed transvestite comedian on the balcony of a cabaret-and-hotel delivered his Mae West impersonation for free. "Move over, honey!" he shouted down to a woman in a halted convertible. The woman ducked her head in embarrassment and put her hand on the arm of the man driving. Around them the shoppers and tourists, variously shocked and mesmerized, or curious and entertained, laughed at the comedian with his cascading platinum wig and his stupendous, unexplainable breasts. Later that night English would see someone being carried on a stretcher out of the side doors of this building and through the wet, falling snow to an ambulance. And he would think of this man on the balcony in his evening gown making jokes about his potbelly, gripping it with a hand that glittered with rings while flapping his huge false eyelashes, and English wouldn't feel equipped, he wouldn't feel grown-up enough, to be told the whole story about this town.

Phil knew any number of people in Provincetown. He was connected all up and down the Cape. Long before the Pilgrims, English gathered, long before the Indians, way back past the time of cataclysms, even before the golden age of the extraterrestrial star-wanderers who had mated with monkeys to produce us all, members of Phil's family had arrived here and opened small dark restaurants with steamy walls and radios chattering and yowling in the kitchen, and had applied for liquor licenses which to this day they were denied because the grudges against them, though small ones, were eternal. What all this meant was that English wouldn't have to go to a motel. Phil had a cousin who ran a rooming house, freshly painted white and spilling winter roses over a knee-high picket fence, where English could stay cheaply.

Phil insisted on carrying English's suitcase up the long stairs through an atmosphere of mingled disinfectant and air-freshening spray into a room that was small but not cheerless. There were big orange ladybugs printed on the white curtains. A faintly discolored portrait of John F. Kennedy hung on the wall above the desk. The bathroom looked harmless—blue sink, blue toilet, blue tub scoured nearly white. "All right, hey, not bad," English assured Phil, but it had every quality of the end of the line.

Now that they'd travelled together and English was one of the family, with his very own room in Phil's illustrious cousin's house, Phil wouldn't accept a fare. English had to follow him down the stairs and out to his half-disintegrated yellow station wagon, insisting. Then he accepted the twenty-dollar bill that English pressed on him, and gripped the new tenant's hand with his, the money caught between their palms. His eyes were moist. They were two of the same sort, men past thirty without a lot to recommend them; but this happened to English every day. He had a feeling they'd stay strangers.

After Phil was gone, English lay on the bed awhile, but he couldn't sleep because it was daytime and also a little too quiet. He wondered if everybody was at work. Then he remembered that it was Sunday. They'd passed a church, he and Phil, as they'd inched in Phil's vehicle down to the end of Commercial Street, the street of shops, and then in the other direction down Bradford, now his street, the street of his home. English hadn't really noticed, but he thought it might have been a Catholic church. He thought he would go to Mass.

In his first few hours on this dismal Cape, before he'd even seen the daylight here, he'd managed to smash his car and put himself in debt to a strange and probably larcenous auto body shop. The idea of a fresh start took on value and weight as he splashed water on his face and, lacking any kind of towel, dried it with the corner of his bedspread, uncovering in the process a bare mattress. If Mass hadn't started at ten, it would be starting soon, at eleven.

It took English only a few minutes to walk there—St. Peter's, a Catholic institution. He hadn't missed the service. Under a sky the color of iron, people were lugging themselves like laundry toward the big doors of the church. A black arrow outlined in silver directed English toward a side door if he wanted to confess his sins.

In a small room next door to the administrative offices, he found a priest bidding goodbye to an old woman and cleaning his spectacles on the hem of his cassock. English backed away as she passed out of the place, and now it was his turn to sit in the wooden chair, separated from his confessor by a partition with little metal wheels.

This moment seemed to have swooped down on him from nowhere. He'd tried several times recently to make a good confession, but he'd failed. The problem was that about a year ago he'd more or less attempted to take his own life, to kill himself, and couldn't get started telling why.

The priest, a small, preoccupied man, made the sign of the cross and awaited the rote utterances, praying to himself in a rapid whisper.

But English had only one thing to confess. "I'm new in town—excuse me . . ." Violently he cleared his throat. Now he noticed the room was full of flowers.

The priest stopped praying. "Yes. Well, young friend. New in town."

"I wonder if—Father, can we dispense with the . . . ?" English waved his hand around, and was embarrassed to find that this gesture included the confessional and the cross. He'd meant only the formalities, the ritual. What he wanted was plain absolution.

"It's a nice quiet time of year to come," Father said in a puzzled tone.

English waited a minute. The flowers smelled terrible. "I just went crazy," he said. "I committed—I killed myself."

"Uh, you . . ." The priest looked up through the partition's screen as if only now beginning to see he wasn't by himself. "In what sense," he began, and didn't finish.

"What I mean is," English said, "not *killed*. *Tried*, I mean. I tried to hang myself."

"I see," Father said, meaning, perhaps, that he didn't see.

After a few seconds Father said, "Well then. You say you've tried to . . . Is there something you've done about this? Have you sought help?"

"I am. I'm—I'm confessing."

"But . . ." The priest stalled again.

English wondered how much time before Mass. Nobody else was behind him. "I mean . . ." he said.

"Okay," the priest said. "Go on."

"The thing is, I'm starting out here, starting over here." English had come too far. He wanted to find himself standing, without having moved, in the fresh air on the green lawn outside. It was December, but the lawns were still green. There were still flowers around town. He felt cut off from them and from all living things. "This suicide attempt is basically—that's the one thing I'm confessing," he said.

"Well then," Father said.

"I wanted to take Communion," English explained.

The priest seemed weighted down with sadness, but it might only have been shyness. "I don't sense much commitment," he said.

"Can't I just—"

"But I think, do you see, given your—lack—"

"I wanted to confess. I wanted to take Communion."

"Of course," Father said. "But—"

"I'll try again," English said. "I'll try later."

He left the place quickly, embarrassment crawling up his neck as he found his way to the door. Somehow he'd succeeded in confessing his greatest sin, yet had failed to find absolution. He felt hurt by this failure, really wounded. He couldn't hold himself up straight. It was hard for him to walk.

But his spirits lifted as he breathed the chilly air outside, where his fellow Christians ambled, most of them ignoring the paved walkway, across the lawn and through the church's double doors. He watched them awhile, and then, temporarily, he granted his own absolution. Self-absolution was allowed, he reasoned, in various emergencies. Wetting his fingers at the tiny font by the entrance and genuflecting once, he walked in among the aisles and pews with the touch of holy water drying on his forehead.

It was larger, more vaulting, than the church he'd gone to in Lawrence. At the front, behind the altar, the middle of the huge wall telescoped outward away from the congregation, making for the altar not just a great chamber that had nothing to do with the rest of the place but almost another world, because its three walls were given over completely to a gigantic mural depicting the wild ocean in a storm. In the middle of this storm a bigger-than-life-size Jesus stood on a black, sea-dashed rock in his milky garment. The amount of blue in this intimidating scene, sky blues and aquas and frothy blues and cobalts and indigos and azures, taking up about half of the congregation's sight, lent to their prayers a soft benedictive illumination like a public aquarium's. The wooden pews were as solid as concrete abutments on the highway, the whispers of those about to worship rocketed from wall to wall, and English's awareness of these things, along with his irritated awareness of the several babies in the place who would probably start their screams of torment soon, and all the boxes and slots for seat donations and alms for the distant poor, and the long-handled baskets that would be poked under his nose, possibly more than once during the service, by two elderly men with small eyes whom he thought of against his will as God's goons, let him know that his attitude was all wrong today for church. But he was a Catholic. Having been here, he would forget all about it. But if he missed it, he would remember.

There were as many as fifty people scattered throughout a space that would have seated four hundred. All around him were persons he thought of as "Eastern," dark, European-looking persons. An attractive woman with black bangs and scarlet fingernails was sitting behind him, and English couldn't stop thinking about her all through the service. To get her legs out of his mind he swore to himself he'd talk to her on the way out and make her acquaintance. Then he started wondering if he would keep his promise, which wonder took him to the wonder of her legs again, and in this way he assembled himself to make a Holy Communion with his creator.

The tiny priest was a revolutionary: "I have been asked, the diocese has instructed us—all the parishes have received a letter that they are not to go out among the pews to pass the sign of peace." He seemed to get smaller and smaller. "But I'm going to have to just disregard that." A nervous murmuring in the congregation indicated they didn't know if they should applaud, or what. A couple of isolated claps served to express everyone's approval. " 'I give you peace; my peace I give you.' " Were they already at that part? The priest came among the pews and passed out a few handshakes, and the congregation all turned and shook hands with those nearest them.

It never seemed likely, it was never expected, but for English there sometimes came a moment, a time-out in the electric, a rushing movement of what he took to be his soul. "A death He freely accepted," the Silly Mister Nobody intoned, and raising up the wafer above the cup, he turned into a priest rising before Leonard English like the drowned, the robes dripping off him in the sun. Now English didn't have to quarrel, now he didn't have to ask why all these people expected to live forever. And then the feeling was gone. He'd lost it again. His mind wasn't focusing on anything. He'd had the best of intentions, but he was here in line for the wafer, the body of Christ burning purely out of time, standing up through two thousand years, not really here again . . . He was back on his knees in the pews with the body of Our Lord melting in his mouth, not really here again. Our Father, although I came here in faith, you gave me a brain where everything fizzes and nothing connects. I'll start meditating. I'm going to discipline my mind . . .

Everyone was standing up. It was over.

He went out the front way with the other pedestrians, not because he was one, although he was, but because he was trailing the woman who'd been sitting behind him. She was easy to keep in sight, but she walked fast.

She was halfway to the corner by the time he caught up. "My name's English," he told her.

"My name's Portuguese," she said.

"No, I mean, that's really my name, Lenny English." He couldn't get her to slow down. "What's your name?"

"Leanna."

"I was thinking we could have dinner, Leanna. I was thinking and hoping that."

"Not me," she said. "I'm strictly P-town."

"Strictly P-town. What does that mean?" he said.

"It means I'm gay," she said.

Had he been riding a bicycle, he'd have fallen off. He felt as if his startled expression must be ruining everything.

She walked on.

"Wait a minute, wait a minute," English said. "You don't look gay. Isn't that against the law? It'd be easier if you gave some indication."

She was amused, but not to the point of slowing down. "I must've been out of town when they passed out the little badges," she said.

"Couldn't we just have dinner anyway? I don't have anything against women who like women. I like women myself."

"I can't. I've got some other stuff to do." She smiled at him. "Do you know what?" she said. "You left your wallet in the church."

"My wallet?" He'd taken out his wallet to make a donation. Now it was gone from his pocket.

"It's sitting on the bench," she said. "I noticed when we all stood up."

"Oh, shit. Oh, great. How come you didn't tell me?"

"I just told you," Leanna said.

English wanted to talk more, but his anxiety was already carrying him back inside, against the tide of people flowing toward Bradford Street. He swiveled left and right, slipping through them sideways and apologizing convulsively, with an energy he'd lacked in the confessional: "Pardon me. Excuse me. Pardon me. Pardon me . . ."

Monday was the day to become presentable, look alive, and appear at his place of employment. Last night's precipitation had been only somebody's idea of a joke about snow; the streets were dry and the air was sunny and fraught with health and the water in the harbor was blue.

Anybody taking a minute to size up Leonard English, as he

passed shop windows and occasionally glanced at his reflection in them on the way to his new job, might have guessed he was no good at sports and lived in a room alone. On each quick examination of his image he changed the way he walked, or adjusted his shoulders, or wiped his hands on his pants.

Maybe he was about to fail to impress his new boss. He was worried. The truth was that he hardly knew Ray Sands, who ran a private investigation agency and who also owned Provincetown's radio station.

English was at a loss to trace his own path here to the very end of the earth and this new career. It was beginning to seem that the big mistake of his adult life had been giving up his work as a medical equipment salesman over a year ago. He'd drawn a fair salary for a single person, and above that a generous commission. He'd had unbelievably good health insurance—Minotaur Systems couldn't have afforded not to give its workers the best in coverage—and a big pension down the line, and plenty of variety in his workday, wandering all around the city of Lawrence and talking with doctors, university people, and hospital administrators.

He'd enjoyed selling. He'd been treated fine. That hadn't been the problem. It was the equipment itself: gleaming, precise, expensive tools that seemed more like implements of torture than agents of healing.

These incomprehensible gizmos had made him tired. They'd seemed to involve him—implicate him—more and more deeply in the world of the flesh. He'd started going to church again, maybe not too regularly, but at least sincerely, on his thirty-first birthday. That was the other world. The two were in conflict. The conflict sapped his strength. He'd found himself irritable, depressed; and then he'd made the decision that had married him to perpetual financial insecurity. Actually it hadn't been a decision. He'd taken a vacation, extended it with medical leave after his silly attempt at hanging himself, and then been let go.

The try at self-murder he classified as an embarrassing phase of development, that is, nothing really serious.

Somehow the spiritual things, questions like what was really wanted of a person and just how far God would go in being God—he couldn't have said what exactly, but he guessed it was the depth of these conundrums, the way he could spend an afternoon thinking about them and never get anywhere but feel he'd made great strides—*something*, anyway, had dizzied him, and for a while he couldn't function. Stepping off a chair with a rope around his neck and hanging there for a minute had broken the spell.

The same mesmerization had overcome him yesterday in the empty church when he'd gone back after his wallet. He'd found it undisturbed on the bench where he'd been sitting, but instead of leaving right away, he stood among the pews like a solitary farmer in a big, plowed field, holding it in his hand. The mural taking up three whole walls was scary now. From inside His blue storm, Christ called out to the believer to sail up against His rock and be shattered like a dish. What concerned English, night and day, was whether somebody would actually do that.

Wondering about Heaven all the time made him drag his feet. After the medical instruments business, and then even life itself, had paled for him so dramatically, finding some new occupation he could settle down to wasn't easy. A stint with one of the temporary clerical services led him eventually to the Lawrence police station, where he worked for nearly eight months, interviewing the victims of crimes. Most of the victims of crimes were friends or neighbors or relatives of the perpetrators, and they ended up just the same, friendly or neighborly once again, still related and exchanging sheepish looks at sentimental family gatherings. But in the meantime, they wanted to be heard. He took down their statements, keeping them to the subject and boiling away the murky waters of personal history until what remained was stuff actually covered by criminal statutes. It was hard work, and thankless. Everybody went away shocked because justice was never done.

Three nights a week, in the hope of turning himself into somebody else, he took classes in radio announcing and studio electronics. He met a number of private detectives at an audio equipment convention in Kansas City, and was offered a job by Ray Sands of Provincetown. Sands was a retired Boston police detective with a one-man private agency, and he was taking English on as a radio DJ and as an assistant investigator, both positions part-time. Mainly, English gathered, Sands expected him to do things with listening and recording equipment—bugs.

The night courses had given English a reasonable understanding of the kind of taping and editing a production studio might require of him, but about the gadgets and techniques of spying he knew next to nothing. He hoped he wouldn't be a disappointment to his new employer. The problem was, he really didn't know the man. He'd met Ray Sands only that one time, a couple of months ago, and the former police detective, who managed to outfit himself like a banker but still pinched pennies like a municipal hireling, booked him unconditionally after one lunch (Dutch treat) in Kansas City and two long-distance phone talks, both paid for by English.

What clinched it for Sands was the idea that English had worked with the police. It meant—English sensed Sands believed this—that English shared that sacred understanding they all had, something to do with the irremedial rottenness of people everywhere. Did Sands really think that just because English had hung around one of their buildings for a year or so, he understood? Because to tell the truth, the minds and hearts of the police were a darkness to him. It made him uneasy to think that a false impression was the basis for his hiring. He certainly didn't want to be a disappointment—not least of all because it might leave him jobless, carless, stranded on a big sandspit with a lot of strangers among whom, it was turning out, were hundreds of transvestites and homosexuals—and he would have a word with Sands about that, too, he told himself as he wandered Bradford Street in search of the address.

He found it on a side street a block from the harbor. Ray Sands lived in a small home with a high-styled entrance—double doors—and a nice enough yard, with a hedge. Out front, stuck in the lawn by the walk, was a sign announcing that he took passport photos.

English wiped his hands on his pants and rang the bell. It was one you couldn't hear from outside, so you didn't know if it was broken and you should knock or if you should wait awhile and see if anybody came, or what. But Ray Sands opened the door right away and said, "Young man, you're late," as if English were dealing with the President. And Sands was dressed like a forgotten President, in a white shirt and dark necktie, and grey pants with suspenders.

"Well," English said, and started to tell about his activities of the past two hours: He'd had to get a sweater, and a watch cap; he hadn't been ready for this unearthly mix of warm sun and chilly sea breeze; he didn't know which shop, a lot of the shops weren't open . . . Sands was taking him inside as he went on, taking him into the photography studio and sitting him on the stool before the camera and tripod, as if maybe Sands didn't know who he was and was bent on taking his picture for a passport application.

Sands looked at him with sadness, less like a stern judge than a kindly doctor. He had that physician's air about him, the slowness of a man robbed of sleep for a century, the kind of subterranean eminence nurtured in the light of hospital corridors. "You don't think ahead."

This was not, for English, a revelation. "You forgot to tell me about all this," he said, waving his hand at the world behind him, all the cross-dressers and all the—for him, a guy from Lawrence, Kansas—all the sexually disoriented people.

Sands followed the gesture and looked at the wall, curtained to make a backdrop for official photos, behind his new employee. "I don't know what you mean to indicate."

"This whole town is gay," English said. "I mean, it's very unusual to a person from Kansas. A whole town."

"You get used to it," Sands said.

"I realize that."

He was trying to think of something else to say, because Sands was saying nothing now, until he understood that Sands was listening to the sounds of somebody moving around in the next room, from which they were separated by a door. The door shuddered as if someone was tugging at it. Sands reached a hand to it and pushed it open, seeming to lower himself—he was a tall man—toward a child's small voice.

An old woman whom English took to be Mrs. Sands, whose pink scalp shone pitifully through her white hair, stood there in some confusion. "Should I make some tea now, Bud?" She was heavy and feeble, with fat, doughy hands. A white lace shawl draped one shoulder and was falling from the other, and she was trying to catch it with a grasp that clutched air. "Some tea for the visitor, Bud?" She smiled like the blind, at a space where nobody was.

"Oh, no, thanks—no tea, thanks," English said quickly.

Sands shooed his wife out with some remark that English couldn't hear and got back to his new employee as if there'd never been any interruption. "I imagine you'd better get familiarized with these recorders."

I don't care if that's your wife, English felt like saying.

"We'll teach you a little photography, too. But that's for another day."

"How about my shift at WPRD?" English said.

"We'll wait awhile. I've got some surveillance for you."

* * *

English picked up his first surveillance subject that evening as she strolled past the Chamber of Commerce, a small building that looked across a parking lot at a long pier made lustrous and a little bit unreal by the lights of Boston fifty kilometers across the Bay. It shocked him that he'd hardly unpacked but was already at work in a world he knew nothing about.

He didn't enjoy lurking and loitering like a figure in a cheap movie, glancing every few minutes at the photograph of a stranger. Long-distance buses stopped here, and maybe he resembled a person waiting for one, but he thought he looked like somebody hiding unsavory ideas.

When she passed by him she said, "Hello," a tiny brunette, jeans and knee boots swaying beneath a jacket of fur, who made him think, for some reason, of dimples. English didn't care that she saw him. As long as nobody guessed his occupation, he could tail the whole town. It was a metropolis of two streets, after all, and everyone saw everybody else six times a day.

The idea was that this woman, Mrs. Marla Baker, had changed addresses recently. Now she lived somewhere on the town's east end. By waiting in a likely place and following her home, English was supposed to find out exactly where.

Meaning to give her a head start, English stayed on the bench. Before he could get up, she went into the Tides Club just this side of the pier, and to keep her in view he didn't have to move at all. As she greeted the man at the bar who sat nearest the door, she shook her shoulders—a gesture to say it was cold outside. There was some discussion with the man, and then apparently they reached an agreement about the weather, because he got up and shut the door.

There wasn't any public exit, as far as English knew, other than the door he was watching; and so all he had to do to pick her up again was sit on the bench. But he didn't. He paced up and down in front of it. He'd never followed anyone before, and even if it was easy in a town where recurring visibility aroused no suspicion, he was still completely untrained in how to stay on top of his quarry; or subject; he liked that word better, subject. He was getting cold, too. How did these private eyes keep from freezing?

And now the night conjured up from the waters a gluey fog. It got in his lungs; he felt diseased. One minimal concession of fate was that they didn't have the terrible lowing of foghorns here that certain films had got him looking forward to with trepidation. The horns of the two lighthouses on the Cape's tip, blinking red and green across the water, were less dreadfully pitched, high and clear-toned, like sweet bells.

The 9 p.m. bus arrived, all lit up inside. Nobody got off. There was no one aboard but the driver. He silenced and darkened and locked his vehicle. "Waiting for a package?" he asked English, holding his book of tickets in his hand beside his dead machine. "Waiting for my ship to get here," English told him. "Happy waiting," the bus driver said.

Now English noticed somebody walking in the lee of shadow alongside the Tides Club, going up toward the little heart of town, but he couldn't make this subject out, except to say she was petite, like his own subject, Mrs. Marla Baker. As soon as whoever it was turned the corner, English jogged across the stretch of asphalt to the Tides, jerked open the door, and poked his head inside—a statue at the pool table chalked its cue, blank faces looked up at him out of a frozen moment—but she wasn't there. He resumed his jogging, up the block and around the corner.

Far down Commercial Street she passed under streetlamps and alongside the illuminated windows of closed stores, visible and invisible, like a ghost. English walked, out of breath, until she took a left. Then he picked up his pace. It was still misty out, and when he took the same left onto a side street, the mist closed behind him. He had seen fog, but had never witnessed a back lane that lurked in it, a red light blurring in it above a fire exit, or these back stairs draped with its still, pink scarves and saying everything there was to say about loneliness. He wanted to call out to Marla Baker, tell her that she wasn't alone and that neither of them was really invisible. But when the lane curved, a tavern came into sight and she went in. He saw her through the window among friends, two women, one of whom squeezed her furred shoulder—he could feel the dew of mist on it with his own fingers—while the other tried to pour beer into her mouth from a mug, and he could taste it.

The three of them, Marla Baker and her two friends, had a drink before they strolled, whooping and laughing together, down Bradford and then back in the harbor's direction, past the town hall. They were going to some kind of show at the Beginner's Dance Lounge, one of the biggest places, in terms of square meters, on the water.

Cars choked Commercial Street, and the parking lot was jammed. Dozens of people lingered outside the Beginner's, making their deals. English's subjects all had tickets, and he didn't. The man at the door, dressed in white tie and tails and wearing purple lipstick and green eye shadow, told him they were sold out. English had to bribe the man with a twenty-dollar bill. "Daisy Craze" was the name of this well-attended extravaganza.

English thought he'd be smart and take a table near the door, but he couldn't spot a single vacant seat. The bar ran along the back of the crowded room, and it looked like pandemonium in that region. People were talking away, a rubble of voices under a sea of smoke, and only those at tables near the stage were paying any attention to the show. In the yellow stagelights an elderly woman—actually a man outfitted as a Spanish dancing lady—leaned on the upright piano and lip-synced "The Impossible Dream" as rendered by the recorded voice of Liza Minnelli, perhaps, over the crackly P.A. system. As the song grew more passionate she stopped leaning against the piano and, with movements gangly and frail, began to emote. She even mimicked the head jangle of the singer's violent vibrato. Below the hem of her dress, a man's gnarled ankles hobbled around in high-heeled shoes. She had a tendency to limp and stagger and lean to the right. But English saw that this was not a comic act. Deep feeling that was partly stage fright glistened in her eyes as she sang the finale: *"Still strove—with his last ounce of courage—to reach—the un-reach-able . . . stars!"*

English was still hunting around in this battlefield for an empty seat. He found one, but somebody claimed it was taken. While people applauded the Spanish dancing singer, English located a chair near the bar, carried it overhead, trying to look as if he belonged here, and put it down where some people squeezed over this way and that to make room for him. He sat partly at their table and partly behind a supporting pole for the ceiling. He had to look on one side or the other of it to see anything. His subjects were only a couple of tables away.

The mistress of ceremonies was the one he liked the best. He'd already grasped that they wouldn't be seeing any genuine females in this entertainment, but just the same she was a real woman, whatever her official gender. She was making a long thing out of introducing the next act, who was going to be Miss Shirley. "And I mean," she said, "this is a fine, fine imitation. This girl has really, really worked on this act." The MC wore her platinum hair in a matronly bun, but she was made up after the fashion of a chorus girl. Silver-sequined eye shadow fanned all the way up to her sketched-on eyebrows. Shivering golden earrings dangled. Her breasts were real. English had heard they did that with silicone injections. Her long midnight-blue and shiny dress clung to her paunch, but was kind. "Miss . . .

Shirley!" she said at last, and bowed off. She was poised and full of grace, and he was rooting for her.

Miss Shirley was only a guy in a blond Brillo-style wig who dragged a teddy bear into the lights and lip-synced "The Good Ship Lollipop," the scratchy original Shirley Temple version. But it was funny, and it made a big hit.

It was an amateur night. One by one they paraded themselves onto the stage and stalled there, brazen and embarrassed. The MC hung out onstage with a tall drink in her hand and said how badly these girls needed to be here, in a town where they could promenade along the streets in dresses, and get up on this stage and hide nothing about themselves. They were all in some kind of club, from places up and down the East Coast, and they were usually under tension, dressing up only in secret, and they needed this respite from the world. Some of them had wives in the audience. They were all living in a dorm-style situation in a couple of the hotels here in Provincetown. "They *need* you to see them," she said. English noticed there were plenty of cross-dressers in the audience, too.

The air turned thick and hot, the applause grew a beard of loud voices and got all out of proportion to the quality of the miserable acts, which were almost all lip-synced. When the record got stuck or skipped, the performer would get wild-eyed, wondering how to cope, but the audience just cheered each one through these difficult moments. English's brunette got up, snagging her fur jacket along with one hand, and was immediately lost outside the aura of the stagelights. He wanted to stay; he was having a nice time. But it turned out she was only visiting the bar behind them to get a drink. As for English, he drank nothing, because he considered himself on duty, until suddenly there was an apparition of a white-coated waiter before him, at which point he crossed the borders of sense, he couldn't have said why, and waded out into the Scotch-and-water.

Next was a person whom English thought of as a cowboy, because by his flung-knee position, as he seated himself on a stool with his guitar, the man reminded English of nothing so much as a wrangler straddling a chair backward in the bunkhouse after a tough ride. His makeup had been washed away by sweat, and his coiffure was only a mess of hair drawn back into a ponytail by the use of a green rubber band. He was decidedly and happily masculine, but he happened to be wearing a Pop Art dress, with lightning bolts and whirling stars all over it, and black high heels, severe and schoolmarmish street shoes. This man played his guitar and sang, without benefit of a professional's recording, a song he'd written himself about how his older sister had started dressing him up when he was a little boy. "And the prison of manhood stepped aside for me," he sang, "and I could do all the things that only little girls could do. I could be loving. I could be soft. I could surrender and be weak." It was a sad song. Everybody was very moved. He was a great favorite.

For English's money, the atmosphere was better than in an actual show. The worst acts were the best, and the good ones were a relief. Just to reward each one for the feat of getting finished without expiring, the audience shouted and pounded on their small, circular tables, everyone crammed knock-kneed around these toadstools at an alcoholic tea party presided over by a steadily more and more inebriated duchess. English himself drank until he felt the floor shift. Everything was happening faster than it usually did—a cigarette seemed to last ten seconds—but the MC was taking a longer and longer time between acts now, seizing this chance to fill everybody in on most of her past accomplishments and giving them the benefit of her thinking on quite a range of issues, including the veiled meaning of their lives. "I had a man," she remembered. "*I* had a man." She raised her hands to put a stray lock of hair back into her bun with perfect movements, holding her elbows forward as only a woman would. "I had a man," she sang with shyness. "But my man got drafted, and do you know, girls, he refused to tell them he was a fag?" Right, English thought, right for you, whatever I mean by that. He was feeling a great affection for all these people. Cut off by the sea from the steel mills and insurance companies who would never know them like this, they obviously felt a wholesome bond among themselves, the closeness of doomed cruisers on a sinking ship—"Do you know what I mean?" he asked one of the people he was sharing a table with, but he didn't know at which station of his thoughts his mouth had got on. "Do you get it?" He'd lost count of his Scotch-and-waters.

The last act was going to be something special—"like I was, my dears, my dears—if you could have seen me!" the MC told them all. She wasn't choked up with grief; she observed with humor the train of years as it left her behind. She conjured up for them her youthful self and presented this ghost as she might have presented a daughter whose loveliness even she was astonished by. "I was the seven*teenth*-highest-paid female impersonator in the world . . . Europe—of course the girls in Europe might have given me a little competition. But don't you know, it might have been the other way, too—I might have given *them* a little competition, don't you know? But I stayed in my own country." She looked at the audience steadily, and English remembered, from his own experience in a high-school production, that she probably couldn't see a single face. "Because I wanted to be Miss America."

And in the same generous spirit, tainted only a little by matronly jealousy, she presented the young person whose future, she assured the audience, was assured.

This last performer was beautiful and smoldering and sexy, in a lacy black corset and garter belt, high heels, net stockings.

First she did a number that was fast and was supposed to be funny, but nobody laughed, everyone only applauded endlessly. She was a gifted dancer. For her second act and the evening's last number, she mimed a version of "My Funny Valentine." English was a little mixed up about his feelings as he watched her, because he felt weak in the arms with yearning. He caught sight of the subject Marla Baker, who was kissing one of her friends while around them the crowd applauded a parade of the night's performers, and he wished them well.

Now Marla Baker was caught in a staring contest with—was it black-haired Leanna, the woman he'd talked with at Mass? —the two of them confessing everything with their eyes, tears streaming down their faces, in a moment of such intensity they seemed to have surfaced into sunlight and been frozen there . . .

Singing the Miss America song, the recorded voice of Bert Parks whispered under the cheering. The Leanna woman had disappeared. English headed for the facilities, seeing that Marla Baker, gazing off now with shiny eyes and not listening to the talk of her companions, still had a drink to finish on the table in front of her.

Three or four men waited to use the john, but they were all so intoxicated, talking about nothing and struggling to make it clear, that he just went in ahead of them. The walls inside were completely papered over with magazine photos of naked boys, thousands of them striking every possible attitude and conveying intentions that, for all their being only photographs, made him uncomfortable. He went into the stall and leaned against the side of it, while his cigarette burned away rapidly like a fuse. Then he was trying to light another one, but the matchbook danced in his fingers and floated off, and the stall pitched forward and knocked him on the back of the head. He washed his hands, which felt as if they were dressed in big fat rubber gloves. His face in the mirror, ringed by dozens of photographed penises, seemed to be still in the process of forming. Over and over again he splashed his eyes with cold water.

When he got out, the sleeves of his sweater were all wet. He'd lost Marla Baker.

There were only a few people left in the place. There was a man trying to write a check at the bar, squinting at the mystery of his checkbook, two young fellows waiting for the man and both of them drumming their fingers with exasperation, there were two women across from one another at one of the little round tables, alone in a sea of little round tables, a bartender smoking a cigarette with a distant look of pleasure on his face, and out beyond the area of light, a waiter circling through vagueness with a dim white rag, as if he were surrendering.

English had no idea what to do. He had a feeling it didn't matter.

As he left the Beginner's he said hello to a young man and a young woman who clung to one another just inside the entrance, and the young man sobbed, "I don't want to die! I want to *live!*"

English would ask people—tomorrow. He would find out where Marla Baker lived just by asking people—tomorrow, not tonight. Tonight he was having trouble carrying out his first assignment, and some difficulty delivering his head out beyond the doors.

Over the next few weeks the several squads of tourists in evidence on his arrival just disappeared. In the whole town only two or three restaurants stayed open for business, their windowpanes filmed with steam and bordered by grimy snow. Brief thaws came often, but Provincetown seemed, in general, arctic and bereft.

His two jobs kept him busy enough, but in the evenings English didn't know what to do with himself. He felt the fires of a deadly boredom. When he didn't have night work he stayed late in the bars with the people whose malfunctioning faces floated above their beers, turning from his own image in the mirror to another one of him in the black window. By this time there were only a few taverns open, and he kept seeing the same terrible people over and over. In the cafés where he ate breakfast, the local fishermen drank coffee and argued about certain financial realities of the industry over which they had no control and about which, it seemed to English, they weren't entitled to have any opinions, or anyway, it began to seem to him, not such stupid ones; and they traded lies and passed judgment on their colleagues and rivals endlessly, until he believed he would get up and go over and tip someone's eggs into his lap, just to see.

He was getting to be a creature of the night, spying till the zero hour, and then on Tuesdays and Thursdays working a shift at WPRD from two until six in the morning. His employment wasn't going all that happily. At the station they had only those two four-hour shifts for him, and he'd been doing next to nothing as Ray Sands's assistant investigator. His one investigation, in fact, still involved tracking Marla Baker—who turned out to be older than she'd looked at first, a middle-aged divorcee—from her apartment to her lover's house and back again, several times a week.

On these occasions the lovers had dinner together, and English recorded their conversations with a mike taped to the window glass. They lay together on the living-room couch till midnight or so, these two bland middle-aged women, and talked, and embraced, and massaged one another with scented oils, and he recorded all this, too, with the same mike taped to the glass of a different window. It was the kind of thing he'd sworn never to be reduced to, but he couldn't remember when, exactly, this oath had been pledged. Everything was softened in the candle-light of their romance, and unknown to them, he skulked outside with the clouds of his breath, adjusting the volume knob with frozen fingers. His ski mittens dangled by little clips from the sleeves of his black leather jacket, two limp, flabby hands that wrung themselves helplessly while their owner went around doing things he disapproved of.

One night Marla Baker and her lover, whose name was Carol, had a visitor. It was the woman he'd spoken to in church his first day in this town and then pitifully invited to dinner—Leanna.

The three of them held a kind of conference in the kitchen. All English witnessed, through a slim parting of the living-room curtain that gave him a view of the archway to the kitchen, were the stove, which slowly developed a face out of its dials and seams, and the torso of Marla Baker, with sweater sleeves pushed back to her elbows. He saw her hands put an orange kettle on the flame and then saw them take it away when it steamed. Under his blue knit watch cap he wore small Walkman earphones, and he heard everything they said. But it was the length of the silences, those clutching lulls in talk, that spoke the clearest.

English had never realized, until he'd listened to recorded conversations, how much time people spend saying nothing, thinking about what they've heard and preparing what they have to say. But in this little gathering, made excruciating by Leanna's presence in a way never quite specified, these three women started and stopped a lot more than usual, agonized through their remarks about the tea, and choked up when they talked about the weather, as if they were making terrible confessions. English pressed his palms against the window to quell miscellaneous distorting vibrations.

After that night, Marla Baker and Leanna started sleeping together occasionally at Marla's apartment. The first time it happened, English climbed a tree and put the mike on a fishing pole, nudging it close to Marla's bedroom window, and he listened. The two women undressed after a while and went to bed. They slept together as sisters might have, giving one another not so much pleasure as comfort. Marla and Leanna, Marla and Leanna—it had a nice sound to it. They'd been lovers once, but it hadn't worked out the way they'd planned. They certainly knew how to let themselves weep.

English spent that evening straddling a branch, the tendons in his thighs at first uncomfortable and then, after a while, really on fire, wondering who was paying for this service, who was ultimately listening to these tapes, to what use was he or she putting them, what was this person like? Later he'd tell himself that if there was a beginning to his troubles, that was it: wondering.

It was almost 3 a.m. He couldn't believe he was sitting in a tree with these items, which it would be impossible to explain if anybody asked: much worse stuff than, there was no comparison with, really, the medical implements he'd been convinced were soiling him a couple of years ago. Hadn't his experience as his own unsuccessful hangman turned his life around? At what point had he gotten this corrupt?

English marked no thread of occurrences leading up to his halfhearted suicide attempt, no clear trail of his own footprints, but he did feel pretty certain that the finish of his employment in the medical world had begun with his introduction to the new surgical stapler Minotaur Systems had developed. This item was supposed to replace the old-fashioned sutures. Basically it was the same thing used around any office, but it was large and elaborate and wouldn't have looked out of place in the hands of an astronaut walking on the moon. English had looked forward to learning all about it at a big sales conference in Chicago. But what should have been a fun and diverting trip to a medical lab near the city had soured very shortly after his cab let him off at the gate at the appointed hour. The laboratory, an offspring or cousin of the Minotaur corporate family, was out by O'Hare Airport in a sea of grass and corn bridged here and there by tiny cloverleaves of Interstate 90. There was desolation in the scouring sound made by distant jets that knew nothing about this place and in the whistling of the wind through the chain-link fence, a wind that also brought him the stink of urine and dog shit and the berserk exclamations of laboratory animals housed right there under the sky. Nobody had told him about this. Dogs running up and down their cages, kittens shivering in concrete corners, stunned rabbits, goats dangling wires from their ears, even a couple of blind sheep standing around in the straw, their eye sockets covered by bandages. English was still trying to swallow the shock of his own presence in a place like this as he was ushered into a room, in the laboratory proper, filled with whimpering, tranquillized dogs on small operating tables. There he was handed a smock and a scalpel and one of the new surgical stapling devices. The tiled floor was full of drains. As a child, he'd been bothered by certain noises in his bedroom closet. Now the closet was opened, and everything he'd imagined inside it came out and revealed itself to be his employer. He waited for somebody to point out how horrible this was. As soon as someone spoke up, he would, too. But nobody said a word. Under the direction of the laboratory's supervisor he took his place before one of the several dozen tables and put on the green operating cap, shower-curtain booties, and translucent surgical gloves that lay beside the drooling head of a fawn-colored dachshund, and, in the midst of fifty other green-garbed members of the Minotaur Systems sales force, he began tearing at this dog's belly with his scalpel, heaving out intestines and other organs and cutting into them and, from time to time, when directed, laying down the scalpel, picking up the surgical stapler, and learning about the variety of its uses.

English had become something of a specialist in the area of sterilization devices. He could talk antisepsis with the best of them. But, because his field had narrowed this way, he wasn't like these other salespeople. They had all spent time in operating rooms and were not only accustomed to the sight of blood and at home with the idea of anybody else's physical pain, but they'd even, a lot of them, taken part in surgical operations on living patients, had taken the instruments they were selling into their own hands and shown the doctors just how they worked. The idea of opening up these dumb, tearful animals didn't faze these veterans, but English's eyes burned and he sobbed deep in his throat, watching his own gloved hands tremble and stab limp-wristedly at gristle. Nobody talked much. Blood sprouted from arteries in brief, graceful ejaculations, like fronds of seaweed, and pattered to the floor or fell across their gowns. The ripped lungs flapped and wheezed, salesmen and saleswomen occasionally exclaimed over the unexpected force of a death rattle and made the kinds of jokes that medical people always made, and the staplers clicked, the scalpels clacked on the Formica, and once in a while, because they were slippery, a scalpel got away from somebody and went tinkling across the floor. English heard all these noises acutely, though his head hurt as much as if his eardrums had burst. The building pitched, humming, back and forth. The grasses outside no longer seemed to lie down in the wind, but cringed before the sexual approach of something ultimate. Like a long curse a jet's sound passed close above the building toward the horizon. That an airport could go about its gigantic business in the same world as this laboratory seemed impossible, unless—and he didn't think this so much as feel it as a self-evident fact—unless all things conspired consciously to do perfect evil.

He couldn't stop this. There was nothing he could do. It wasn't his fault. This dachshund was finished, no matter what. The dog was already scarred down all four legs, and just above its tail and on top of its head two bald patches had been incised for the planting of electrodes. There was some undercurrent here that, even more than his job as a Minotaur salesperson, it was his nauseating privilege, his instinctive duty to do whatever the creatures who weren't dogs were doing to the dogs.

With the same blind gesture of childhood games like pin the tail on the donkey, he pushed his scalpel into what he hoped was the poor animal's heart, and it expired like a balloon.

The thing was, why had he submitted so mindlessly, why hadn't it occurred to him at the time to stop, to object, to get away? The experience gave him, in a way he couldn't explain, some slight appreciation of what rape might be like for the victim. And now, like a woman with a gun in her purse, he waited for somebody to try again. He wasn't going to let it beat him twice. He would do whatever he had to do.

When Marla and Leanna had fallen asleep, that first night, English climbed down from the tree with his bag of tricks and his fishing pole. He'd been aroused, even in the cold, by the sight of naked women.

On the way home he threw the tape cassette in a dumpster, and later he told Sands, "I got nothing." He told him, "I may be an idiot, but I'm not an acrobat." He told Sands he wouldn't work up that high, out on a limb. There was too much for him to juggle up there.

He might have wished that he'd turned from the butter of moonlight on the harbor to see her standing there with the sea taste on her cheek, but as it happened she was in the drugstore on Commercial Street, buying something which she tried to hide from English when he said hello. Feminine protection evidently. She was dressed in a sweatsuit. She'd come from an exercise class. She smiled and seemed to give him the benefit of the doubt.

Gusts of wind took their words away as soon as they'd stepped out the door:

"Hello—"

"Hello—"

"Didn't I—"

"Yes—"

"Right, a few weeks ago, at Mass—"

"I told you we'd meet again—"

"Let's get a cup of java," he said, private-eye-style, guiding her into a doorway out of the weather.

He got the idea that she was laughing at him. "Java," she said.

"That's right. Java. I thought you spoke Portuguese."

"Is that Portuguese?"

"You tell me. I don't speak Portuguese."

"What was your name again?"

"Lenny English. And you're Leanna, right?"

"How did you know?" Had she forgotten she'd told him?

"Things like that get around." He liked that answer, but she seemed unimpressed. "I work over there at WPRD," he said desperately.

"Oh? Yeah? Have you got a show?"

"Well, I do classical stuff from 2 to 6 a.m., Tuesdays and Thursdays. And also I'm a production engineer."

"Oh, 2 to 6 a.m., oh, I'm asleep by then."

Sometimes you are, he felt like telling her, and sometimes you're not.

Leanna insisted they go over to Fernando's, a café and bar clotted with hanging plants, and everywhere you looked a sign that read THANK YOU FOR NOT SMOKING, a phrase that always seemed to resound in his head, like a dental tool. When they got there they went through a tangle of decision-making before taking a place by the window. English didn't care where he sat; he hated the whole restaurant.

He started right in. "I've changed addresses eighteen times in the last twelve years," he told Leanna. "I lived in Lawrence, Kansas, that whole time. I'm a nice person, but I have a lot of inside trouble."

"Inside trouble. What is that? Inside trouble."

"Unsound thinking. Getting myself all worked up over nothing, you know what I mean." If you told people these things right away, they discounted it all. Later you could say, I warned you. "I smoke cigarettes," he told her.

"That's okay," she said.

"I eat meat."

"And you're aggressive in conversations."

"That's true. Yeah. Okay, I sometimes am."

"That way you don't have to respond to anyone."

This happened to be the truth. He looked around. "They have any coffee in this place?"

"When you're on a bus, nobody sits near you because you look too lonely. I bet you're lonely, but not because nobody wants to know you. It's because, really, you don't want to know anybody."

Her accent wasn't New England; she spoke in the way of stewardesses: "Are fline time wull be wen are en fifteen mennets." He thought it made her sound unintelligent.

"I'm not that lonely," he said. "Really."

She seemed not to have heard him.

"There's a difference," he insisted, "between solitude and loneliness."

Leanna raised her eyebrows. "You're the loneliest person I know."

The waitress, a large woman dressed in jeans and flannel shirt like a lumberjack, was staring down at him as if in support of Leanna's assertion.

"I guess I'll have whatever she's having," he told the waitress.

He wasn't getting any less irritated with this restaurant. These places felt underdecorated if they didn't have all the accoutrements of a subtropical swamp, including fish from outer space in glass tanks of water and fat little palm trees in big clay pots full of dirt, and a menu on which every kind of item—even tea, even ice cream—was something he'd never heard of. And he was irritated with himself, too. Here was this beautiful woman giving him a little of her time, and he couldn't think of anything very charming to say.

In a minute he said, "You're good at interpretations, so what about my love life? Can you interpret that whole mess for me?"

"You tell women a lot of lies, but at the time you're saying them, you think they're true. Right? I can tell by your expression I'm right."

"Well," he said, really embarrassed, really unhappy, "I can see we're not going to hit it off."

"You think you've been involved a lot, but really the story on you is that you've just been into a lot of indiscriminate random fucking."

And she looked so sweet! Hadn't he seen her at church? "Do you know a lady named Marla Baker?" he asked—because he wanted, in any way he could, to crack her smile.

"You know I do," she said, "or you wouldn't be asking."

"No, no, it's just a name—there was a call for her at the station. She's not in the book."

"She moved across town."

He couldn't think why he'd started this, or how to get out of it. Lamely he said, "Well, you've got my past all scoped out, don't you?"

"You're a type," she said.

"A type. Am I your type?"

"You're predictable. Not overly funny."

"Oh. Yeah. Predictions. So what about the future? Are you kind of like gifted with that knowledge, too?"

"Oh, you'll probably doodle along just like you are now, until you set yourself on fire because you're smoking one of those cigarettes of yours in bed," she said, "and then you'll die."

A bad prophecy. He himself had imagined something similar. "I mean, I was talking about the future of my love life. Not if I'm going to burn myself up in bed."

"You mean you were trying to flirt?"

English sweated a lot. He sweated at parties where he was lost, at interviews for jobs he didn't want, at those times when he met strangers who used to be his friends. "I'm sweating."

"Do you take honey?" She started doing businesslike things with their two pots of tea, which had just arrived, giving out a fragrance like detergent, while he mopped his face with his napkin. He thought it was very gracious of her.

Her manner was straightforward, but she was physically quite languid and—modest, English believed. She talked low, she kept her left hand in her lap and gestured delicately with the right one, or lifted her cup, which she didn't bend down to, but raised up to her lips, and she had this quality he'd seen in many young girls, and a few women, and which had always made him feel he was being tortured invisibly, this quality of seeming not to weigh even one ounce. And she was having a great time, she was delighted. He burned to be responsible for that. But he knew he wasn't.

"What," she said when she saw him watching her and failing to drink his camomile tea.

"I was trying to think what I want to say."

"And what is that?"

He was sure the tea wasn't all that bad. It was only that his stomach was in knots.

"My fear level is pretty high," he said.

"I'll bet it's pretty high all the time," she said.

"This isn't my usual kind of conversation at all," he said.

"If it's all too new to cope with, then don't talk." She took a sip of tea. "Drink tea."

"Am I so funny?"

She drank her tea.

"Am I such a fucking joke?"

She put down her cup. "Now you're pissed."

"I was trying to get someplace with you."

"I got that."

"But I'm a joke, it's a fucking joke that I come on to you, just because I'm not a woman? Because if it is—I mean . . ."

"You don't know what you mean."

"Yeah. No. I mean, it's wrong"—he sensed his own biases were showing—"wrong to be so prejudiced, is what I'm getting at."

"I'm not prejudiced, I'm gay. I told you I was gay."

"Then how come you're having coffee with me? Tea, I mean. Tea."

"Because I'm thirsty."

With his napkin English blotted his forehead. "You're stepping all over me in this little talk. You've had practice. You've said all this before, and I haven't." This silenced her. "I never have." He pushed his tea away, and his spoon. "The one who's playing games here is you, and I'm being honest for a change." The place before him was clear. "And anyway, why have I been sitting here pretending I like camomile tea? In other countries," he told Leanna, "they soak their feet in camomile tea."

She smiled at everything, like a person at the circus. "Lenny? Or Leonard?"

"Two people meet," he said. "They each have three or four qualities they can show each other, you know the ones I'm talking about, the ones that always get them by. For the woman it could be that she makes jokes all the time, or she could be kind of self-effacing. The man could be scientific and easygoing. He could show her he likes her jokes because he has a good sense of humor, and he could deliver some compliments. That shows he's not going to beat her up, like the other guys did. They tell each other things like, how old, what are your hobbies, I work at the hardware store, I'm going to be manager someday . . ."

"Are you telling me about a movie? Have I lost my place?"

"What I mean—this is just another one of those conversations, if you ask me."

She looked hurt. "I don't—"

"What you are, and what I am, and who's who at the zoo. What you are is a dyke. And I'm a failed pimp."

"I wish you success." She toasted him with her cup of tea.

"Then what?" she asked him after they'd sat through a minute of uncomfortable silence.

"What? What then what?"

"After they reveal all this stuff," she said, "then what?"

"Then—nothing, I guess. I guess the first conversation is over."

"And so what about the second conversation?"

"What do you mean? It's the same."

"But how do they get close? How do they decide they want to make love?"

"That stuff, all that goes on sort of behind the scenes. That goes on in their hearts."

"And what are the conversations like after that?"

"When? After what?" he said.

"After they make love, after they're lovers."

He saw she wasn't fooling. She really had no idea.

"Have you ever been to bed with a man?" he said with great fear.

For a beat he didn't think she would answer, but only gaze

at him until he simply—ceased. "Not in the way we're talking about," she said.

Now he was speechless. He groped for the thread . . . Something about what lovers said. "After they're lovers, the conversations are the same," he managed to tell her, "but there's something sort of different about them."

She wasn't talking now. English felt toyed with. "Come on," he said. "You knew all this."

She laughed. "Have you ever been to bed with a man?"

"What? No! Me?"

"Then I guess I know as much about it as you."

True. But he only said, "Can't we talk about something else?"

"We met in church. There's that whole side of things."

"As long as I'm being honest, the stuff that starts happening after that subject gets raised mostly bores me."

"Then what were you doing there that day?"

"Slumming."

But she wasn't having any. "What were you doing there? Are you so scrupulous? You don't look like a compulsive Catholic."

"I'm not." What was the point in hiding? "It means everything to me."

"The Church? Or church attendance?"

"Not that. Not even the Church. That's what I mean by boring stuff. I don't care about infallibility. I'm not really interested in abortion. It confuses me, all that shit. The Pope confuses me. I just—" He thought he might as well. "There's really only one question."

"What's that?"

"Did God really kill Himself?"

Leanna wasn't smiling now. She was staring at him, but softly. "Who are you?" she asked him.

Whatever she meant by the question, he didn't want to answer it. He wiped his face with his napkin, and in reference to the warmth of the place said, "Man."

"If you took off your jacket, you'd be cooler."

"For some reason, I usually keep it on. I don't know why."

"It's your armor. You're a knight, huh?"

"I'm a knight of faith," he confessed suddenly. He'd never said anything like this to anybody before.

She looked at him. A frail light shone out of her, this he would have sworn. "I know you are," she said. She sipped her tea, but he happened to know her cup was empty.

"When straight people get together," he said before they parted that day, "the man gets the woman's phone number."

"Hey, what—doesn't he have a phone book?"

"At least the guy gets her last name."

"Sousa."

"Sousa?"

"It's Portuguese. I told you about that."

"Well, Sousa has never been my favorite name. In fact, the only one I ever heard of was this person who wrote 'Be Kind to Your Web-Footed Friends.' "

"That wasn't me."

He stood up, laying down a dollar for the tip, and in a gesture of parting Leanna reached over and touched his hand. "Leonard."

He was so entranced, he was so charmed, so captivated—rolled out flat, dreamed into, shone upon—that when she said his name, English started to live.

After one conversation he was ready to marry her. In fact, he'd been infatuated with Leanna since the night he'd seen her naked and putting her former lover's hand to her lips, in a dim, warm bedroom, in consolation for their mutual failure. "We've got to let this door close," she'd said to Marla Baker that night, "before any others can open for us." He wanted to be naked like that with Leanna. He wanted Leanna to put his hand to her lips. He wanted Leanna to say something like that to him.

During those first few weeks in Provincetown, English had only one other case. A boy ran away from home, and English went in his Volkswagen, now repaired but no longer the same as it used to be, to show the boy's photograph around the Hyannis bus station. But when he walked into the small, crowded depot, the runaway was there himself, sitting on a bedroll and looking through a comic. English told the boy who he was, though he wasn't supposed to, and asked the boy where he was aiming himself. The boy said he was going back home for Christmas. Figuring to save him the bus fare, English gave him a lift to his doorstep in Provincetown, but for this service Ray Sands charged his parents an extra twenty-two dollars.

As for the radio station, WPRD: in that world he was a ghost, in and out in the darkest hours. Nobody knew him but the air shifter who left when English came, and the other one who arrived when English left, the first usually weathering a blitz-krieg of self-administered esoteric chemicals, and the second almost always hung over. Sometimes English worked in the production studio very early on Wednesday mornings, and so he was also indefinably acquainted with that day's two-to-six air shifter, a white Rastafarian who played Jamaican reggae music and spilled things and never wiped them up. It was the kind of station, and nobody tried to disguise it, where self-respecting disc jockeys were never found. The floors were muck-stained and the trash accumulated perpetually in the corners, the equipment was very nearly Edison-era, the records were sloppily catalogued and put back on the shelves all wrong—which meant, in a collection of several thousand recordings, that they were lost forever—and there were low-rent signs and manifestations all over the walls: schedules, charts, useless maps, scrawlings of employees' offspring, postcards from the listening public, most of them patronizing and some actually exuding pity, cartoons about radio life torn out of magazines, including one from *The New Yorker* sketched by the artist right there in WPRO's announcer's booth, which meant he thought this outfit was probably good for a laugh; also notes about idiosyncrasies that had suddenly cropped up in this or that machine, notes concerning car pools, babysitters, and things for sale, cryptic notes between DJs about, English guessed, drug transactions, anonymous notes of the character-assassination kind, generalized laments about the equipment, or the cataloguing, or the lack of team effort, or the floors, and breathless rules hastily developed thanks to the slovenly few: ALL MONITORS AND SPEAKERS ARE TO BE TURNED DOWN AFTER 10 P.M. NO GUESTS UNLESS THEY ARE ON THE SHOW, IE BEING INTER-VIEWED WITH PRIOR PERMISSION!!!

During his shift English stayed there alone, playing hour-long classical music tapes over the air. Most of his time he spent in the production studio with a mixing board, rerecording the conversations of Marla Baker, smoothing out the volume level of voices that had come and gone through the rooms of love. I'm quitting tomorrow—I'm quitting tomorrow—but he was hooked. For one thing, he admitted to himself, he was zapped by all the gadgetry, obsessed with the idea of clear audio. But more than that he felt, sometimes, that in hearing these most private revelations, these things lovers said to one another when they were alone, he'd found the source of a priestly serenity. Listen, he wanted to say, I don't judge you. You comfort me, whatever you do, arguing, lying, making stupid jokes. However small you are, however selfish, I'm there, too. That's me. I'm with you.

He was fascinated with how Marla Baker and her lover Carol

easily communicated in the most garbled sentences about little things that didn't matter, and then failed, over and over again, to make themselves understood with the clearest statements whenever it came to the really important things.

"Well, I'm just *angry*," Marla would say.

"But—I don't understand. It doesn't make sense," Carol would say.

"Please," one or the other would say, "please, let me explain the whole thing again."

Backing the tapes up, starting them forward, pushing up the treble, filtering out the clinks: I'm not alone, I'm never alone, he told these voices of people who'd forgotten they'd ever said such things and were now fast asleep; I'm with you.

Ray Sands invited English to his home for an early dinner on the afternoon of New Year's Eve. English said no in his heart, but his mouth said, "Okay." Which is about how those two generally operate together, he thought forlornly.

He'd worked the Thursday two-to-six, and sleeplessness made him feel soggy and gritty behind the eyes and put a sorrowful taste of cigarettes and coffee in the back of his throat. He kept feeling, as he walked the block and a half from his rented room to his boss's house, that he needed to wash his hands.

It was a cold, bright day. A recent snow, partly melted, had frozen over again. The air smelled of refrigerated sea muck. This seaside dampness seemed to lurk, staler and halfway warm, in the hall behind the double doors of Ray Sands's house as he let English in. The guest was embarrassed because Sands was all dressed up—that is, not much more than he usually was, but his suit was dark and he wore gold cuff links. With discomfort, as if shedding some part of himself, English took off his leather jacket. He wore a white shirt and a necktie.

"Good of you to come, Lenny!"

English had never seen Ray Sands even mildly cheerful before; it's fair to say he'd never seen his employer even abysmally cheerful. But nothing was as usual today. Instead of going left through sliding doors into the messy office, where Sands generally lectured English on equipment, standing still before him while English sat on the stool for people being photographed, today Sands took his dinner guest through the sliding doors on the right, into his home, where everything was tinkly and rich. Intricate white lace draped the tables. The floorboards shone deeply. In the windows crystal prisms dangled so that faint rainbows stained the gauzy curtains. And on the dining-room table were silver goblets, and a big silver tureen in which reflections lay like brilliant postage stamps. English was surprised. He'd assumed that all retired police detectives were dead broke.

"This is beautiful," he told Sands.

Too low to hear clearly, one of WPRD's rich-voiced afternoon classical announcers spoke from a sound system on shelves against the wall. A mild spicy odor had found its way out of the kitchen, which lay toward the back of the house.

"Thank you," Sands said. He was still smiling, displaying a very plastic-looking set of false teeth. "Can we get you a drink, Lenny? We have apple juice and cranberry juice. Or maybe you'd like to join me in a beer?" He was already heading for the kitchen.

"Sure, yes, I'd like a beer," English said.

The furniture was white and stuffed and printed with a pink-and-blue floral design. All of it looked brand new. Even as he was admiring it, Mrs. Sands revealed herself to be the robot caretaker of all this immaculateness, rattling and clucking through with a yellow square of cheesecloth, saying, "Hello. Hello. Hello."

English said, "Hi, Mrs. Sands."

The old woman ignored his greeting. She appeared to be

searching for dust, fussing over square micrometers where maybe some of it had landed. She was still preparing the scene. She seemed to be under the impression more guests were coming, but nobody else ever came.

Ray Sands poured beer from a can into a big frosted glass mug as he walked out of the kitchen. "Lenny, my wife, Grace. This is Lenny English, Grace."

At that instant Grace looked at English with narrowed eyes and said, "William."

"Leonard," English corrected her. "Lenny."

His employer handed over the mug of beer, and English raised it in a kind of toast, but Sands hadn't gotten one for himself after all. English smiled at him, and Sands nodded, and Grace, who seemed frozen now and terribly alert, said to English, "The lawn. And somebody they should fix the front screen. It should be fixed immediately." She was apprising anyone within hailing distance.

"The front screen?" English said.

"Lenny, why don't you sit down?" Sands asked.

English hadn't pegged it as the type of furniture you actually sat on. He put a very tiny portion of his rear end on the edge of the nearest overstuffed chair, resting his beer mug on his knee and holding it by its handle.

"Wow," he said, "it's really a beautiful day, isn't it?"

He wanted to smoke, but there were no ashtrays in sight. While he was thinking of the next thing to say, he drank down his entire beer.

Grace headed back to the kitchen. "Lint," she said. "Marks on the walls. Fingerprints everywhere." She walked sideways.

"A lovely day," her husband agreed.

Then English was lost, and he wanted to go home. Not to his room with the unmade bed and the picture of John F. Kennedy on the wall, but to his family's farmhouse in Prairie, Kansas, and to his childhood, and to his dead mother and father.

* * *

Grace stayed in the kitchen with the food, which turned out to be roast beef, while Sands and English talked, fairly easily, about things having to do with WPRD. They named names, recalled episodes, chuckled over the mistakes of others. Sands gave English all the beer he wanted, and English found he wanted a lot. English asked Sands about the complicated business of getting a radio station started in a small town. How happy he was when Sands decided to lay out all the details for him, applications, permits, licenses, appearances before boards of idiots and commissions of dunderheads, so that for his part he only had to nod and go, "Oh, really?" or "Wow, fascinating," or "Oh, I had no idea."

The hostess ran a race between the kitchen and her big dining table, faster and faster, moving a mountain of food one plateful at a time and continually talking to herself: "*That's* not where you go. You go *here*, and *you* go *here*, and where do *you* supposed to go, where do *you* supposed to go?"

She was a mystery to English. Throughout the dinner—which was very good, he thought, and she evidently had no trouble concocting things among burners and timers and bells that jangled a person's mind—Grace would fog over and leave the world around her, but then suddenly grow sharp and decisive about issues that just weren't real. When she said something crazy, Sands was deaf. When she talked sense, he responded as if absolutely charmed.

"How is your place?" he asked English. "Your apartment."

"Oh," English said, "it's very nice. It's not an apartment, exactly, more like a room. Everybody's very nice."

"Who's nice?" Grace said.

"I mean the people around me, the other roomers."

"You get to know them?" She leaned forward with an interest that seemed quite false.

"Well, you know—they come and go, I guess. But there's

two or three who've been there as long as I have. We say hello, we sit in the foyer down there and talk sometimes." This was a lie.

"You should get to know your neighbors," Grace said. She was about to wipe her hands on her apron, and then, apparently just realizing that she was wearing it, she pushed her chair back, stood up, and reached around behind her back to untie it, clawing upward at the bow behind her neck with some small alarm. On the front of her apron was the slogan *When It's Smokin' It's Cookin' and When It's Black It's Done*.

Ray Sands dabbed at his lips with his napkin and then said, "Grace. Here. Here." He stood up and loosened the bow for her. They both sat back down. Grace was still wearing her apron, and now she wiped her hands across the breast of it.

English said, "This is—*wonderful* stuff, Grace. Really. I didn't expect to get a home-cooked meal any time soon."

"Thank you very, very much," she said.

"We knew you'd been on your own all month, so we thought we'd better have you over," Sands told him. "I realize your schedule doesn't give you much chance to get acquainted around town."

"Well, I just have to thank you," English said, suddenly actually feeling grateful. "It's a really nice gesture."

"Doesn't Polly—what's her name, now?"

"Polly—I can't remember her last name," English said. Polly was one of the receptionists at WPRD.

"Right, yes. Doesn't she live in the same rooming house?"

"I've never seen her around there."

"Maybe it's another one," Sands decided. He seemed unaware that his wife had stopped eating anything and was now staring at English with a kind of sinister, amused recognition—one thief to another.

"A nice lady," Grace said. "I like to know her."

"She's really a very nice person," Ray Sands agreed.

"Right," English said. "I'm sure she's a very nice person."

"I mean take the time." Grace was still looking at him with a smoky knowledge in her eyes. "I mean really know her," she said. "Really."

"Well," Ray Sands said. "And isn't there some dessert?"

This question pulled the rug right out from under her. "Dessert?" she said.

"I believe you've got some dessert for us?"

"Dessert."

"Yes, you do."

"I do," she said. She seemed to be travelling through a long tunnel to reach this dinner conversation. "And I got something else!" She stood up and took off her apron without any trouble and went, taking the tiny steps of a bulky old woman, through the living room and out through the sliding doors. Her dress was gay and printed with flowers, like the upholstery she passed. English saw that she wore knee stockings rolled down to her ankles and huge black shoes that tied with laces. He heard her going up the stairs: *clump*, clump; *clump*, clump, getting both feet firmly on each stair step before trying the next one.

Outdoors, the sunlight was leaving the world. Ray Sands walked through the living room and dining room, turning on the lamps.

Now English had no more polite remarks to deliver. He watched the dregs of dinner grow cold while Sands went into the kitchen and came out with some ice cream in three tapered sundae dishes, and three long spoons, keeping pretty quiet himself.

By the clumping of Grace's big black shoes, she was just overhead; now she was coming down the stairs again, and now she was back in the living room, carrying a green gift-wrapped package just about the right size—English was trying to guess

—for a truly massive cigar, and in her other hand a color photograph in a gold frame. Grace set the picture on the table, right in front of a chair, as if its subject were joining them for dessert: a young man with a fat face, a mustache, and clear blue eyes. He wore a hunter's red cap.

She put the gift before her husband.

"How wonderful!" Sands said. "And I've got something for you, Grace."

Hidden behind the couch he had a fair-sized package wrapped in alabaster gift paper with shiny red stripes on it and a green bow tied by a professional. He set it before her and they both opened these gifts with a thunderstorm of paper and appropriate small cries of thanks. Grace's was an espresso coffeepot. Mr. Sands got an engine for an electric train.

Now English was afraid he'd overlooked some custom of exchange. "I'm sorry I didn't bring any presents for you guys. In Kansas we don't give presents for New Year's, not that I know of."

"It's not a Massachusetts custom, either. But it happens to be our forty-second anniversary."

"Our son," Grace said, pointing at the picture sitting across the table from English.

"We give thanks to God," Sands said, "by giving gifts to each other."

English couldn't believe his ears.

"We can't give anything to God," Grace explained, "so we give gifts to each other."

"That's—really great," he told them both, not sure to what the hell he himself was referring.

"Bud got a personal friendship with Bishop Andrew." It seemed she was talking to the photograph. "The Bishop!"

"We're not going to help you with the dishes," Sands let her know. "I'm going to show Lenny my trains."

Grace said, "He gonna show you the *trains*."

"Oh, good. Good," English said.

"We'll be back down in a minute."

"Oh," Grace said, "good."

Sands didn't give him a tour of the upstairs, which English didn't want to see anyway. Instead, he took English directly to a tiny room filled with his electric train set and switched on a hooded lamp hanging, somewhat like an oppressive sun, over a landscape set on plywood and held up by sawhorses, with a little margin of space to walk around it in. The room smelled like wood.

As Sands put his new engine on the track and sent it whirling around the circuit, a figure eight with an S in the middle of each circle, English got the notion that WPRD was really just an extension of his employer's zeal for such contraptions. Sands didn't treat his train set like a toy. He was calm and scientific, making sure everything worked, track switches and so forth, before he hooked a few other cars to the engine.

"I've had this setup for twenty-five years," Sands said.

Now Sands let him turn the dial up and down on the transformer, making the train go fast and slow.

"We've been in this house, I guess, oh, seven years," Sands estimated for him.

Rather than feeling the mild interest or mild boredom he usually experienced when faced with other people's stupid passions, English felt his heart rising in his throat. Now that they were alone, he wanted to ask Sands what he thought they were doing, spying on innocent citizens.

The only light in the room shone down on the train. The train hissed and clicked over the track past minuscule barnyards and brief main streets—church, post office, general store—bounded at either end by nothing. It went over a bridge where it was summer and through a blue-and-white mountain where it was winter. English found that if he kept his vision narrowed to clock nothing but this journey alongside little cows and tiny sheep and miniature frozen townspeople and farmers, it was almost as much fun as a ride on an actual train. The disappointing part was coming around again to find the figures always in the middle of the same drama, over and over. On the other hand, he saw how that might sometimes be a comfort to a person's mind.

Sands took over the controls and showed him how to back the train into a siding and under a water tank without any water in it. Then Sands put some water from a dropper into the engine's smokestack, and plopped in a white pill from a bottle he kept in a leather box beneath the table. As he sent the train on its way now, it gave out puffs of white smoke; also, he pushed a button that made it whistle.

Although English knew it was his sacred duty as Sands's hireling to resent him, he saw that his boss was no monster. Just like his train, Sands checked through a set world, one circumscribed by the scratchy records of his radio station, and the dull shimmer of the backdrop curtain in his studio, and his demented wife's dusting and polishing of totally false memories—"We don't have any children," he told English at one point. "That picture is one of my nephew. He lives in the Philippines"—and it was Sands's job to step out of this zone now and then only to bear witness to adultery or to ascertain that missing persons were truly and forever lost. "Bishop Andrew," he said, "has never visited me. I don't know where she gets her ideas. I don't know what's wrong with her."

This was too intimate for English. The threat of a sudden unmasking, of revelations so embarrassing he couldn't stand them, got him onto the subject he'd been afraid to raise. "Mr. Sands. Don't you ever wonder about what we do?"

Sands glanced at him and then was reabsorbed by his train.

"I mean—I heard you talking about God, and"—English was nervous, couldn't get his thoughts straight—"how does that tie in with the nature of our work, is what I'm asking about."

"It's a tough job," Sands said, turning off his train.

"I feel bad about spying around on Marla Baker," English said.

"It's a very difficult business."

These sideways answers made English feel weak. "Do you have any idea what kind of information I'm gathering here? I mean, for what purpose? Is it legal stuff? Is it a divorce thing, or what?"

"Judgments as to the *kinds* of information are things we just don't make. What use the client makes of it, whether these things are good or bad—well, your best bet is to stop following that line of thought. Stop thinking. Look at it this way. We deal in information. Any great involvement in what we're passing along would be like the mailman opening your letters for his own amusement. Try and see yourself in a role like the mailman's."

"This woman's sexual preference is going to be used against her."

"That's a fair assumption."

"You want to be a part of that?"

"Things are occurring. You're recording those things and listening to those things, and passing the information along."

"Well, the information I'm passing along to you right now is, I think this woman's sex life is going to be used against her."

"I've already stated I'm cognizant of that." To English he seemed so dry. He was like paper. His skin, everything.

But Sands wasn't just a case of personal emptiness, English could see that. He had some inner power to be mild, it showed in the way he dealt with Grace. He accepted her blandly and totally. English saw how you could love somebody like that. After a number of years none of the usual things would matter.

It was hard to come up with a judgment against one or two activities of an electric train enthusiast who knew how to love without hope.

And so his disappointment in himself, for abetting Sands in his spy life, couldn't be too firm or entire. He didn't know what to think.

That night, after he'd said goodbye and gone home and done nothing for a while, English sat down in the overstuffed chair with a loose-leaf notebook and a pen. Opening the notebook to the middle, he wrote across the top line of the page

You don't know me

and looked at those words for a while. He began to write again, stopped writing, leapt up, rifled his top drawers, and found an envelope and two aging, brittle stamps. Then he sat down and finished the note he'd started.

You don't know me, therefore I don't feel a need to tell you my name. I just thought you should know that your husband is having you followed by a private investigator around town. He's been getting information about your life.

English wrote three more words—"Happy New Year"—but crossed them out. He read the note. As far as he could see, it delivered what he wanted to get across. He tore the page from the notebook. He folded it into its white envelope. He put a stamp on it and walked five blocks, thinking that he didn't want to move people and change people, failing to think how they might be moving and changing him, to the post office, where he dropped the envelope in a box out front. It was his first use of this post office.

1981

Within a week his subject, Marla Baker, had moved away. English's duties as a private eye were nil, but his boss, Ray Sands, found more work for him at WPRD.

Essentially, on the production end of things, at WPRD he did just what he'd been doing in the cold midnights outside Marla Baker's windows: he taped other people's conversations. But now he was right in the room with them, they saw him, he was no spy. After they went away he edited out embarrassing slips of the tongue and overlong silences, dubbed themes and intros and outros onto either end, and tossed down the reels in the Special Programs in-basket. English found it all pretty dull stuff—half-hour chats between WPRD's big-yawn personalities and their baldly uninteresting guests, who happened to be goofball artists, authors of books about birds and clams, or has-beens the listener would be surprised to learn were not yet dead. Sometimes English helped train new staff arrivals. These had to be frequent in order to keep up with the departures.

One new arrival English worked with was a Portuguese man named Smith, not an unusual name among Portuguese fishing families, it turned out, because many of them had adopted the names of their British captains when they'd first jumped ship on the Cape and taken up their lives here, far from home. All these name changes had happened in the murky past, but to English this gentleman sounded as if he'd just stepped onto the pier. Maybe he'd come here two days ago and only then adopted the name his American relatives had used for generations; English really couldn't guess, and there was no finding out, either, because Smith had his own way of trying to communicate, and it didn't work. Over the air this wasn't a problem, as he broadcast in his native language.

Around the records and equipment the new man had a hunched, respectful deliberateness of which English approved. Smith was portly. But he had a blubbery quality, too. English imagined they still called him by his childhood nickname around the house. English sympathized when sometimes Smith forgot and left the switch for the announcer's mike in the wrong position—it was supposed to be On when he was talking and Off when he wasn't, and it sounded simple enough, but everybody got it wrong sometimes at first, trying to do two or three things at once and very aware the whole time that people were out there listening and possibly considering you some kind of a geek, or worse. When Smith made this little error he invariably looked as if he was about to surrender all control. "Oh! I'm making, iss—diss wrong! Too wrong!" He had a bald head, doctorly reading glasses he was always donning out of nowhere, a fringe of hair more literally a fringe than English would have hoped to see anywhere outside a cartoon, and a checked golfing cap that he deeply cherished. "I'm wear a het on my had," he told English, "because I'm don't"—he rubbed his smooth head—"you see? Iss bowled." He displayed his checked cap. "You see?" He wore his wristwatch on the outside of his sweater sleeve, set off like fireworks against the orange knit. "Issa new—brain you," he liked to tell everyone. There was a digital clock on the announcer's board and a wall clock on the wall, but when he wanted the correct time, Smith always went into a huddle with his watch.

On his first delirious night at the controls, he opened his program with a 45 rpm recording of a Portuguese orchestra doing their country's national anthem, after which they played the American national anthem, managing to make them both sound exactly the same. Next Smith read the intro to his show from a little yellow card he held before his face with a trembling hand, but his mike was still switched to Off. When he was done reading he turned it to On and desperately asked English a few incomprehensible questions that went out over the air.

While Smith read his introduction to each song from one of his yellow cards, pushed the button that set it spinning, and then cued up the next record on the other turntable with the sweating vertigo of a person under fire, one of the newsmen— for English's money there were too many newspeople around the place—taped a phone interview in the hall closet with a Vietnam veteran about Agent Orange. Acoustically the closet was the only place, because the phone company had refused to wire the production studio as long as the station was in arrears. "And why did they do that!" the newsman was saying. He felt he had to shout. "What was it exactly that they told you!" Smith liked to keep the speakers in the studio turned up high. The music of his homeland carried him away. He was moved to tears by a ballad, a typical one of tootly violins and a passion-wrung male voice begging violently in Portuguese, except when every now and then it sobbed in English, "Hoppy birthday— to you—my dolling . . . ." "It sounds like you were getting the runaround here, am I right?" the newsman cried. Smith looked at his watch, at the wall clock, at the digital clock. He was getting alarmed. The timing on his play list must not have been working out. Time was his conqueror. When the song was done he talked in a choked, halting fashion to the audience, holding no yellow cards now, clutching the microphone by its neck. English sensed he was confessing his incompetence and apologizing for his whole life.

Before too long, the interview in the closet was over. Berryman, the reporter, was leaning against the glass window of the announcer's studio looking drained of blood. English motioned to him to come on into the studio, though there was hardly any room, if only to stop him breathing on the glass like a kid who needed a nickel. Berryman was tall and pale, with the look, to English's eye, of a real juicer, just the kind of washout you'd expect to locate in one of the closets around here. Everyone at WPRD was either just starting out in the radio business or completely finished. There was nobody in between. "I just got fired," Berryman said.

"Bullshit."

"No. No. Ray Sands was just in here, and he fired me."

"You must've misheard him. He must've not recognized you and he must've said, 'You're hired.' "

Smith turned and asked a question, but now he couldn't say anything intelligible because his bald head was tuned to Portuguese. He might have been requesting permission to explode the station. English nodded and smiled, rather than make him feel misunderstood.

"What'd he fire you for?" English asked Berryman.

"He was standing in the fucking hallway," the reporter said. "He was waiting for me when I came out of the fucking closet. He said the fucking interview was hogwash. He pronounced my fucking fate."

"Hogwash? What has he got against hogwash? I mean, hey"—English pointed at the day's small stack of Special Programs tapes—"Baba Ram Dass. Check this out, Berryman—'The Nicest People on Cape Cod.' And anyway, when did Sands even get a chance to hear the tape?"

"He didn't hear this tape," Berryman said. "This is part two. He heard part one. He heard it last week, on the air." Berryman held out the tape, a cassette. "This is part two. He doesn't want to hear part two."

Smith, trying to get one record stopped and another started, now developed the notion that he was being asked to play this tape. "No, no, no. I'm play music en rahdio—very"—he went through a bunch of gestures that got nothing across, picked up his play list, and ran his finger down along the titles—"I'm make diss, to will be—very *nice*."

"I don't believe anybody ever got fired before at WPRD," English told Berryman.

"He said the whole report was hogwash. I mean, as if he actually gives two shits."

English was hardly paying this chat any mind—mainly he kept his eye on Smith, communicating wordlessly with the new arrival through nods of the head and the way he held his body, letting Smith know he was still there, still helping. And yet what passed between him and Berryman turned out to be important. Things were coming swiftly into his mind along various paths, like spears. But— Fired, tough luck for the unlucky, was all he thought at the time. "Well, Berryman, I'll buy you a drink," he told the ex-reporter.

"I happen to be drunk already," Berryman said, "but something like that might be arranged."

"Right when this shift is over. How about a cup of coffee?"

"Fuck you," Berryman said. "Hogwash."

They were sitting in a basement place on the East End, Berryman's idea of a bar. English preferred a spot about a half block away that had brighter lights and a little chromium. But tonight it was Berryman's party.

Smith was with them and seemed to grasp that he and English

were consoling Berryman for the negligible loss of his job. Smith's face was expressive. English had never seen anybody before who actually "furrowed" his brow. Smith pushed his lips toward the rim of his glass like the bell of a honeysuckle, and what he did was, he quaffed.

"So tell me about this tape," English said, he hoped sympathetically, to Berryman.

"But the point of it is that there's nothing to *tell*, English. 'Nam vets, Agent Orange, it's last year's stuff. But a phone interview has a certain immediacy, so you do a phone interview. What does Sands want, a big scoop? We can't even make a long-distance call, man, because his credit's trashed."

English was ready to get going. It was a bar with dim lights and a faint stink, where the big mistake was a rug that harbored the damp. The customers drank resolutely. It wasn't eleven yet, but he saw men and women already forming tender alliances of the kind that had to be hurried through before they rotted —his kind, as a matter of fact. After a while he couldn't stop himself. "Let me tell you about this woman I got the hots for."

"Are you buying?" Berryman said.

"Who's been buying so far?"

"Mr. English. One of the gainfully employed."

"Smith." English waggled his empty glass.

Smith caught the bartender's eye with a raised finger, then stirred the finger around among the three of them.

"Her name is Leanna Sousa," English said. "Leanna Sousa, Leanna Sousa, Leanna Sousa." He'd never been able to drink —two was his limit, maybe one.

"I didn't get the young lady's name," Berryman said.

"Leanna Sousa?" Smith said. "Sousa?"

"Right. Yeah. Sousa—Portuguese."

"Diss a lady that she have one hotel? Sousa Hotel?"

"We didn't get around to what she owns."

"You guys are so close. You go so deep," Berryman said.

"It wasn't that kind of conversation."

" 'It?' Are we talking about one fucking conversation with the dyke owner of a dykes-only hotel in one of the homosexual capitals of the world? What religion are you?"

"Catholic."

"You're about to suffer worse than a Jew."

"I'm crazy about her. Her hair is pure black."

"Oh," Berryman said, "oh. Why didn't you say so in the first place?"

"If I could get you to see what I see in her, then I wouldn't feel so alone."

"You're not alone, English. I'm right here. Buy me a drink."

"You're right there with the snotty remarks. You're above it all. But you know what they say? Empty people float upward."

"My glass is almost empty," Berryman pointed out.

"Diss woman," Smith said. "Because she—the family feel terrible."

"Yeah, I can dig it," English said. "She's non-traditional."

"She's a dyke," Berryman said. "That's okay for her, that's okay for me, but it's not okay for you. I've seen these reclamation projects. I've seen them fail." He crossed his eyes, trying to look at an ice cube while he drained his glass of bourbon. "Big deal."

"Reclamation? I wasn't talking about reclamation. Hey, I would never ask a woman to change herself for me."

"For Christ's sake, English. You don't have to snow me. We're none of us gentlemen here."

"I wasn't snowing you." But he was. This fact soured his view of those around him.

Smith put his hand on English's arm as English got up to leave.

"You're not taking off?" Berryman said.

"I am. I think I'll go listen to your farewell tape. Part one."

"It turns my stomach to see people have two drinks and then just . . . leave," Berryman said.

Smith made a point of shaking English's hand, taking it in both of his, European-style.

It was only that English was curious about Ray Sands. Because English worked two jobs for him, to English he was actually two bosses. English would have admitted that, around WPRD, he himself had a voice in the universal shock and disgust at the avarice, cowardice, and stupidity of the boss. But as Sands's only assistant in the detective trade, English had seen his house, eaten his roast beef, talked with his prematurely senile old wife, and played with his toy electric train; and the underground of Ray Sands, the lightless shafts—how deep did they go? Even on a sunny afternoon, standing outside his home in a blue parka and one of those hats that dads wear fishing, trimming his hedges with electric clippers, as English had found him doing one day, Sands seemed very mysterious and almost invisible. Maybe it was just that he was one of those people who'd been grownups when English was a child—shrouded, and heavy-laden with matters English hoped would go away before he had to learn about them. Anyway, why shouldn't he be interested?—as when once he'd looked through his father's bureau drawer and found more silver change there than a child knew existed. Looking at it he'd wondered so hard what it must be like to own so much shiny money that he'd stolen it all. Not that he meant to steal anything from Ray Sands. But he wanted to spy on the person he was spying for.

There were signs on the second floor indicating a radio station was housed here, but the linty rooming-house atmosphere of burned-out naked light bulbs and eerie trash in the hallway would get anybody thinking that these placards—WPRD 103

FM and SHHH BROADCAST IN PROGRESS!—were holdouts from some unrecollected age, like the one on the stairs that said CAUTION—FRESH PAINT!, a claim that was, by his reckoning, more than one hundred percent false. In the hallway there were two doors to WPRD, and he took the first into the station's front office. That was one-third of the place, and the rest was the production studio and the announcer's studio and the bathroom. No janitor had ever been at work here. They looked like the premises of an outfit that was almost ready to be inaugurated or one that had very recently closed.

He was a little surprised to find Berryman's phone interview right where it should have been in the tape library, which was really a closet in the front office of WPRD. Part of him had expected it to be missing.

He listened to it through headphones in the production studio. It was just your average interview, nothing remarkable about it that English could see, aside from the awful peaks-and-valleys volume—Berryman shouted in his ear, while the replies from Wilkinson, the head of 'Nam Vets for Cape Cod, sounded like a small bee in a jar. Side effects of Agent Orange, Wilkinson said, were turning up in the veterans who'd used this herbicide in Vietnam. Wilkinson spied a conspiracy to resist all the evidence that this chemical was dangerous. Everybody was in on it, the American Legion, the Vets Administration, the President, Congress, the John Birch Society, other right-wing outfits. "Dow Chemical and those guys," he said. "Any chemical company, whether they manufacture it or not. Insurance companies don't want this information passed around. People are still using it right here, there's chemically related stuff being used along the roadside, right out here on Route 6. The right-wingers, these poor suckers the Truth Infantry—you better edit that out," he said.

"Edit what out?" Berryman asked him loudly.

"Don't you know who you're working for?" Wilkinson asked. "Edit that out, too." But Berryman had edited nothing out.

Ray Sands was flat on his back. "Today you're the investigator," he told English, who was feeling, for reasons he couldn't put a finger on, proud to be admitted to the sick man's bedroom. The room didn't smell of medicine or a stale convalescence. Sands was dressed for business in a shirt and tie, but instead of a suit coat and street shoes, he wore a quilted blue robe and bright yellow slippers. He lay propped up by pillows on the perfectly made bed in a sunny atmosphere, while English got the idea that any taint of illness here emanated from himself.

He neglected to take the white envelope Sands was holding out to him. "I don't know the first thing about missing persons."

"You've done it before," Sands said. "You did a fine job of work on the Charlie Hendler thing."

"But really all I did was drive to the Hyannis bus station. I mean, it was just a case of staying between the lines on Route 6."

"This is the address," Sands said, giving the white envelope a shake. "Go there, talk to Mr. and Mrs. Twinbrook, and get anything he left behind with numbers on it—address book, bills, letters if they'll let you take them, diaries, appointment books, any such material. Bring it to me, and we'll go over it together."

"But what do I ask these people? What kind of information is supposed to help? See, I don't know that stuff."

"There's really nothing to it, Lenny. Ask them what you'd ask if they were the parents of a friend, an old friend you were trying to track down. Who does he know? What does he do? Where does he go, what places did he frequent, where would you find some friend of his or some acquaintance who might have further information? A good deal of the time, you'll find they know just where the person went, but they don't want to make certain of it themselves. The daughter's run off with the gardener, and so on. In this case, the son."

"I'm not ready for this."

"I'm here to assist you. I'm your assistant now. Just talk to the Twinbrooks and just keep bringing them around to the subject of their son. If they mention people, places, or numbers, write those down." He wiped his lips with the back of his hand—it wasn't like him. "Names and numbers. Names and numbers. Make of car, year of manufacture, license plate, passport number, age, height, weight. Recent photos. What we're going to do is compile a list of facts about this man, and a list of people for you to contact, and a list of places for you to visit . . ."

Now his boss seemed to be at rest, or in thought. English was sitting in a stuffed chair by the bed and didn't mind waiting forever, except that he wanted a cigarette. He hoped Sands didn't have cancer or something like that. What if it was cancer? And the guy didn't even smoke.

"There's a trick to all this," Sands resumed, "that's what I want to say. When you're talking with people, especially the strangers you'll be interviewing later, your attitude has to be that you just don't care. Your only interest in life is to gather information that will locate. You're blind to anything that might compromise the people you're talking to. Anything that's illegal or strange. Nothing matters to you—that's what gets people to open up. You want names and numbers, not stories. Take the same attitude you did when you were working for the police in Kansas. You don't care, you don't judge."

"Couldn't you just phone them? The Twinbrooks, I mean? Couldn't you just give them a call?"

"I intend to do that, if it becomes necessary." Sands melted back into himself visibly. Now he really did appear ill—holding a precious motionlessness on the bed, he looked out at English as if from a cage. "I've got to take care of this respiratory condition."

English accepted the envelope bearing the penciled address of the couple who couldn't find their son.

What do you mean, he wanted to ask, by respiratory condition? But Sands was old. It might be serious. English decided he didn't want the details.

On his way out, he paused at the bottom of the stairs and stood at the door to Sands's office and photography studio and looked in. The stool stood before the dark backdrop curtain, a tripod without a camera on it stood before the stool, Sands's desk stacked neatly with the paper of commerce waited before the window where the curtains lay wide open, admitting daylight and fearing no examination. Of course, he told himself. What would I be looking for anyway? A swivel chair addressed the desk and was occupied only by a pale green tennis ball. He left, avoiding Grace Sands, whom he heard around the corner of the opposite door, puttering in her living room.

Mrs. Twinbrook turned out to be small, and she didn't look quite right in a turtleneck sweater. "I hadn't expected such a— youthful detective." Her face was heavily powdered and looked frozen. It had been the business of the years to make her features heavy and changeless, but her voice was kind.

More than once, on TV, English had seen just such a woman in just such a crisis, and the TV woman had always worked something around in her hands, a pen, a scarf, her own blue-veined fingers, but Mrs. Twinbrook only gestured, maybe a little weakly, with hers. "This is the dayroom, that's the parlor," she said, moving past these rooms too swiftly to let them be anything but names in his ears.

"Let me show you the lower level, Mr. Sands." She led English beyond the dayroom and down some stairs into what constituted a whole extra house. They skirted a row of rooms like compartments on a train—a study, some sort of sewing room, a bedroom—each with a picture window looking out on a garden filled with sculptures in the snow. It was thawing, and a big rock and a birdbath, and the stands for delicate metal works of art, were edged around with the black wet of the winter lawn.

"Actually, I'm not Mr. Sands. I'm Leonard English, I'm just the assistant. I'm the one you talked to on the phone yesterday."

"Oh. I thought you looked awfully young. I'd understood Mr. Sands was retired, and I—naturally—" At the door of the last room, she held him off. "And where is Mr. Sands?"

"Taken ill. He'll be going over the information and planning my moves."

"Good."

"I stopped by the address you gave Mr. Sands," he told her. "The lady next door hasn't seen him lately. But she says somebody's come by once or twice—a man, she said. And there's no mail in his mailbox."

"I have his mail," Mrs. Twinbrook said. "Gerald's been picking it up—Gerald Senior, my husband. There's not much."

"If you don't mind, I'd like to take a look at it. I don't know, return addresses might tell us something."

"Of course. Remind me before you go."

Now was the time to start asking questions, but he couldn't bring the words out.

"This is my son's studio. He works here a couple of days each week."

It was small and looked more a place of storage than a place of work. Paintings, most of them no larger than dinner trays, were stacked against the walls, and above them hung more paintings. Cardboard boxes filled with rags and paper, and paint-smeared glass jars, each with a shock of brushes, cluttered the floor. There was hardly anywhere to stand or walk. The big window gave it all a sense of light and space that was false— an element of dust, a museum quality, lay on the air. By the window stood a large collapsible table with drawings and pencils all over it.

"Does he actually paint here?" English was sidestepping objects to get to the table, but he was distracted by the paintings hanging on the walls on either side of him. Now that he was in the room, a tincture of oils took hold of his breath. "Did he do these pictures in this room?" One of the paintings suggested Miami Beach, as English imagined that place, with tall buildings overlooking a shoreline blotched with umbrellas.

With every further statement, he felt his next one would be a confession of his complete inability to know where to begin.

"Jerry paints outdoors," Mrs. Twinbrook said. "I believe he sketches in here, or rethinks portions of his canvases. He's very, very meticulous. He believes in the absolute power of detail. I want you to look at this man's elbow." She laid a coral fingernail against the brown flesh of a sunbather in the scene he'd been studying. All the figures were simply rendered. To English the elbow looked like the joint of a stove pipe. There were no faces on this beach. The half-dozen bathers in the foreground were all looking away. "That elbow is *leaned on*, wouldn't you have to agree?" The man reclined in an oval of umbrella shade, his maroon bathing suit slashed by the sunshine.

English was at a loss when it came to elbows, but he had no trouble recognizing, in some of these paintings, the eerie Cape light. On overcast days the sun might be just a brighter patch in a grey sky, but its effect would smolder anyway on the hills and occasional white buildings of the countryside and on the water, so that the world seemed to lie straight under a blowtorch; and yet things cast no shadows. English had guessed that the light collected somehow on the waters and made a brightness in the air, even under clouds—just in the air, a brightness not otherwise locatable. Jerry Twinbrook had caught that light and let it fall through these paintings. "I've been to this place." English pointed at the two landscapes flanking the one of Miami Beach. "Herring Cove, right? Just outside P-town."

"You see," she said.

English could only nod. See what? He was supposed to be asking questions, but she expected him to pay attention to this stuff first. He felt sorry for Mrs. Twinbrook, because she looked, by her clenched interest in this room, like bricked-over despair. She herself had the same black-and-white quality as her walled back yard. Her turtleneck sweater was thick and snowy, but her hair was a shining, artificial black and her skin was dark— as a matter of fact, it came to English, she was suntanned.

"I'm just taking all this in." He tried to sound like an expert, a genius of the faintest trails. "Now, these look like they were painted indoors." At the level of his knees, various interior scenes leaned against the walls. He saw what she'd meant about elbows—the people in these somber pictures were mysterious, seated around tables or standing in doorways, and they had no faces, only blank ovals, but in the way they held their bodies the people were alive.

English looked at the drawings on the table, carefully moving each one from on top of the others so as not to smear them or disturb something—evidence maybe. He wasn't a judge of art, but these seemed to be only doodles, geometrical shapes scratched on rough heavy paper, studies of chairs and torsos, practice at the cast of a shadow or the angle of a view. None of it was information. He was wasting her money as he handled these sketches. And yet he felt a prickly discomfort, as if he were learning more than he wanted to know about this lost person.

"You see," Mrs. Twinbrook said, as if English would grasp what eluded her husband, "my son has a gift."

Her husband had been driving away just as English had arrived, and he'd paused only long enough to give English an impression of a pink, shaven face as he'd rolled down the window of his Lincoln to say, "Are you the detective?" English had gotten out of his Volkswagen and started across the gravel driveway toward him, but already Mr. Twinbrook was rolling up his window. "He can't paint and he's probably good for nothing, but we love him. Find him."

"I will," English had said. I can't, he had thought.

Once back in Provincetown, English parked his Volkswagen behind his building and walked along Commercial, toward his bank, before he returned to Ray Sands. On the darkening street, where lamps were starting to take over the business of making things visible but where a little daylight clung to the air, English watched two boys going home late from school. It was almost Valentine's Day, but Halloween was what they were talking about, and one of them suddenly tossed down his books and raised his arms to demonstrate, for the other, how big a pumpkin had been. This pantomime had a curious effect on English—he was amused and heartbroken, watching this kid posing like a ballerina, making a circle the size of a lonely vegetable with his empty arms. The wind blew out to sea, and the air was cold and fresh and so vacant that every object, even the pumpkin that wasn't really there, stood out boldly and seemed to mean something. You are here, he said to God, and then from nowhere came the hope that he was wrong, that the grain of wooden phone poles and the rough stones of the courthouse were taking place on their own, and that nothing would ever be asked of him.

"English! Leonard English!"

It was Berryman hailing him, hanging out the door of a café. "Let me treat you to a coffee and pie! I'm a working man!" The voices of chilly patrons behind him called, "Close the door! Shut the door!"

English was happy for Berryman. "Who made the mistake of hiring you?"

"The archrival—our weekly newspaper." Berryman, for once, looked more alive than dead. He guided English along a path through crowded tables to a booth in the rear. "It's all different nowadays. I load the copy into a word processor. I'm setting the type as I write the story." His eyes were clear; on top of being cheerful, he was sober. "I'm a technologically advanced human being," he said without irony. It was as if his cynicism had crumbled to powder and drifted out of his nature.

"I'm also doing great," English said. "I have a date tomorrow night with Leanna."

Now a little puff of the shed self clouded Berryman's eyes. "Wonderful."

"*She* asked *me*. I stopped by her place, her big hotel there. She's got her own apartment in the back. She sleeps on a water bed."

"I don't want you to confide in me, English. Pardon me," he called to a waitress. "Apple pie and coffee for this pitiful person."

"Nobody's confiding in you. I didn't get *in* the water bed."

"Ask me about my new job, would you?"

"Okay," English said. "What was your biggest story so far?"

" 'Tree Falls in Road.' "

"Far out," English said. "Do go on."

"Never mind," Berryman said. He told the waitress as she set down English's pie and coffee: "My friend here is paying for himself."

"Why didn't you tell me about Leanna? Has she got it made, or what? Stereo, big color TV, water bed—"

"I'm of a generation that doesn't talk about these things."

"Listen—"

"It's unbecoming. How old are you?"

"Listen—"

"It makes my skin crawl. You're too old—"

"Listen: she's got a hot tub. A sixteen-room hotel with a hot tub out back, and no guests. It's the off-season."

"How old are you, English?"

"Old enough. I'm not a virgin. But I think Leanna is."

In Berryman's face the attentiveness, which had been draining away, stopped dead. "You're unbelievable," he told English. "You're crazy." He laughed, a rare thing.

"Point me out somebody who's sane around here."

"You've got no brakes, the cliffs are waiting—"

"This is just how I commonly do it. I just go ahead. It won't kill me."

"Not every time," Berryman said.

English was angered by this voice of reason, but the feeling quickly failed and a damp gloom came down around him in this buzzing restaurant where he felt himself among Germans, strangers, grownups. "It's on you, because I'm broke," he told the reporter, and got up to leave. Struck by a thought, he leaned over the table. "I was wondering," he said. "What's this Truth Infantry thing all about?"

"The who, now?"

"The Truth Infantry. You know."

"I never heard of it." Berryman's face changed and brightened, and he hoisted his chin to greet some new arrivals.

"You lush," English said.

"Only on weekends." Berryman's attention was elsewhere. English shouldered past customers waiting for seats and got to the street.

English was on his way to the bank because he needed cash for his date with Leanna. It was all her idea, she'd been the one to do the asking, and it wasn't right, somehow.

Everything seemed to be reversing itself like that, a woman asking him out, most others ignoring him while the men seemed to look him over, this strange hush at evening, as if it were dawn, and even the buildings seemed to be going in the wrong direction, this small old bank on a shop-lined and window-crowded street by the sea, for instance: every building around here seemed to be receding into the historic past. The wooden floorboards English crossed as he entered the bank must have been two centuries old, but the ceiling was given over to the idea of a contemporary St. Valentine, with glittering silhouette hearts strung across the air and tinsel drooling down. There were candy hearts in plastic cups by the tellers' windows. "Can I have a heart?" English asked, and at the same time the young lady asked him, "Is it cold out?" "What?" they asked each other. "What?"

"You talk first," he said.

"What can I do for you today?" she said.

"I'd like a candy heart, and I'd like one of those counter check things, because I lost my checkbook."

"Oh, you lost it. Have you reported it lost?"

"It isn't really lost," English said. "It's just missing. It has to be in my room someplace."

"Well," she said, kidding around, "then it isn't missing, is it?"

"It must be, if I can't find it," English said.

She laughed, and started punching out a check on her machine. "What's the name on the account?"

"Don't trust this man. Would you sit beside this man on a bus?"

He turned around toward the voice. "Leanna."

"I saw you from the street." She reached past him and lifted a couple of treats from the cup. "Let's go to the movies in Hyannis."

"I thought we were going tomorrow."

"Let's go tonight, too. Let's go both nights."

A signal he couldn't read, something in the hesitation of her hands as she held a tiny sugar heart in the fingers of each and looked completely uncertain about herself for once, made him want to say yes. "I'm supposed to work, but I'll make it quick."

"Oh, are you working at the station tonight?"

"I have to talk to my boss about something. I don't think it'll take too long. I'll pick you up at your place in about an hour."

"Don't eat," she said. "Let's have dinner. I'll let you bullshit me all you want."

English had been surprised to find himself in possession, after a single afternoon on the case, of Jerry Twinbrook's mail—a letter, a bill, and a bank statement. As an interrogator he'd fallen short, getting nothing in the way of names and numbers. Mrs. Twinbrook had wanted to talk only about paintings, mentioning important figures and styles and periods as if they were things he found in the papers every day. She'd seemed as anxious to locate her son in the history of art as she was to find him in time and space. "Maybe I should go back and talk with the father," English suggested to Ray Sands. "The father seemed a little more down-to-earth."

"Don't worry about it," Sands said. "It's typical. There's never any information from the people who suddenly can't find a family member. Nothing in the way of hard facts, in any event. If they don't have documents, they don't have anything." He laid his head back against his stack of pillows. He was dressed in pajamas now, he was pale, there were medicines on the nightstand and a flat dark outside the bedroom windows, in which hovered the reflection of his bedside lamp. "Families communicate a lot less than they think they do," he said.

English stood nervously in the room, went over and closed the curtains without asking. "This one's from an art gallery," he said, handing Sands the envelopes one at a time. "Here's a bill from Blue Cross. And this looks like a bank statement."

"That's the one that tells the tale." Sands opened the bank statement first.

English crossed his hands behind his back and waited, curious to find out how much Jerry Twinbrook made and how much he spent.

But Sands wasn't interested in those numbers. "New England Telephone," he read as he lifted one of Twinbrook's checks up to the light. "Take it." He flipped through others. "A tavern; a tavern"—he held each check close to his face—"same tavern, Walker's Inn; Hammond Office Supply." He turned this last check over. "That's in Marshfield. So are these taverns," he said, consulting the backs of those checks.

English looked at the payment to the phone people: seventy-two dollars. "Where's Marshfield?"

"It's between Boston and the Cape, on the Bay." Sands flipped through more checks. "Phil-Hack Realty, also in Marshfield. This man's bank and his house are in Orleans, but his life seems to take place in Marshfield." He turned the check over again. "Dated January 3." He handed it to English. "Now, nothing is certain, but if you told me you guessed that to be some sort of monthly payment, I'd have to agree."

English was lost. "Monthly payment for what?"

"For real estate, young man. A house, a piece of land. Possibly an apartment, if this agency handles rentals."

"But he lives in Orleans. I stopped in and talked to the neighbors. They know him. He comes and goes. That's where he gets his mail."

"Perhaps he's moved." Sands looked amused.

"Now what?" English said.

"Do as much as you can over the telephone. Call these taverns, call Phil-Hack Realty, see what they have to say about Gerald Twinbrook. You can call the taverns tonight. They'll be open. Use the phone in my office. Make a note of the calls. If you get no help, try the two art galleries."

"What do I say?"

"Identify yourself and tell them you're a detective—not a private detective, a detective. Don't identify your client. Just say you're trying to reach Gerald Twinbrook, Jr., on a routine matter. Give them a description if the name isn't familiar. Did you get a description?"

"His mother says he looks like the people in his paintings and he has brown hair."

"And what do the people in his paintings look like?"

"Tall and skinny, is about all."

"He was in Walker's Inn twice last month, and at this other one, what is it—"

"The Ends."

"At The Ends at least once. They know him, I assume. They cashed his checks."

"I'll talk to them right away," English said.

"Fine. But before you call anyone, find out if by any chance he has a telephone number in Marshfield. It's possible you might be able to call Gerald Twinbrook himself."

"I'm amazed." English was telling the truth. It was something to see this detective indicate the blank space named Gerald Twinbrook by surrounding it with facts—like the pumpkin the school kid had surrounded with his arms, a while ago, on Commercial Street. "I could get to like this job," English told his boss.

"Names and numbers." But Sands didn't look as triumphant as he might have. He waved English away from his sickbed. "Go. Go," he said softly.

"I'll be right back." English was glad to leave.

Downstairs he turned on the overhead light in Sands's office-studio, drew the curtains, and sat down in the swivel chair to play with the tennis ball that had been lying on it while he called the two taverns in Marshfield.

Both bartenders knew Jerry Twinbrook but hadn't seen him in at least a couple of weeks. Evidently he was missing.

English put the tennis ball back where he'd found it and travelled up the stairs to report this news to Sands. But the detective was asleep, with his hands folded over his groin in an attitude that made English feel sorry for him, and English left him alone.

Grace Sands, however, was awake and active. He found her just inside the front door with a feather duster, stroking the two umbrellas that jutted from the ceramic umbrella stand. "I got a million things to do," she was whispering, "a million things. A million." In a worn grey dress with a white scarf tied around her head, she looked like a charwoman.

"Hi again, Grace," English said.

"Bud is sick upstairs," she told him. She'd said these very words on admitting him half an hour ago.

"Yeah, I just got done talking to him. He's looking better."

"I—is he gonna be all right?" Worry crumbled her soft old face. "What am I gonna do?"

"He'll be fine."

In English's perception the lines of power in this household suddenly reversed themselves. He felt the presence of Sands, sick and asleep in his upper chamber, held aloft by the concern of this woman.

And then a curious impulse struck him, an idea he realized he'd been having all along. "Maybe you should go upstairs and see if he needs anything," he suggested to Grace.

"Oh . . ."

He wished he hadn't said it.

"Oh, all right." She looked around like a person hopeless of finding one small item in a huge storehouse.

He wanted to take it all back. "I suppose he's all right," he told her. "Really." But it was the wrong way to put it. Grace was preparing herself for the ascent, growing visibly heavier with the weight of determination. "Maybe," he said, "I can find out if there's something—I could bring it to him, tea or whatever." English was desperate for her not to go now. He'd only wanted to have a look in Sands's desk.

But she didn't seem to hear him and hefted herself upward, one step at a time.

English moved into the office while she was still only halfway up the stairs. He slipped open the desk's center drawer and found pens and pencils, a screwdriver, loose paper clips, a small kitchen knife, two worn gum erasers. In the two file drawers on the right there was nothing to catch his eye—they were just files, what had he expected? There was no file called "Truth Infantry," nothing about "Agent Orange." Everything seemed to be labeled "Correspondence." "Correspondence—Harold & Fine," "Correspondence—State Street Bank." "Correspondence —BPA" turned out to be letters to and from the Boston Policemen's Association.

That drawer was only half full. The lower one held files about John Hancock Insurance, T. Rowe Price investments, correspondence about a prize for the biggest fish, sponsored by the RCEB—Retired City Employees of Boston. A folder labeled ET CETERA was empty.

Behind the folders, in the back of the drawer, were stacked three blue-black American passports: William Michael Pierce, George Terrence Morris, Gregory Arn Shahan. The picture had been pried from each one. English thumbed them through, squatting on his heels by the open drawer, suddenly light-headed and unable to read, and then put them back stained with the sweat of his hands.

Things he'd seen at the movies prodded him to a nerve-racked microscopic study of the drawers he'd opened. Had Sands put a piece of tape or thread across their seams, in the hope of detecting any tampering? He picked up the tennis ball from the swivel chair and rattled it—for God's sake, it was a tennis ball, a tennis ball. In the single left-hand drawer he found two more tennis balls, and a couple of chewy rubber toys with tin bells inside, for pets.

He left fast, and outdoors, as he found a cigarette, he promised the dark street that he'd keep his nose out of other people's desk drawers and other people's business, their phony passport business, or whatever it was.

As he waited in his Volkswagen beside Leanna's building, English rolled down the window to let the cigarette smoke out and let in the chilly smoke of wood stoves in the houses up and down this quaint street of trees. He checked the contents of his billfold and prayed over his gas gauge, that it stay above Empty round-trip. In Leanna's apartment the light went off. The hotel was dark now—three floors of historic wooden architecture, with assorted outbuildings named for famous women, most of them entertainers and none of them saints. "I got about thirty bucks," he told Leanna when she reached the car. "Don't break me."

"It's Dutch treat," she said. "Is money tight?"

"I had car trouble on the way up here in December. The repairs ate up all my savings."

They drove in what was for English a nerve-unraveling silence to that part of Hyannis, fifty miles down the Cape, where two shopping centers faced each other across the highway. "We'll never find this vehicle again," he told her. In the parking lot the million cars of late shoppers diminished from horizon to horizon. In his mind, the Cape's population exploded. He'd thought himself almost alone on this peninsula, but now he felt crowded.

It was almost eight, but all the stores were open. English and Leanna found their way across the random paths of citizens into the mall, past one goods-glutted window after another, and down into a tiny basement restaurant something like a cave. "Are we dealing with Italian or Mexican?" English couldn't tell. Candles in Chianti bottles on the tables and sombreros stuck flat against the walls mixed up his expectations. "It's omni-cuisine," Leanna told him. "Shopping-centeranian, I guess. But the food's wonderful. This is the best table, right here."

"Is there more than one?" His eyes were getting used to the dimness.

He had it in mind to locate a phone and tell Sands that Jerry Twinbrook was well known in Marshfield, a report he felt he'd promised to make quickly, but he got interested in the cocktail menu instead. "One margarita. Just one. *Uno*," he told the waiter, who was elderly and dressed in a black uniform like a miniature cop. "Two," Leanna said. "*Dos*," the waiter said, enjoying himself.

"I have to watch out about how much I drink in this town," English confessed to Leanna. "One of the cops on the late shift gave me a warning."

"When was this?"

"Well, it was the car trouble I said I had. Actually, it was more of a small wreck. The guy said he wouldn't give me a breath test because I wouldn't pass, but he made a few promises about keeping his eye out for me in the future. No telling what shift he's working now."

She looked happy, and covered his hand with hers. "You're kind of always in the wrong lane, aren't you?"

"In this case," he said, "that was exactly it." He leaned closer. "Is it okay for me to tell you you have beautiful eyes?"

She laughed. "You think you're so sexy."

"Animal magnetism is all I have."

"All you have," she said, "is a black leather jacket."

Because Leanna was so enthusiastic about it, they both ate chicken cacciatore. "You're right, it's real good," English said. "But I believe they threw the ass end of this chicken in here." He raised a piece on his fork to show her. "The Pope's nose."

"The Pope's nose?"

"Yeah, the tail. That's what they call it in Kansas, anyway."

"That's anti-Catholic." She appeared serious.

"You know what I'd do if I was the Pope? Every time I ate chicken, I'd ask loudly for the Pope's nose."

"You're not funny. You're too perverse."

"And then I'd eat it."

They drank white wine and English felt tired. He had a sense of dead water all around him. "Why are you with me?" he asked her.

"I haven't got anything better to do," she said, and he saw that she was only being frank.

"And why are you with me?" she asked. In the candlelight her eyes seemed dark, sacred. Her face was soft and disappeared, when she leaned back out of the glow, into a blankness like that of the faces in Jerry Twinbrook's paintings.

"It's because of your face," he said.

It seemed she'd heard it many times before. She let the subject die in a short silence. "I wanted to ask you something. I was wondering what you meant about being a knight of faith. Remember?"

A cold wind blew through the room but nothing moved. "I don't know what it means." He felt terrible. He needed something funny to say. "I just have the feeling I am one."

"It's from Kierkegaard, right?"

"That's not where I got it. I heard a priest talk about it, I think. I don't remember exactly."

"Are you going to mop your face with your napkin now?"

"Yeah," he said, and he did.

"I'll tell you my secret, if you'll tell me yours."

"What's yours?"

"Is it a deal?"

"Only if I think your secret is worth it."

"Lenny, is it a deal? Whatever it's worth."

"Okay," he said. "You first."

"I'm tired of the gay life. I just keep getting hurt. That's why I'm with you."

"Is that it?"

"Ever since I saw you at Mass that day, I've known it was going to be you."

"Because I was at church?" It shocked him that he could talk, because all the sensations he'd felt when he'd first had tea with her, lightheadedness, a great momentum, a vision that she was made of air, were coming over him again. "I'm not that religious."

"I know. That's the only time I've ever seen you at Mass."

"Because I'm still recovering from it," he said. "One shot lasts a long time with me. I'm serious."

"I believe you." For a minute she just watched his face. "So what's your big secret? What is it that makes you so— closed up?"

"It's just crazy," he said. "A crazy feeling."

She said nothing, but only held on to the stem of her wineglass, her left hand in her lap, and watched him.

"It's this crazy feeling that I'm being called," he said finally. "But I'm not listening."

"Called to the priesthood—is that it?"

"I don't know. I told you, I'm not listening." He felt as if his heart would break now. "I'm running away."

She said, "Don't you want to know what it is?"

"No," he said.

"What do you think it is?"

"For all I know," he said, "I could be the Second Coming."

She didn't receive it as lightly as he'd tried to send it. "But, Lenny," she said with great tenderness, "don't you see that's crazy? It's a delusion."

"I told you it was. I said it was crazy. But I'm still running away, no matter what. Maybe the idea is just a fantasy, but the fear is for real."

"But if it's just some kind of delusion, then what's there to be scared about?"

"I'm scared it's not really a total delusion. It could be just a blown-up version of the truth. Like"—maybe he was making a fool of himself, but it was started now—"like a kid who thinks his mother's calling him to come inside and be the man of the house, when really she just wants him to clean up his room or something like that. But she's calling, that's the thing, she's calling." He felt the world loosen around him. It was as if the small restaurant suddenly gave him all the space he needed.

Leanna seemed very moved by all this. She laughed, but her voice was hoarse. "Whoever's calling you, don't go in, okay? Stay out here with me for a while."

"Yeah," he said. "Definitely."

There was a sweet shyness between them now, a moment that didn't live through the little conversation with the waiter, the declining of dessert and the business of paying the check. English conceived that he hadn't, from the start, ever been in charge of this romance, if that's what it was, and he gave up. Waiting for the change and thinking nothing at all, he hit on the idea that the way to deal with this woman, with his time on this eerie peninsula, maybe with his whole life, was to stand back and look at it as he would a painting he didn't understand and probably couldn't appreciate. Climbing up from the dark underground into the decadent glitter of vending, he watched this shopping center as he might one of Jerry Twinbrook's beaches, the arrested moment of it, and he thought he caught the somber heart of each bright color, the moons, so to speak, of which these colors were the suns, the softer actuality that Jerry Twinbrook had known about for a long time. He was wrenched by a thought: I've got to find that guy. It was a necessary thing.

Someone was calling him. "Somebody's calling you," Leanna said, catching him at the edge of the walk before he stepped out into the vast parking lot, where they didn't need to go— the theater was just across the mall. "Lenny English!" It was Phil, his landlord's cabdriver cousin, lounging against a black limousine-like taxi. "Where are you, in another world?"

"How are things?" English surfaced from his dreams. "You're on the early shift tonight."

"I'm on two shifts, man—it's the prime of my life, time to move, time to make money." Phil drew English close, his arm over English's shoulders, and put his head down as if he were going to say something about their shoes. But he had something to say about Leanna, who waited on the walk and looked at the window of a store. "Lenny English," Phil said. "There's only one way I can tell you this: That woman there goes after girls. She don't go after men. You hear what I'm saying?"

"Yeah."

"Do you get the underlying meaning?"

"She's a dyke."

"Can you handle it that I told you that? Are we still buddies?"

"She's just a friend," English said, embarrassed. "But listen, I'm glad I ran into you."

"I'm glad I ran into you, too, man. I been rooting for you. I know it's tough in a new town."

"What I wanted to ask you about," English said, "you're a 'Nam vet, aren't you?"

"Yeah, yeah, yeah—how'd you know?"

"You have that quality," English said.

"What. I'm a little zoned, maybe?" Phil was concerned.

"No, no, it's just, you know, that quality."

"Yeah, I get it," Phil assured him. "Right. Right."

"I was wondering if you know this guy Wilkinson, I forget his first name. He's head of 'Nam Vets for Cape Cod."

"Wilkinson? Sure. Yeah. I know everybody, man."

"What about the Truth Infantry?"

"Truth Infantry?"

"Yeah."

"Truth Infantry? I don't know. I'll find out. Get back to me, okay?"

Leanna was stepping over to them, and so English wanted to change the subject. "Have you ever heard of the artist Gerald Twinbrook?" he asked Phil.

Phil seemed to think he was on the spot now. "Gerald—yes, I have. I have. I'm familiar with his work."

"You know him? Do you have any impression of him maybe?"

"Gerald Twinbrook?"

"Twinbrook, yeah."

"Twinbrook . . . No, I don't." Phil's tone was that of a person being interviewed. "I, uh, it sounds vaguely familiar, that's about it."

"This is Leanna."

"Hi, yeah, I know you," Phil said.

"You know me?"

"Well, what I mean, you know—I don't *know* you," Phil said.

"Phil. That's Phil."

"Hi, Phil."

"Get in touch with me, man. I'm in the book."

"Good deal," English said.

"I think we're late. We're going to the movies," Leanna said.

"*The Red Shoes*," Phil said. "See *The Red Shoes* immediately."

"We are," Leanna said. "That's the one."

"You're gonna *love* it. I cried," Phil told them.

"I'll give you a call," English said.

"I'll answer," Phil told him as they hurried off.

They were late for the film and had to go all the way down to the second row. English got very edgy sitting beside her and thinking only about the dark, and about sitting beside her. Within two minutes, the movie was embarrassing him. Was it too stupid? Was it possible she wasn't enjoying herself?

Then he remembered that he still hadn't talked to Ray Sands. "I need all the change you've got," he said as softly as he could. "I have to call Provincetown."

"Okay." She gave him her coin purse out of her handbag.

"I was supposed to tell my boss something. I have to call him."

"Okay."

Halfway up the aisle he realized he could have asked her if she wanted any popcorn—they'd been in too much of a hurry coming in. But he couldn't go back now. I'll get popcorn, he thought. Buttered, medium-size. He pushed through the doors into a small panic of kids and patrons entering and leaving the other movies in this place. He felt much better here, where the pandemonium was outside him, than he did in there shoved up against Leanna's warm breathing silhouette, where it was all in his heart. I am a grownup, he declared to himself, cutting in front of two little boys wearing paper 3-D glasses, who were about to use the pay phone by the ladies' room.

"What's the 3-D movie?" he asked them as he deposited seven quarters. But they were mad at him and wouldn't say.

Grace answered.

"Mrs. Sands. It's Lenny English. Is Mr. Sands awake by any chance? I think he was expecting me to tell him something, but he was asleep—"

"I don't know," she said. "It's terrible!"

"Terrible," English repeated.

"Bud's sick! What am I gonna do!"

"He'll be okay. Don't worry—"

"Bud's turning purple! He got vomit all over him!"

"Wait a minute. Hold on," English said. "Is this for real?"

"Who are you! Why you did this to Bud!"

"Try and—wait. Wait a minute. Can I speak to Mr. Sands?"

"Bud fell over—he got a face like a *beet*!"

"I'll talk to him tomorrow," English said before he could think of anything else to say.

"Yeah! Okay! Tomorrow!"

Grace hung up, and so did English.

He dialed the radio station, because Sands lived nearby and maybe somebody could run over and check on him. His palms were slick with sweat because he felt he might be in a position to make a terrible mistake, something fatal. The line was busy.

Before I do anything, English thought, I'm going to get some popcorn. As he waited at the counter, another twelve-year-old wearing white paper 3-D glasses that were crooked on his face told him, "Hey, your jacket looks 3-D! It's wild!"

"Shut up," his sister said, grabbing the back of his neck. "God." She looked up toward the heavens.

"It *is* 3-D," English said. "*This* is 3-D." He was annoyed, even frightened. "*Real life* is 3-D." He got his popcorn and the lady laid his quarter change in a spot of melted butter on the glass. Before I do anything, he thought, I'm going to go to the bathroom and wash my hands. In the bathroom he splashed his face with water and forgot all about his popcorn, knocking it with his elbow and spilling half of it into the neighboring sink. He heard a man talking to his child in one of the stalls: ". . . or I'll take you home *right now*." I have got to function, English told himself. "That's the last time we try that," the man's voice proclaimed. Wiping his hands and face with paper towels, English heard them passing behind him toward the rows of sinks and mirrors and the exit. The faucet went on and he could hear the father saying, "That's disgusting." English asked himself, Why am I listening to this? I've got to think.

False alarm, English decided.

But he couldn't let it pass. He wanted someone to reassure him, he wanted to feel at ease. He hurried back to the pay phone, clutching his half-empty bucket of greasy popcorn. The line at WPRD was still busy. And now Sands's home phone only rang and rang and nobody picked it up.

I'm calling in a false alarm, he told himself, dialing the operator. "I don't know how to say this," he told her. "I think there's an emergency in Provincetown, but I'm not completely sure about it. Could you get the police to check on it?"

"I don't understand what you mean," she said.

"I just—" Speech deserted him. He couldn't explain. "Please connect me with the Provincetown police," he said. "It's an emergency."

"I'll connect you," she said, and rang them.

Someone answered. "Whoever you are," English said, "do you know Ray Sands?"

"Who am I talking to here?"

"I'm his assistant. Leonard English. I'm in Hyannis, I just talked to his wife, and she says he's very sick. Could you check on him? Do you know him? He lives on Cutter Street. If he, you know, if he needs an ambulance—"

"Ray Sands? Sure, we'll check it out."

"Great. Unbelievable. Thanks."

"You're entirely welcome," the person said.

English put the phone back: I'm done. It's out of my hands. He left the bright lobby where nothing made sense.

In the darkness he found Leanna and handed her what was left of the popcorn. "I don't want this," she said. He hunched down in his seat and began eating it himself. "You make a lot of noise," she whispered. "Don't eat with your mouth open. Look at her outfit," she said of the woman on the screen. "What a fox."

For two minutes he tried to settle into the movie, but it was like watching a film within a film. He was very much aware that the people on the screen were larger than the people in the theater, and that their statements came out of loudspeakers and echoed from the wall behind him. Someone was dancing and people were applauding. "Weird things are happening," he whispered to Leanna. "I gotta make another call."

"Are you a drug dealer?" she whispered. "Because you sure spend some time on the phone."

This time there was somebody to answer at Ray Sands's house, a policeman who identified himself quickly and English didn't get his name. "I called about an ambulance earlier," he told the officer. "I wanted to find out if Ray Sands is okay."

"Who is this?" the policeman's voice said.

"I'm his assistant, Leonard English."

"Your boss is pretty sick, Mr. English. He's on his way to Cape Cod Hospital right now."

"Cape Cod Hospital? What's wrong with him?"

"It looks like a heart," the policeman's voice said, "but I wouldn't diagnose."

"What'd the ambulance people say?"

"That's what they thought—a heart. You're his assistant? You pretty close to him?"

"No," English said. "I'm not."

"They were doing CPR on him, the whole routine." Now he heard the excitement in the policeman's voice. "I'd say he wasn't too alive when he left here."

"Well," English said, "okay. Thank you."

"You're entirely welcome," the policeman's voice said.

He stood in the aisle, bending down to speak to Leanna. "Listen, I'm all fucked up. There's an emergency."

She looked at him and turned back to the screen and then looked at him again. "You mean urgent business, or a real emergency?" She looked at the screen.

"My boss is having some kind of heart attack. Where's Cape Cod Hospital?"

"It's here, in Hyannis. Near the airport. Don't you know where Cape Cod Hospital is?"

"Show me, would you? I'm completely lost."

English couldn't get the attention of the emergency room's clerk, a well-kept young man doing twenty things at once, gesturing to an orderly and searching through a cream-colored filing cabinet while holding the telephone receiver between his shoulder and his jaw and saying, "Yeah—right—yeah," into the mouthpiece. Surrounding the clerk in his office, which was nothing more than an oversized cubicle, what appeared to be patients' charts cluttered every surface. There were charts on the floor covered with the prints of shoe soles. The waiting room English stood in was glutted with patients and their relatives and friends, all of whom seemed to be holding bloody rags against their faces. English tapped on the cubicle's wired-glass window again, this time more forcefully. Behind him a burly man in a bloodstained down-filled vest was explaining to the others there how his wife had been injured. "First I kind of pinned her with this arm," he told them, "and then I went to work on her face with my elbow." When he dropped his red soft-drink can in the midst of gesturing with it, he started to cry, saying, "Now I spilled my fucking Coke. I just plain lost my *head*!" He marched across the hall into the trauma room and English saw him in there examining the features of his wife, an immense woman sitting on one of the high, narrow gurneys with her legs dangling. The man looked into her eyes, now blackened, and into her sutured face. He fell to his knees before her. Meanwhile, "You're going to be all right," the clerk said into the telephone. "You're going to live forever." Children were screaming, men and women wept, and Coca-Cola spread out over the floor and under the plastic chairs. One man, sitting stock-still in the middle of all this, gripped a hunter's arrow in his fist and stared at it. English felt this was no place to come for help. He wanted Leanna, but she was in the ladies' room.

The radio on the clerk's desk started beeping. The clerk answered. A kazoo-like voice lost in spitting static spoke to him. English couldn't make out a word, but the clerk was astonished by the message. "What's your ten-twenty? What's your ETA?" The radio's voice crackled back at him. "Shit," the clerk said. He seemed to notice only now that he was still holding the phone receiver in his hand. He hung it up and then immediately lifted it again, looking at the intercom on his desk and surveying its buttons helplessly. He dialed a number on the phone and said, "This is ER. We got a heart arriving in about—less than ten minutes."

"I think I know that patient," English said to him through the hole in the glass.

The clerk ignored him. "Yeah!" he said into the telephone. "Page it now!" He examined the intercom again, but seemed to have forgotten how it worked. He began yelling, "Helen! Helen!"

"That's Ray Sands," English said through the hole. "He's a detective, and I'm his assistant."

"Okay. Okay," the clerk told him.

A nurse, tall and heavy, came out of the trauma room across the hall, walking crab-footed and seeming in no hurry. "What are you screaming about?" she asked the clerk. But at that moment a voice came over the public address: "Dr. Heart, emergency room. Dr. Heart, emergency room."

"You're kidding!" the nurse said. "I got seven patients in the goddamn trauma room. Get in here," she ordered the clerk.

"There's coffee under the desk, Officer," the clerk said to English. "Keep it a secret."

English stepped from the waiting room and through the door of the cubicle by way of the hall, as the young clerk elbowed past him saying, "Help yourself," and followed the nurse into the trauma room. Together the clerk and the nurse began wheeling startled patients on their gurneys out of one of its doors and into the hallway, down near the fire exit, where they left them.

Leanna was back now, standing in the waiting room on the other side of the glass. "Did they put you to work?"

"The guy thinks I'm a cop," English said.

But he was so dazed by this emergency that he couldn't hear himself. Under the clerk's desk was a coffeepot and white Styrofoam cups, one of which he filled, bending over and, as he did so, feeling that his back was vulnerable to some vague hostile thrust.

People from another part of the hospital swiftly hauled past his cubicle a portable EKG machine on buzzing plastic wheels.

In the midst of movement, English felt required to move. He stepped from the cubicle and saw, far down the long hallway, a flock of doctors and nurses running toward him, covering their breast pockets with their hands as they ran.

"I'll be over here," Leanna said, and disappeared from view, passing deeper into the waiting room's stunned turmoil.

English was breathing hard and witnessing events in small, frozen frames, as from the window of a journey. He was drinking his coffee. It was still hot. He'd just taken a sip and put down the cup, and the fingers of that hand were still warm, and he still tasted the artificial creamer on the tip of his tongue as the ambulance pulled up outside, its dying siren lacerating the air. He smelled medicine and heard a dozen conversations at once. As he moved toward the sliding doors of the emergency entrance, he felt himself tearing away from these details and felt the strands of them being burned from his person. The doors slid open, cold air blew over him, and he ducked aside to make way for the ambulance men rolling the wheeled stretcher into the hospital, moving as fast as they could run. One pushed the stretcher, one covered the patient's mouth with his own mouth, the third pressed on the patient's chest with both hands. Ray Sands, dressed in his pajamas, the shirt of them torn open, was the patient. English followed along into the trauma room, where the man performing mouth-to-mouth turned to vomit in a sink along the wall while a nurse put a respirator mask over the patient's blue face, and half a dozen medical people, like the fingers of a fist, closed in on the stretcher.

English stood and watched for several minutes, seeing nothing, while people in white smocks went to and fro around the stretcher and came and went from the trauma room, speaking in low, urgent voices. When he felt the strength returning to his arms and legs, English left and went back to the clerk's cubicle, nodding absently to an ambulance attendant—the one just pushing the stretcher—who loitered in the hallway now, holding a cup of coffee in one hand and in the other Ray Sands's set of false teeth.

The clerk had his intercom working. He talked into it and the telephone both at once. "Anybody you need?" he asked the intercom, and the intercom answered, "Anesthesia!" "Anesthesiologist," he said into the telephone.

By this time there were medical people all over the place, many of them without a purpose, it seemed. They spilled out of the trauma room and into the hallway, where confused patients tried to sit up in their mislocated gurneys and demand an explanation. A nurse rushed out of the trauma room just as a priest was rushing into it, his black garb billowing behind him. They banged into each other. The girl was thrown against the wall. She recovered, started off again, abruptly halted, wheeled, and hurried back through the doors behind the priest. English and the clerk, leaning together close to the intercom, listened to the clunking sounds of a machine giving Ray Sands's heart stiff electric jolts; and then they heard the steady whine the EKG emitted when it was taking a flat reading. There were so many similar sounds, the dentist's drill, vacuum cleaners, the high test tones of radio stations; and in his weightlessness and complete openness to all sensation English understood deeply, for an instant, that this was music. Over the intercom came a girl's breathless voice asking, "What medication? I forgot, I forgot—" "Couple of aspirin, and call me in the morning," one of the doctors said, and those gathered around the corpse broke into laughter over the priest's rapid monotone and the music of the EKG. The clerk shut down the intercom. "All over," he said into the phone, and put away the receiver.

Looking up, English saw Grace Sands standing on the other side of the glass, next to a policeman. She was crying out, and her face was as she'd described her husband's: like a beet, swollen and shiny. She seemed not to have heard the clerk's pronouncement. She'd mistaken him for a doctor. "He *gotta* make it, *please*, he *gotta*— *Doctor, do* something!" She broke loose of the comforting and restraining hand of the policeman, who stood behind her with the flaps of his winter cap turned up and flopping like a mongrel's ears and making him look even more at a loss, in the face of a widow's torment, than he probably already was. "Make him *well*, *please*, you *got*ta, you *got*ta!" Her features were so changed by panic that English wouldn't have known her except by the mist of white hair around her head, and also by her apron, which he recognized from their New Year's Eve dinner together, the back-yard barbecuer's smock with lettering on it: *When It's Smokin' It's Cookin' and When It's Black It's Done.* The clerk seemed to read this slogan carefully, and then slid aside the glass between them and offered her a box of Kleenex. "Oh, thank you, Doctor," she whispered, "thank you, thank you," staring at the Kleenex and never touching it.

A real doctor, a tired old man, came into the waiting room. Grace saw him and clamped her lips together over her sobs. Wordlessly, he took her elbow with one hand while giving the policeman's shoulder a friendly squeeze with the other, and he guided her from the room and into the hallway to talk to the priest. The clerk opened and closed one file drawer after another. "Where are those death certificates?" he said.

The phone rang and the clerk stopped his search to answer. "They're all done," he said. "They'll be coming back in a minute." English felt thirsty, and then suddenly saliva flooded his mouth and he thought he'd be sick. "Deceased," the clerk said, and hung up the phone. Out in the hallway, the new widow started screaming at the priest and the doctor.

English caught sight of a beautiful woman with long black hair. Then he saw it was Leanna, looking as if she belonged right here in the middle of all this. She seemed to know exactly what she was doing, but she wasn't doing anything except standing by the water cooler with her arms crossed before her.

The nurse called Helen came in and sat down heavily in the chair beside the clerk's desk, sticking her rubber-soled shoes out in front of her and chewing viciously on a lollipop. "Got rid of half our patients," she said, and English noticed for the first time that many of the injured, even untreated ones, were gone or were leaving, no longer impressed, maybe, with their own contusions and abrasions. The clerk, standing beside the filing cabinet, began to tremble. English could see it plainly. Helen was also shaking as she showed the clerk where to find a death certificate, and English noticed that she chewed up and swallowed her lollipop stick. English lit a cigarette and inhaled deeply. When he turned to rest it in the ashtray, he found two others, both his, already burning there. The widow sobbed loudly in the hallway, while the priest spoke reassuring phrases. Helen went back into the trauma room to cope with the patients whose ordeals had been interrupted. The hospital was quiet again. English wondered if a human soul drifted along these corridors now, but he found—much to his alarm, to his great anguish—that he doubted it.

The clerk's tiny office seemed to be the crossing point of any number of paths in this hospital. Within the space of a few minutes, doctors, custodians, orderlies on break appeared one by one and asked, "How'd it go?" and were told, "Deceased," and wandered off. Leanna slept softly in one of the waiting room's cheap plastic chairs. English stayed around, thinking he should talk to Grace Sands, but all he was able to say was "Grace—" as she passed by, flanked by the policeman and the priest, and then she was gone.

The automatic breath and rattle and thump of the entrance's sliding doors repeated at intervals, letting out the people who'd been a part of this death, until the clerk's cubicle and the rooms around it were as still as the moment before a concert. But English stayed where he was, half sitting on the clerk's desk, because he knew he couldn't handle a car. "Taking a break?" the clerk asked him.

English nodded.

"That guy looked old for a detective," the clerk said. He glanced at what must have been Sands's chart. "Born 1915."

"He's retired," English said. "Was. Was retired."

Helen came and leaned in the doorway, looking jolly. "Had enough excitement tonight, Frank?" she asked the clerk.

The clerk looked at the clock on the wall. "Wow. Only thirty-two minutes to go."

The phone rang. The sound echoed all over the building, it seemed. It woke Leanna, the only person left in the waiting room. English was going to say something to her, anything, but she looked around and then closed her eyes again.

"Everything went real smooth," Helen was saying on the phone. "Deceased," she said. "Deceased. I think he was basically DOA." She was looking at Sands's chart. "It was his fourth coronary." English was more than surprised to hear this: he felt betrayed.

"The mortuary people oughta be around any time now," Helen told the clerk. "Help me get this man's clothes off, would you?"

"Me?" Frank said.

"Everybody's gone. Sue's at the snack bar. Andy's down at CIC. Come on, it goes with the territory."

But the sliding doors sounded again as soon as they'd gone into the trauma room, where Sands lay, and Helen had to come out and greet two new arrivals—one of whom English recognized, a Vietnamese man from Provincetown. "What seems to be the trouble!" Helen asked, stooping down to this foreigner and enunciating loudly.

Frank came out of the trauma room. "I'll take this man's chart," Helen told him. "You get back to work." She was getting a kick out of Frank's discomfort.

"Could you give me a hand, Officer?" Frank asked English, indicating the trauma room.

"Actually—" English said.

"The morgue'll be here any minute. I've got to get his belongings together."

English followed him into the trauma room.

Except for the body, it was empty of people—a space full of white examining tables, machinery, and high cloth partitions left at incidental angles.

The body was dead, it was not alive in any sense at all, and the face was other than any living person's, the eyelids pinched into sockets that looked empty and the toothless jaws wide open and the lips forming an astonished "Oh!"—but the flesh was heavy when English lifted the legs so the clerk could pull off Sands's pajama bottoms, and the flesh was warmer than his own when he raised the bare legs so the clerk could remove Sands's shit-stained boxer shorts. "I guess you've seen a lot of dead bodies," the clerk said to English, "but this absolutely spooks me. It really does. It's not in the job description."

Resolutely, as if charged with this office among men, English began dragging the left arm from its pajama sleeve. "I'm glad to be alive," he said. Together, because it was very heavy, much heavier than it should have been, they reached behind Sands's neck and raised the torso, and the clerk pulled the shirt out from under it. Ray Sands lay naked and grey and large between them. English felt an unbearable thrill in his chest, as if it were empty of everything but a clear light.

Helen appeared at Sands's feet. "Get some dividers around him, you guys," she said. "I have to bring this man in."

"What's his trouble? A fight?" Frank asked.

"No. His foreman drove him over from the factory. Foreign body, left eye," she said. "I'll call his doctor." She left Frank and English to roll three cloth partitions into place around the body.

The Vietnamese man came in, escorted and then politely abandoned by Helen, and sat on the next gurney. English said hello to him. They were hardly acquainted, but the man was something of a personality, Provincetown's sole Asian refugee, Nguyen Minh—"Fwooy-en," it was pronounced. He'd been a pilot for the South Vietnamese Air Force and had flown hundreds of missions, though he looked even now not much older than a boy. In the war's last days he'd stolen an American helicopter and guided it out over the China Sea toward some destination he'd believed worth reaching, taking along as many others as it would carry. But the helicopter had been shot down, or its fuel had run out, or its engine had given up, and all these people had gone down in the water to sink or swim. A few stayed afloat, for two days, and were rescued by the U.S. Navy. Now Nguyen Minh sat on the edge of the high gurney, his hands between his knees and his black tennis shoes dangling down, and stared at the cloth partition protecting him from the sight of death. The skin around his left eye was puffy, and the eye had turned pink. English was comforted by the presence of this small, patient man, because he himself had never touched, or even seen, a human corpse before. "How long have you been working at the factory?" he asked Nguyen Minh.

"About tree yers," Minh said. He formed his words carefully, as if he had a peach pit in his mouth.

"Do you like your job there?"

"I have a machine," Minh said. He smiled. "Die cast."

"You got something in your eye?"

"Some piece of metal." He shrugged. "I don't know."

"You'll be okay," English said.

"Maybe so."

"Do you ever wish you could go back to Vietnam?" English was nervous asking the question; it felt like prying.

"They're all dead there. My parents, and my brother, too, and all relatives. It's no good there."

"Was your brother a pilot?"

"He was a monk."

"A Catholic?" English was astonished.

"No. Buddhist." He smiled. "My brother did the self-immolation."

"Jesus Christ," English said.

"No," Minh said. "Buddha."

"Do you know that guy Nguyen Minh?" English asked Leanna as he drove the last mile into Provincetown. "Do you know that his brother was a monk, a Buddhist monk back there in Vietnam, and he burned himself up?"

Leanna reached her fingers to the back of his neck and stroked the locks of hair and eased his muscles, for a few minutes, until he turned off the highway and into Provincetown. "Let's go to the Beginner's," he said. "I want to get a couple of beers and dance with my shirt off."

He felt easy in the atmosphere of Provincetown now, its boarded-up windows and its silence of waiting post-something. English himself was still dizzy, and the Beginner's was the outward image of him, the dance floor shiny under changing discotheque illumination and pounded by gigantic speakers, but occupied by only five or six people who swayed, out of their minds with drink, in stationary circles; a place frantic and lonely both at once, eddying pointlessly in the wake of last summer. English didn't take his shirt off, but he threw his jacket aside and drank a Cuba Libre in three swallows.

"Suddenly the trouble is," he told Leanna, "I'm not too sure about life after death."

"What?" she said.

He couldn't hear her for the rising insanity of "Cruisin' the Streets," but being heard wasn't the issue, not at all. "The Resurrection of the Body seems like a crock. That guy was so *dead*." Impatiently he signaled for another drink, scooping the air over his empty glass.

He danced with a woman, and then Leanna danced with the same woman; and then the three of them danced together, he and Leanna sandwiching the woman between them and smiling at one another over her left shoulder. "Who is she?" Leanna asked him when they were done—the song didn't end, one blended into the next relentlessly, all at the same relentless beat; they just stopped dancing when they were tired.

"I don't know her," English said, "but let's take her for a ride in your hot tub."

"I don't operate that way."

"You're operating that way right now."

"I'm dancing."

"Let's all sleep together. I'm lonely," English said.

"I have to know the person first."

The woman was from Michigan, but looked European. She was overweight in a bouncy way, and didn't like interrupting the smooth flight of her evening, or even opening her eyes, to answer English's questions. " *'Bye, baby, see you around*," she mouthed as the stereo speakers blasted the room with these words, and she danced away and danced back toward them with a face peaceful and bathed in moving colors and sang, "*Remember me as a pink balloon . . .*"

"This music leads to violence," English said to her. "You want to go sleep in a hot tub with us?"

The huge female voice of the record spoke: her love was *alive*, it was like the sea . . .

"You've had a bad night," Leanna told him.

"*Aaaaah-ah-ah-aah-oh!*" the great sound sang.

"I just want to, I don't know, blow it," English said. The woman danced, short and squat, alone behind her closed eyes. Disco trumpets rose, choral voices rose, it was like Heaven; silence opened and a rivulet of chimes fell over the steady beating of a great heart . . . Ah shit, ah shit, English thought, not you.

In the overheated lyrics of rock and roll he often heard the sorrows and pronouncements of a jilted, effeminate Jehovah, and this song made even grander, more awful claims than most, suggesting that Her love was profoundly uncontrollable and maybe not actually friendly—

Not you, I don't know you—

—as inexorable as the ocean eating the sands of the Cape from under his feet, willing to take forever, if necessary, to drown him. Nothing would lift him from the waters: "Ain't No Mountain High Enough" it was called.

Infinite disco love boomed, a wounded woman calling forth these bits of light to swarm over the walls. Her love was alive? It was monstrous. "I'm not here," English said out loud. "So shut the fuck up."

Not you, not you, not you— Crackling dance-hall lumens circled these headless idiots in a whirlwind. Voices—angels—saints— "Fuck it," English announced, "let's just blow it."

The bartender was pointing him to the door. Leanna was crying. The woman was laughing, glass lay in shards across the puddles of the bar and changed colors. Not you, not you. "Not you, goddamnit, not you . . ."

Leanna and one of the bartender's friends helped him out into the knives of winter. "Time for Disco Inferno," English said. "Let's get serious."

She was having a hard time getting his clothes off as he tilted in the kitchen's doorway and tried to kick away one of his shoes. His sight was still twisted and the rhythm still beat against his head. "Endless disco," he told her.

She was crying. She punched his chest. "Goddamn you," she said. "Where did you get that leather *jacket*, anyway?"

"It was given to me," he said.

They stepped, both of them naked and English feeling incredibly *white*, into the small yard behind her apartment. There was old snow beneath his feet. "My feet know," he told her, "but my head isn't getting the message."

"Here's the message." She swept a bulky black cover from the hot tub, stepped delicately in, and pulled him by the arm in after her. "I don't want to fool around. I don't want to touch you." They sat naked across from each other in the wooden vat, attended by hardened drifts of snow, while warm camomile-scented waters churned around them, around her breasts, and the vapors of his mind revolved and dervishes of steam passed between them and the stars froze in the untroubled night above.

English woke the next morning while it was still dark. His hands felt of grease, and the hair on his forearms was matted with it. Groping for his pants and cigarettes he knocked over a bottle on the floor by the bed, the action of whose water-filled mattress made him feel queasier than even he had a right to. He cut on the lamp. Filippo Berio olive oil. She'd given him a massage. He got a Marlboro lit. He wasn't sure that smoking was approved of here, but Leanna was still sleeping and he assumed, because he'd spent the evening in a hospital and looked down into the face of a corpse, that everything was permitted. She was under the sheet and blanket in a lump, all but her sleep-softened face and dark tangles. They hadn't made love last night, or any sense. He watched her long enough to make certain she was breathing.

In the kitchen he found yesterday's *Boston Globe* on the counter and yesterday's coffee in a glass pot. He washed his face, hands, and arms at the sink, but got into his pants with his legs and buttocks still oily. In the papers he read about a murdered nun, a woman killed by unknowns in Brazil, and it started to seem to him, as he smoked cigarettes and drank cold coffee and imagined and imagined her last moments, that if what he imagined was true, then the earth was uninhabitable. This fear passed through him slowly, as though he'd eaten of it, and he cried. By the time the sunless daylight had come, the feeling had rarefied into a spacious hatred attended by the stink of brimming ashtrays.

There was no sense waiting for Leanna to wake up, no use wondering how she felt about him, in a place like this.

After dressing he went downstairs into the hour when paper-boys might be delivering, but the street outside was empty. The seats of his Volkswagen were chilly and brittle. He shut the car door softly. There wasn't any place open where he'd find break-fast, and so he told himself he'd go without it as a respectful fasting before Mass. It was the first he knew he was going. But he didn't mean to go to St. Peter's here in Provincetown and confront the figure in the mural beckoning from its rock in the storm. He'd been back there once, on an afternoon when the pews stood naked, and had discovered that the figure wasn't Christ at all but somebody completely different, St. Peter it would stand to reason. In that case, he was just beckoning you into the folds of the Church, not into the storm. But please, don't beckon me at all, not this early in the morning. English started the car and drove out to the highway and moved off down the Cape.

He didn't see the name of the town he entered some miles later. On an unreal Main Street like the one in Ray Sands's elec-tric train's landscape he found a Catholic church, Our Lady of the Waves, and also a café that was open, where he decided to have breakfast after all and wait for Mass.

At five to eight he stood before the heavy doors of the church feeling no hunger. The wooden entrance offered a Southwestern-style bas-relief severally and gaily colored and depicting Christ, looking quite a bit seedier these days, unshaven rather than bearded, his hair not flowing but unkempt, stalled beside some wooden flowers and keeping out of the way of orange slats of wooden sunshine. The crowds in the summery Cape atmosphere he'd never seen might move easily through this doorway, but English, with his mind on Ray Sands and murdered nuns, could hardly put his fingers on the handle: Jesus sheds His heat like tin upon you, spreads His tropic love, His Florida, on the army smashing in the faces of His brides. If we were truly as alone as that. He pushed through the doors to take Communion. There was never any explanation, never any consolation, but everything could be laminated by a terrible endorsement.

The interior was cozy but unheated. A blue sponge of Holy Water in its receptacle just inside the door was frozen solid. But he heard people talking in a room off to the side, and then it occurred to him that, of course, they often had the poorly attended dailies in some smaller room. He probably could have saved gas by going to St. Peter's and still have evaded the call of its patron saint. He headed toward the voices.

In the tiny room he took a seat among old ladies in a row of folding chairs. The priest was just donning his vestment by the makeshift altar, and his head, round-faced and middle-aged, came up through the neck. "Yes," he told them in tones faintly Irish, "he attended church regular."

One of the women said, "It's a shame."

"Was there an evening service last week?" another said with worry. "I missed it, I didn't know—"

"A meeting of the choir," the priest said. "And he dropped dead right there by the door."

The others clucked and ohed.

"He turned to his wife," the priest said, "turned to his wife and told her, 'Martha, this is it.'"

One of the women was also a witness, and said, "And then he keeled over, just like that. I feel so sorry for his son—you know, the son lost his own son last summer, and here, six months later, his father. What a world."

The priest was lighting the candles. "Doesn't he have something to do with basketball? The son?"

"He coaches. He coaches down South. They were in Albuquerque for the championship."

"That's right." It was coming back to him now. "He couldn't be reached to tell him all day."

The others all shook their heads.

"That was a close game," Father said. "North Carolina won it at the last buzzer." He took his place behind the altar and lifted his hands above the chalice. "The ball," he said, "was still in motion."

But a late arrival, another old woman, was just coming through the door. "Did you see Pavarotti on Channel 9 last night?" the priest asked the others, politely waiting a minute to begin.

At the homily, Father said, "I don't usually give a homily at the morning service, but I should say about Simone Weil, because I was in a discussion . . . You know Father Daniel, he's here from Lynn for a while, he mentioned Simone Weil, and it's very interesting, she never joined the Church. But you could say she was very much in the Church, very concerned about suffering. She was a little like Joan of Arc, you know, she got an idea in her head and that was it: she wouldn't give it up, starved herself to death. She said she wasn't going to eat any more food than the people in Hitler's concentration camps, and this is the thing about faith, or about conviction. She died. For what it's worth," he said. "Just something to think about. We're blessed with plenty to eat in this country. We read about famines in the Bible," he said, "but . . ." He paused to show he'd finished with the homily and began the Eucharist.

Hung over and unsorted and fatigued, English couldn't pay

attention to the Eucharist and heard only the most disquieting phrases, "This is the cup of my blood" and "We eat your body and drink your blood."

Afterward, as he turned his car onto the highway, English met a cloud of rain that must have been pouring water down for some time, because the police directing traffic around some roadwork were dressed in bright orange Day-Glo slickers.

Simone Weil. He'd heard of her, didn't know much about her, wasn't particularly interested. Who would be? Hitler had killed millions, and by her gesture of starvation she'd managed to raise the count by one, that was about all you could say for her. Still, if the message arrived, and you believed it came from God . . . Vague hints beyond the periphery. An aroma opens onto an avenue. Messages issue from the toast, *Kill your captain* . . .

A storm was a bad thing, because English's windshield wipers didn't work. The cops' raincoats looked like blowsy neon through the strings of rain. TOWN OF WELLFLEET, their car insignia read.

It was the hometown of Phil, the cabdriver. English turned around up the road and drove back to the town's café to wait out the rain and call him.

"You're right around the corner," Phil told him on the phone. "Look, man, I can't talk—you wanna drop around here? You play cards, man? Poker?"

"I'm flat-ass broke anyway," English said.

"Good, good, then you don't have to spend ten hours with these guys, and what happens is, you end up that way anyway, right?"

Phil was upstairs in an old yellow house not four blocks north of the church where English had just tasted God's flesh. The apartment door was already standing open and the hallway smelled of stale smoke. Phil had been up all night, too. He met English at the door, burned-out, giddy, and hoarse.

"I am so far ahead, man," he told English, "so far ahead." Impatient voices called him from the kitchen, and he led English in to where several men, easily pictured eating pigs' feet in a barroom, sat around a table covered with cards and cash.

English drew himself two glasses of water in quick succession from the faucet, standing at the sink and looking at small-town back yards out the window.

"I hate to gloat, you guys," Phil said. "I hate to gloat. I *hate*—to *gloat*. So what brings you around here, Lenny?"

"I was at church," English said.

"Excellent," Phil said. "Good for you."

"Third Street," the dealer said. "Ace, never hurts. No help. Nuthin. Possible flush, hearts. Two sixes. No help. Sixes bet."

"You want a beer, man? Church is over, right?"

"I don't drink in the morning unless I'm hung over," English said.

"Your bet, sixes," the dealer said.

"You hung over?"

"Yes," English said.

"Hey. Hey," the dealer said.

"O-*kay*," Phil told him. "Two."

"Call."

"I'm out."

"Fold."

"Call."

"Four."

"Flush, my ass," Phil said. "Six."

"Shit."

"Yeah, ditto."

"I call."

"Fourth Street," the dealer said, giving Phil and the other man their fourth cards. "Bust the flush. No apparent for the sixes."

"What'd you wanna see me about?" Phil asked English.

The dealer rapped the table. "Come on. Sixes."

"These for the taking?" English indicated a forest of bottled beer beside the sink.

"Help yourself. What'd you wanna see me about?"

"Can I tell you something without you getting a terrific resentment?" the man dealing asked English. "We're trying to have a poker game here."

"Remember I was asking you about something called the Truth Infantry?"

"Those guys are mostly in New Hampshire," one of the other men said.

"The winners want to talk, and the losers say, Let's deal," the man in the seat next to that man said.

"Listen: bet or check," the dealer said.

"They're like—paramilitary," Phil said. "Two dollars."

"They're all up around Franconia. I gotta see one more. I call."

"See what? You only *get* five cards, man. Your flush is busted."

"New Hampshire?" English said.

"Yeah," Phil said, "all except your boss. Know what? He's the head of it. The Generalissimo of Jive."

"Fifth Street," the dealer said. "Another heart, too late. No help for the sixes."

"You mean—Ray Sands?"

"Oh yeah," Phil said. "Stewart, Stewart, Stewart," he said, shaking his head sadly at his opponent. "Two dollars. Yes, yes, yes," he said to English, "Raymond Sands. Which means that you," and English hoped he meant the other man, "are gonna get fucked in both ears at once."

English drove back into a town fallen on by drizzle, but the town might as well have been in flames. If he was the assistant to the deceased head of a paramilitary squadron, in what sense, he couldn't help wondering, would he now be viewed as the head of it? Phil had lost his hand of poker to a pair of nines, much to the satisfaction of his friends. "Kicked in the head by Karma," he had announced. The sight of a police car in the A&P parking lot thrilled English like a drop through the dark.

His eyes were full of sleep. The shine of rain on the asphalt blurred abnormally, looking less liquid than electric. His strength for the day was spent, yet it wasn't noon. He had appointments at the station's production studio, but he imagined he'd just skip them, go home, and leave this world for one of dreams he wouldn't quite recall when he woke again.

But first he stopped to look in on Grace Sands.

Grace came to the door red-eyed and generally disarranged, wearing the same clothes she'd been wearing last night at the hospital. "The operator," she said. Her lips quivered wildly and she gestured behind her at nothing.

He put his hands into his pockets. "Grace."

"The operator is rude."

"Grace," English said. "Do you know who I am?"

She looked past him, over his shoulder, and then turned to peer into the living room she'd just come out of. "I'll make some tea," she said.

"Very good."

"Sit down!" she cried as she left him standing in the hall. "What you call it—the couch. I make some . . ." At the far end of the house, where her voice had faded, he heard a faucet going on.

He went to the desk in Sands's office and took the three blue passports from their drawer, and then stood still in the middle of the room, not a pocket anywhere in his clothing big enough to hide them.

With a pencil he started a rent in the lining of his jacket, ripped it wider with his fingers, and stuffed the three documents out of sight; then walked, his elbow jammed awkwardly against their bulk because he'd torn a hole large enough for them to fall out of, across the hallway and into the parlor.

Sitting back on the flowery divan, English closed his eyes and listened to a singing along his taut wires while Grace disturbed the kitchenware. Now that his eyes were shut, his vision was acute: across a curtain of phosphenes he watched primitive, shrunken heads devolve into faceless splashes.

"So. So. So," Grace said, coming back with a tea service held out before her.

"Oh. Here." He took hold of the coffee table with both hands and moved it three inches to the left, pointlessly.

"And you going on a trip," she said, setting down the tray.

He studied the two small cups, the unadorned white teapot, the bowl of sugar and pitcher of milk, the plate of lemon slices. "Not to my knowledge."

She took her place across from him and poured him out some tea. "Bud gonna be along real soon." Some sort of unpleasant thought crossed her face. She put her hands in her lap and looked at them.

"Very tasty." English sipped his tea.

"I don't remember all the numbers, and she's rude," she said. "So rude I'm not gonna talk to her, that kind of person."

After a moment she looked at him in fear. "Are you waiting for your photograph while it's developing?"

English sighed. He felt his lower lip trembling as he touched it to the rim of the cup.

"Bud got a personal friendship with our Bishop, Bishop Andrew."

English said, "I'm glad."

"The Bishop, our Bishop, you know Bishop Andrew? He visit my Bud personal last week. Lenny," she asked him now, "where's Bud?"

"I beg your pardon," he begged her.

"Do you think Bishop Andrew gonna come?"

English set down his cup. "I don't know, Grace." He put his hands on his knees.

"I hope so. The Bishop himself, I be very honored to have him at the funeral."

She wiped her nose on the hem of her apron. "To speak at Bud's funeral."

He closed his eyes on the idea of people standing around a grave and this poor woman trying to fathom it all. What kind of funeral was that? "I don't have to go, do I?"

It simply came out. He wondered if he'd actually said it.

"Oh no, no, no. You go ahead, you finish your tea," Grace told him. "You stay till your picture develops."

Lovemaking was a rare, shy, false thing between them. They never did much more than kiss sweetly while naked. "I don't know," he said, "why I can't get it up." Naked and sitting Indian-style amid the bedclothes, Leanna asked him, "If you're not worried about your sex conduct, and nothing else is wrong, then what's bothering you?"

"What sex conduct?" English said.

Leanna wasn't a virgin after all. She and Marla Baker had wanted a baby once, and they'd hired a man to make love to both of them. Neither had gotten pregnant, and so all Leanna had bought for fifty dollars was her deflowering in an airport motel.

"Yeah, I paid for it, too, the first time," English admitted. "Twenty dollars." He ran a finger from the crook of Leanna's elbow down to the frail bones of her wrist. "It was a black lady with needle marks."

"We almost got back together," Leanna said. "But Marla went to New York because her husband was having her followed."

Suddenly English wanted to leave his life. "Who was following her?"

"Marla's a tough lady. She's older. It was a father thing. She's too old for me."

"Just one, okay?"—English was lighting a cigarette. "You almost got back together?"

"Blow it out the window," Leanna said. "Open the window, baby."

He crouched naked by the window he'd opened and blew smoke through the screen out over the empty parking spaces of the empty hotel. It must have been past 3 a.m. They slept together all the time and didn't sleep. They were lovers, and they didn't make love. It was one of the strangest things that had ever happened to him, and in a couple of senses it wasn't happening. "What was her husband having her followed for?" he said.

"Oh, it's a whole complex thing. They'll never get divorced. He keeps compiling evidence against her, and she keeps letting it fuck her mind all around. Marla reacts. She was in P-town as a reaction, and she's in New York right now just as a reaction to his moves. We practically lived together the last three summers, and she wanted to hide it from him. Deep down she thought it was sick to be gay. But," she said, "you're only as sick as your secrets."

He watched the street, dipping his ashes into his hand. "I never heard that one before," he said. "As sick as your secrets."

"It must've been a private eye from Boston. Marla wanted to catch him. She went crazy, looking over her shoulder all the time. She put on a black raincoat and snuck around outside her building one night. It got so weird," she said, "it got so scary."

By the open window he dangled his cigarette from his lips, and put his arms around himself against the draft.

"Last summer she finally decided not to go home. We were going to—I don't know. Then she met Carol; then . . ." Her thoughts drifted off on a sigh. "You start to think, Who is this guy? If it was a guy. It could've been a woman. They have women detectives now."

"The truth is—" English began.

"We'll never know the truth."

"Maybe that's right," English said in despair, "maybe that's best."

"What's bothering you?"

"Do I look like something's bothering me?"

"You look like you're hiding and peeking out the window. You're an uptight, late-night DJ."

"There's something I'm supposed to do. But I'm not doing it."

"You're guilty before God. You should go to Confession."

"No," he insisted. "I should go to the police."

"The who," Leanna said.

"Sands was into some kind of passport thing, phony passports, and I was like—his secretary, part-time. But I didn't know anything about it. It looks bad. It just looks bad."

"If you haven't done anything, why go to the police? Let them come to you if they want."

"Right, that's just it. But somehow it won't sound so logical if it turns out I *did* do something. Like, I'm an accessory. Then I say, Well, I didn't know, and they say, What didn't you know? I mean what, exactly, didn't you know? You know?"

"I know you're only as sick as your secrets."

A phrase came back to him from somewhere. "Sick unto death."

The sheets whispered and Leanna came across the bedroom to embrace him from behind where he squatted with his chin on the windowsill. She ran her hands along his shoulders and arms and cupped his buttocks in her hands. "I wouldn't worry about it, honey man," she said into his ear. "A smoker's Karma is to die from cancer, not from secrets."

"Kicked in the head by Karma," he said.

"Where are you going?"

"I gotta go. I'm going home," he said. "I need some sleep before I go to work."

That night, he prayed. He threw off the blankets in the small, sleepless hours and put himself on the floor by the bed.

English didn't kneel in prayer each night out of habit, but fell to his knees on rare occasions and in a darkness of dread, as if he were letting go of a branch. To his mind, God was a rushing river, God was an alligator, God was to be chosen over self-murder and over nothing else. He thanked God he had two arms and two legs, he thanked God he had two jobs and some variety in his life, he prayed to God to let him make love to Leanna. Satisfy these yearnings, he prayed, or take them the hell away. He didn't pray anymore for faith, because he'd found that a growing certainty of the Presence was accompanied by a terrifying absence of any sign or feeling or manifestation of it. He was afraid that what he prayed to was nothing, only this limitless absence. *I'll grow until I've found you, and you won't be there.*

Whenever he found himself praying, he knew he was at the very least jammed up inside, probably crazy. He got up off his knees and put his clothes on, and his shoes, and he sat in the room's only chair with the room's only book, *Best Loved Poems*, reading the index of first lines in the back. Nothing grabbed him. *Tell me what to do.* He spun the pages out under his thumb, but the poem he turned up had nothing to do with his situation, and anyway, he wanted guidance, not literature. Tennyson, Lord Byron, you had to be in the mood. Somebody cleared his throat in another room, somebody downstairs dropped a shoe, somebody wrenched a spigot somewhere and the pipes cried out, but for five seconds, ten seconds, English couldn't believe in these people. A familiar thought came to him, one he didn't like: What if there's really nothing? Suppose I'm all there is? What if there's only a child telling himself a story, and the story is the child, and the child is me? I've got to stop living in these rooms alone. I've got to pray because I can't stop thinking these thoughts. Prayer is my home. God is inside it. Coleridge is also there. Walt Whitman. The end of the world. And the deep, dark secret of my life. It's a case of answering the door and being entered.

Outside his door, some men argued loudly over nonessentials as they stumbled up the staircase. Checking his watch, he discovered that it was 1 a.m. as they hurled themselves, from the sound of it, against the door across the hall.

He was an hour late for his shift at WPRD. He was in trouble. In his mind he pictured his attendance record at the station, discounting absences during the day following his employer's death, and tried to convince himself it wasn't a bad record.

It appeared to him, as he got into his pants, that the men outside were backing up violently against his door in order to get momentum for their forays against the one across the hall. In a minute they'd break down the wrong one. And in fact it was happening. He watched in disbelief as his lock tore through the door frame. A fist shoved a pistol in English's face, and a man said, "You ripped off my TV, my stereo, and my bag, man, and you put it in the yard and got your car, and my sister was *home*, man, she *saw* you. I recognize you. You're the same fuck I chased outta the yard Tuesday, man, Tuesday night. You rip-off bastid. You came back."

English said, "I . . ."

"You're coming with us."

"I didn't," English said.

"Come on, thief. You're coming, or I swear to fuck I pull this trigger."

"You're wrong," English said as the man shoved him down the stairs by use of the gun. "Just look at me." There was another man behind them, he noticed now. "Look, in the light," English insisted. "I'm not the guy. I'm not." His feet kept slipping out from under him on the stairs. "*Look* at me." His feet were bare. He didn't have a shirt on.

"Louis," the man said when they were standing by the car.

"What?" the man behind them said.

"Goddamn it, come around me!" the man said. "Open the fucking door, man. Get in the back," he told English. "Get in the back, get in the back. *Louis*, goddamn it, get in the back! I'm standing on the street here!"

English sat in back, the gun no longer trained on his flesh. "Jesus, Jesus, Jesus," the man said, starting the car and trying to steer with the pistol gripped in one hand. English hunched forward with his elbows between his knees. The man next to him was breathing hard.

They were already passing the A&P on the way out of town. In a second they'd be on Route 6. At this point, to English, shivering in back without a shirt, Route 6 stood for the end of everything.

"Listen, please, there's a mistake," English said.

"*One* word." The driver whirled around as he accelerated onto the highway, bringing the pistol's mouth right up against English's scalp. "*One* word and I promise I'm gonna do it."

Louis, the man in the back seat next to English, said, "I like your style."

"You think I wouldn't? I'll do it right now, you want me to show you?"

"Yeah, right," Louis said.

"Okay." The tires cried as the driver slammed on the brakes,

and grated as they bit the gravel shoulder. "Okay. Right now."
But the car regained the highway without stopping.

"Shit. Jambo," Louis said.

"Fuck I wouldn't."

"Just drive right."

"You think I don't know how to drive?"

"Okay."

"No. No. I'm asking you."

"Okay. Okay."

"Hang *on*, man. *I* know how to drive. See this?" Jambo
wiggled the steering wheel. "That's how you drive, brother."

"That ain't how I drive," Louis said. "I do it much different."

"Hey, listen, man," Jambo said. "Okay. What about the time
I took you to the fucking Zone to cop and you said you were
gonna turn me on because it was my wheels, man, and I skipped
work, man—"

"Okay. Jesus Christ."

"I risked my parole for you, man, because you said you were
so fucking sick—"

"I told you, I appreciate it," Louis said.

"And then, hey, listen"—he seemed to be talking to
English—"I'm sitting there in the car and the place is hotter
than shit, which nobody mentioned, this fucker here never told
me the Man's cruising by every two seconds, I'm on parole, not
even supposed to leave Newton: two! *hours* I'm fucking sitting
there pissing my pants. And then so this *cocksucker* comes out
finally, this *cock sucker*, he comes staggering out with his eyes
pinned and like fucking puke all down his shirt, man, and
says"—Jambo affected deep, moronic tones—"*Hey*, man, like
Jesus the fuckers *fried* me, man, but I did you a big fucking
*fav*or, man—tell this guy what you gave me, Louis. Come on,
you think you're such a fucking saint."

"Oh, shit, never mind. I *told* you—"

"This tiny little fucking glassine envelope with fucking *dust*, you know little bits of *dust* stuck in the corners, man—I mean he shoulda throwed it in the trash, right? *Dust*, man. *Two hours* and he brings me the *garb*age after he shoots his arm full. You gave me *dust*. I risked par*ole*."

"Hey, *Jambo*—listen to yourself."

"And now you wanna pull this fucking bullshit, telling me you done me big fucking favors, man."

"Do you hear yourself?" Louis said. "That's all I have to say: Do you hear yourself."

"Yeah, I hear myself."

"Then that's all I have to say," Louis said.

Jambo turned around in English's direction. His face was a darkness. But English had the impression that he was trying to communicate something out of his eyes.

"Turn around, turn around, turn around—Jambo, you hear me?" Louis said.

"What's the matter?"

"You were almost off the road. Don't you realize anything?"

"I'm driving, man. I'm driving this car."

"Okay."

"I'm driving."

"All right!"

They drove for a long time down Route 6. Then the street-lamps revolved overhead as they turned into a town. A number of thoughts swarmed through English's skull—as to his duty now to observe the scene and memorize landmarks, as future evidence—like wild horses over a hill and down and out of sight.

He felt carsick, but couldn't stop watching as the light of streetlamps passed repeatedly over the driver's chest and wide neck.

Jambo stopped the car on a tree-lined street in front of a building that might have been a church or a village hall.

The little town seemed locked down for the winter. Nothing moved on the street except the brittle wind. Jambo lit a cigarette and rested his forearm on the steering wheel, never letting go of the pistol.

"Whatsisfuck got hit right here, last winter. Dead," he said. "He refused to look both ways."

Louis rolled down his window. "You cold?" he asked English.

"I don't have a shirt," English said.

"That's what caused me to ask," Louis said.

"Louis," Jambo said, stretching convulsively to dip his ash out Louis's window, "don't talk to the guy."

"It was just about the temperature."

"I mean it, man. You're better off. Just be like a doctor. Surgical."

Louis changed the subject. "Nobody's here, man."

"Give me a list of your other famous discoveries," Jambo said with disgust, starting the car.

"Where are we going now?" Louis said.

Jambo turned off the car again. "Fuck if I know."

English closed his eyes and counted to one hundred. He started over at one again.

"There was this nurse in detox?" Louis told Jambo with shyness, as if trying not to brag. "And when I got out of there she said, 'Come on over.' So I went there and they were having a *party*. So, I was feeling pissed off, because it's like, when she said, Come over, I thought she meant, you know, come *over*, just *me*. But anyway . . ." He cleared his throat, and stopped talking.

Jambo laughed. "Me and this guy I was in the service with, Eddie Martin. We picked this whore up and I said, 'Eddie, get in the back seat, she's gonna blow me in the car.' Whoosh, whoosh, whoosh!" He imitated a vacuum cleaner.

English put his head between his knees. Louis pulled him back up by the hair.

"Whoosh! Whoosh! Oh, baby. 'Five dollars,' she says." Jambo smacked his palm loudly with the pistol. "Bam! How's that for five dollars? Out cold! And Eddie says, 'What'd you do?' He come around and starts jerking off right over her, she's out cold: 'Best I ever had!' " As Jambo tasted this memory again, bouncing up and down in the driver's seat and repeating, "Best I ever had!" and miming the rapid hand flutter of masturbation, English started to cry, squeezing out his voice in a whisper so as not to be heard.

In a few minutes, the headlights of another car washed over them.

"That's him," Jambo said.

He turned around and nudged English upright with the gun. "This is a 9 millimeter Browning automatic." He forced the barrel between English's legs. "I don't wanna hurt nobody," he said.

"A pickup truck ran him down, man, and he died right there, right out front," Jambo was saying, "died with over a thousand dollars in his wallet."

In the light he turned out to be a wide-faced blond man.

English thought this must be a very old public restroom in what must be a basement. The floors were concrete. Mildew streaked the walls. The urinals were metal, and in a distant area of shadows there appeared to be shower stalls. Equipment hung from the walls—ropes, mops, brooms. A tang of cleanser.

English himself sat in a wooden cane-bottom chair talking to a man who wore a gigantic novelty hat of furry silver-blue velvet, nearly a yard in diameter.

"Am I on LSD?" English asked.

* * *

The man indicated Jambo, who stood over English. "Some items are missing. Why did you steal things from this person's house?"

"I didn't. You—there's a big mistake," English said, and Jambo came around with the flat of his automatic pistol on the side of English's ear. "Tell me what to do," English said. "I'll do anything." In the ringing of his head, the words sounded like fuzz.

He looked at Louis, who stood aside watching Jambo out of wounded, soulful eyes.

The man lifted the brim of his colossal hat and wiped the perspiration from his brow with the back of his hand. "Get me a chair," he said, and Louis brought him a wooden chair.

He sat down in front of English, very close, and leaned forward into English's face. "Some items are missing. Do you know what I'm talking about?"

"I promise—"

"There is no mistake. Think back. Some items are missing. Do you know what I'm talking about?"

"I swear to God, I swear to Christ," English said, "I don't know."

"What did you take?" the man said.

For God's sake, what did I take? he asked himself. If they said so, then he'd done it.

"Think."

The dawn burst. "The passports?"

"The passports. That could be a part of it, the passports."

"Oh, God, the passports."

"Your word. Passports is your word."

"This is a really—it's a bad situation," English said. "They're gone."

"That's just what I told you to start with. We're getting nowhere." The man stood up. "Are we getting anywhere?"

"Yes," English insisted, "yes, we are. You didn't say anything about passports. I told you passports."

"Who said anything about passports?"

"I—look—you're not *asking* me anything. Just ask me and I'll tell you. Anything."

"Where are the missing items?"

"They're down a sewer opening at Cutter Street and Bradford. Practically in front of Ray Sands's house. I thought if they—I didn't want to get in trouble. They were lying around. He died. I thought somebody, you know, lawyers—maybe I'd be an accessory." He thought he should look higher than the man's knees, that self-respect required it, but he couldn't. "Did you know Ray Sands had a heart attack?"

"I don't know what you're talking about," the man said. "Ray Sands. Passports. It's a mystery."

"But you said—" English said.

"Items."

"Right, you're right. You didn't say anything about anything. You're right."

"Items."

"Right, you're right. I'm sorry."

"Are you a tough guy?"

"Me?" English said. "No, no."

The man turned away and English was afraid he was readying something that would hurt.

"I was in a fight once," English said, "in a bar. I got knocked off the stool, right off the stool, one punch. Not much of a fight," he apologized. He longed to please these men, to amuse them. "How many cards are there in this deck, anyway?" he said, crying.

Louis was saying, "He dudn' know nuthin. Can't you see he don't know fuck?"

And the man in the huge blue hat pointed at himself and said, "This individual thinks he knows something. The problem is you, the problem is your attitude."

Louis punched English twice in the mouth, once with each fist.

"You're like a kid who doesn't want to wash his mommy's car," the man told Louis. "How can this person feel encouraged to share?"

Louis made a noise like a pig. Perhaps he was laughing.

"Man, this is so wasted," Louis said.

"Watch!" the man told him. He came near and spread his fingers on English's scalp, and hooked his thumb into English's left eye, right where the tears were flowing out.

"You are a disappointment," the man told Louis.

English felt defeated. He had so very little, and he wanted so much to give. "Here's what I know. Ray Sands was supposed to be the head of something called the Truth Infantry. I swear to God in Heaven I don't know anything about it except that, what I just said. I found three passports in his file drawer and they looked phony, so after he died I threw them down the sewer in front of his house. Almost in front. Right around the corner. I don't know if they washed away or if they're still there, because I don't know about the sewers in Provincetown. I'm telling you every— I'm telling you everything. You have it all, all of it, I'm not holding anything back. I'm scared because you're acting like I must know more, something about something else, but I'm just—nothing. Nobody. See? I'm so scared of you, look, I'm even peeing in my pants. You guys are in the Truth Infantry, right? That's okay, I don't know you, I'm not gonna tell. I promise to God. I believe in God," he said, "I believe in love," and even as he said it he knew he would never forgive himself: "I love you."

* * *

All the way back down the Cape in the car not a word was said. English was glad of it. Perhaps Jambo and Louis felt it, too, a bleary discomfort following their unreasonable intimacy.

They let him off in North Truro, and he walked through that tiny community and along the trail of seaside motels into Provincetown, about three miles, wearing no shirt or shoes. He did not experience any kind of chill at all. By the time he reached his neighborhood it looked to be quite late, maybe near dawn. The streets seemed very much an epilogue. The universe had lived its history. By now his feet ached, and his naked chest was frozen as senseless as an iron shield. From now on, whenever he wanted to, he had the power to kill himself. But he put it off a few more minutes.

At home he shut his room's broken door as best he could and sat in the only chair and rested with his feet up on the bed, looking at a book. After a while he had to use the bathroom. While he was in there he dropped his clothing around his feet and stepped into the shower. The pipes sang relentlessly, and the handles of the spigot in their white gloves seemed to hold themselves out begging as he washed the blood away.

It was growing light as English climbed the hill to the rear entrance of Leanna's hotel. He turned at the top of the concrete steps up to the back yard: the town before him looked truly inanimate, a collection of innumerable tons of stones and boards. Out on the harbor the small blue ice floes were turning pink. The night's darkness had sunk down into the water, just under the glimmering surface.

Often Leanna forgot to lock the back door. English turned the handle and thought for a second that she had, for once, remembered. He tried again with more strength and found himself inside, next to the laundry machines, looking into her kitchen, which he entered, and where he poured himself a glass of milk.

The living room, doubling as the bedroom, was full of the odor of her sleep. English stood just inside the aura of her dreams, sipping his milk and unbuttoning his shirt with one hand.

Leanna had had almost all her hair cut off. She was sleeping on her side and looked like no one he knew. Panic clouded his feeling: he'd come into the wrong room, found the wrong person, and now he could only have the wrong words; even his hands and his face felt wrong. But in a minute she woke up and smiled at him. She'd combed her hair back in the manner of a young hoodlum. Now it was tousled like a baby's and made her gaze more confused and beautiful. He came close and sat beside her.

"What happened to you?" she said.

"I didn't even know it was you," he said.

"Your face looks—fat, terrible, I don't know," she said.

Feeling no place to begin his story, he said, "I hit the steering wheel. I had to stop suddenly."

Here in the candlelit world of the bed he was all right, lying with Leanna in the soft glow of the sheets, beside the pack of Marlboros, the grimy ashtray, the half glass of milk. Men had beaten him up. He'd stepped through a curtain into a world of meat, a slaughterhouse. Oh, God, I am a mess, he thought.

Suddenly, though she was touching him, he knew for certain that Leanna was going to get rid of him tomorrow, or even die tomorrow, and fear moved a finger around in his stomach.

"I love that saxophone," he said.

They were naked. She was stroking his back with oiled and scented hands, moving them toward the heart, always toward the heart.

She paused, wiped her hands on the white towel, and leaned

forward over his head, supporting herself by a hand between his shoulder blades, to turn up the jazz on the machine.

"*Gato* means cat," she said sadly. It was a Gato Barbieri record.

She bent down and kissed the side of his face.

"It looks like you were in a fight."

"A fight?" he said.

"You're going to have two black eyes."

He turned over beneath her, she rising a bit to help this maneuver, and now she sat astride him lightly, groin on groin. They'd been like this many times by now, uselessly.

"I don't know much about you," she said.

"You know everything I know. Maybe more."

She watched him silently.

"I grew up on a farm."

She watched him. "What was the worst thing you ever did?" she said.

"Why do you want to know?"

She only watched him, running her thumbs along his collar-bone.

"One time I tried suicide."

"Suicide?"

"It was a mistake."

She slipped down beside him and drew him close. "You tried to kill yourself?"

"I didn't succeed."

"How old were you?"

"About one year younger than I am now."

Away from the window, down out of the light, her face was too dark for him to see.

"How? What did you use?"

"Death by hanging," he said, "was my sentence."

He kissed her falsely, trying to draw them both into some kind of interlude. But she drew away.

"Did it feel sexy?"

"What."

"Did it feel sexy when you killed yourself?"

The question frightened him, and he tried to drop back into his interior thoughts, scramble in there for an answer, something flip, something silly—

And then she asked, "Did you come?"

He tried just listening to the saxophone. She watched him— staring right through his mind, he had a feeling, down his throat and into his groin.

"Did you come?"

They touched. It felt hot. He was hard. She wouldn't let his eyes go.

"Did you come? While you were hanging, did you come?"

Right now he almost had the power to say that he'd really killed himself. That his life on earth had stopped and then started somewhere else—here, now. That he'd hung himself, died, and been brought here to wait for God's word. God's charge, the task that would bring Lenny English back from the dark.

"Go ahead," she said.

He moved partway inside her.

"More," she said.

She put her arms around him and held him tightly. "Oh!"

He stopped still, though he wanted to move inside her.

"Who are we?" she asked.

"I don't know. Leanna, I don't know."

"Rock. Slow."

"I'm afraid to."

"It's all right."

"Just slow," he said. "I swear."

He didn't know which of them was the maiden and which the seducer. He thrust more deeply, all the way in, and it didn't actually matter.

"But why is it you?" she asked him. "Why isn't it somebody else?"—and he knew what she meant, he understood that nobody mattered, that love was just making love, calling to itself out of the void, and they might be kissing, they might be touching, they might be lying face to face and staring at each other in wonder, but there was nobody home—nobody but love, so why is it you? Couldn't it be anybody? Only you, Leanna, only your lips of fever and moss, and don't ever let it stop. Only you. You're the only nobody for this nothing in the world.

He stopped, breathing hard, his life roaring. He'd killed himself, gone blank, and wakened: here, now.

The saxophone ceased. The needle left the record, abandoning them to a silence

—which he broke finally by saying:

"Yeah."

—which he shattered completely by saying:

"I did. I did come."

She pulled him to her again, and he kissed her. She reached down between her legs, where he was, and put him inside her again. They watched each other, staring each other down. He felt ashamed and alive, he felt *seen*. On her parted lips a mysterious, an unspeakable question trembled. Or was it an answer? He kissed it away. Rising up into the window's view, he let a little daylight touch his closed eyelids.

He opened them. Leanna was his lover. The morning burned his eyes. It was getting on April, but no April he'd ever seen. Colder and harder than March.

Since Sands's death two months ago, English had been staying at Leanna's hotel. What he liked about it was that he wasn't on display here. Far from it. He was practically in hiding. As long he was around the place, he had to keep entirely out of sight of Leanna's friends. "Suppose," she explained to him, "some of your straight friends found you in bed with a man?" He didn't bother telling her he had no friends, straight or otherwise, except for her.

He didn't explain where the marks on his face had actually come from, or why he wouldn't go home. And he knew she didn't ask him about these things because there was something, despite their animal closeness in the bed, that separated them, something like a jagged line down the comic-strip panel showing that they weren't there for each other but only talking on the phone. Then why was he convinced that hiding beside her was the only thing keeping him alive?

He saw each working day dawn and stayed in bed. He smoked cigarettes and watched the light move down the sides of buildings. Eventually it got dark outside, and Leanna came back to bed.

Sometimes he felt they'd been there together among the mussed sheets so long he didn't know what season it was—he thought it was summer, that he'd met her on an afternoon sapped and lulled by sunburn. Sometimes he stood in the kitchen after they made love and stared out at the rotten leaves on the black vinyl cover of the hot tub, and at the snow patches disfigured by blue shadows, and the things he saw seemed to change and simultaneously stay the same, as if clouds passed swiftly over whatever he saw, even the walls and blankets.

The weather kept him in, too—the wind and the rain, the howls and tears of the world. A week into April it snowed deeply, half-thawed, and froze in a cold snap. A second winter hardened around their slow island. But the edges of this island were frayed.

Leanna said one morning, "I have to talk to a cop. My gun is missing. I think Tucker took it. Did you ever meet Tucker? He stole it."

English turned down the radio and stood naked beside it. "I," he said, "I didn't exactly know you had a gun."

"Well, I do have a gun, but it's missing. That's why this cop, Eddie, is coming over."

"What do you mean? What kind of gun is it? You mean you have a handgun?"

"A .32."

"Jesus. I didn't know you had a gun."

"Well, I have a gun. This is a hotel, and I'm the only one around."

"You have a license and all that? What do you need in Massachusetts, anyway? A license or something?"

"It's registered. It's legal."

"Except it's missing?"

"I'm pretty sure Tucker took it."

Lately anything to do with violence, even sirens on the television in another room, caused dread to congeal in globules in the back of his throat. "Is this person, this guy Tucker, is he a Vietnam vet, do you happen to know?"

"I don't think Tucker's a veteran of anything, except reform school or someplace like that."

"And so what is his connection with you?"

"He was working around here. He was staying right over there," she said, pointing out the window at the little cabins named for famous ladies, "but now he's gone and my gun's gone. The money's all here, though." She was sitting at her desk with the telephone, the message-recording device, the bunch of slots for keys, the drawers, the cash box. It was eerie to see her among these things and to know that some of them hadn't been used or even touched for months. It made the hotel seem all the more closed.

He was satisfied that this stolen gun and this thief Tucker had nothing to do with the people who had injured him. But when you thought about it, in the general flow of events nothing could be viewed as separate from anything else, and this point-less theft was another wave of evil dragging him out over his head.

English considered these things on his first day outdoors, when the sun, which had burned away most of the snow on the streets, came over the roof and started on the footprints he'd left in the frost covering the shoveled walk. He was sitting on the wooden lip of the hot tub. Under the black vinyl the waters burbled and hiccuped. The air smelled of woodsmoke and a mix of things that had been trapped for a while under the snow. Leanna put her head out the back door. "Flush the drugs," she said.

She was followed out onto the patio by a fresh-faced, uniformed policeman.

The sun struck English's skin at that moment, raising goose-flesh. The air stirred the crumbled leaves in his hand. Through an open window came the tinny sound of Boston's only country-Western station. All of a sudden it was spring.

"It works, but it's not paid for," Leanna was telling the officer. She meant the hot tub.

English felt uncomfortable around the authorities. He supposed it showed right now in his lack of anything to say.

Leanna was talking about the thief who'd stolen her gun. "He was an unhappy person. I talked to his mother on the phone once."

Though nobody had asked, English said, "I never met him."

"What about the .44 I sold you?" Leanna asked the officer.

"I've got a Browning that shoots better, but otherwise, it's my best one," the officer said, as he wrote down notes on a pad.

Later, after the officer had written it all down and gone away, and some clouds had blown in from the sea and the light had withered, English went inside and started washing the dishes. "Are you in the firearms business?" he called out.

She came in from the living room, where she'd been doing

her accounts. "In my whole life I've owned two guns, and I've sold one."

"I was just wondering."

"Will you relax?"

"Sure thing. Yes, I will."

"Why don't you go out?"

"I will. It's spring."

"Go."

"Lend me some money. A few dollars."

"I'll lend you all you want. But if you want to feel like a person, you'd better get a job."

"I have a job."

"Really?" she said. "When was the last time you showed up around there?"

"I called yesterday. I've got a production date tomorrow. Big bucks." But he wasn't thinking about his work at WPRD. He was thinking instead of Gerald Twinbrook, Jr., the missing person, and his detective's vocation.

"I need to make a couple of calls right now, too," he said. "Long distance."

"Dial away," she said, and left him with the phone.

For a minute he watched her at work out back, sweeping twigs from the iron lawn furniture.

It was spring, and he was making a fresh start. He got Mrs. Gerald Twinbrook, Sr., on the phone.

She'd forgotten who he was. Then, when he reminded her, she said, "We've got another agency on it, Mr. English."

"He's still missing, then."

"It's been four months. We're resigned to the worst."

He cleared his throat needlessly. "Oh. I'm sorry to hear that."

"I called almost every day for a week. I talked to . . . to *Mrs. Sands* several times, but she was very . . ."

"Right, right," he said.

"Anyway, a lady from her church finally answered one day

last month and explained to me that poor Mr. Sands had had a *heart* attack."

"Yeah, it was—it was weird," he said, thinking it was the wrong word.

"If only I'd heard from you a little sooner."

"Yeah, yeah. So you took it to another outfit?"

"In Boston, yes. Carter Investigations."

"I'm fired."

"*Well*, I don't know if I would say *fired*. Perhaps you can work with the Carter people. I wouldn't go so far as to speak for them, you understand, but I would certainly insist they consult with you to begin with. And that's just what I've already told them. Any progress you've made, and so on."

"I haven't heard from anyone."

"It's not for lack of trying on their part, Mr. English. They've been phoning your office without any luck. They tell me—"

"I wasn't around. This whole thing—I mean, Mr. Sands dying, that whole business—what a thing, really. I've been beside myself."

"I understand, Mr. English, truly I understand, and believe me, I'd like to help in any way I can, but *our* concern, of course, is with—"

"Pay me if I find him."

Mrs. Twinbrook emitted a number of syllables, I, uh, we, well—"Certainly, uh, Mr. English. Yes, you see, but we already have the Carter agency—"

"Only if I find him. Only if I get results. Is that fair? That's fair, isn't it? In fact, it's totally unprofessional. I mean—"

"Well now, Mr. English, if you find my *son*, you will most certainly be *paid*."

"I just want an excuse to find him." An inexplicable rush of sentiment dizzied him and wet his eyes. "Don't ask me why. This whole thing has got me—I have to do something."

"You were Mr. Sands's assistant. Are you actually a licensed detective yourself?"

"Of course I am," he said. "Should I bring my license with me next time I see you?"

"Don't you carry it with you anyway?"

"It's kind of big. It hangs on the wall," he guessed, never having seen one.

"All right. Please understand you are not working for us, Mr. English. It's just that I don't want to discourage you if—if you should be successful—"

"If I should be successful in the efforts I am not making for you."

"I'd have to let that be the final word."

"I'm fired but I'm not fired."

"Now you're speaking past the final word, aren't you."

"Okay. Okay. You'll be hearing from me, Mrs. Twinbrook."

"I'd rather you communicated with the Carter people. All right?"

"Because I'm not giving up. It's that simple."

"Goodbye." She hung up. He didn't know whether to characterize that as actually hanging up on him, in the rude sense, or what. He decided it was just a decisive end to an indecisive talk, and promised himself he'd be more decisive in the future. Which was now.

He dialed Jerry Twinbrook's realtor in the hope of getting Twinbrook's office address.

Before he could change his mind, someone answered. "Phil-Hack Realty: Bob Edwards."

"Hi, listen, excuse me, my name's Leonard English, from Provincetown."

"Provincetown! How are things up that way? You getting some of this warm front across the Bay there?"

"Yeah. Yeah. We've hit a thaw. I'm convinced it's spring."

"Well," Bob Edwards warned him, "wait till you hear it from the ducks. The ponds are still frozen down here."

False laughter tore itself from English's throat. He rubbed away his sweaty palm print from the desktop.

"So what can I do you for, Mr. English?"

"Well, Bob, I'm kind of interested in the Twinbrook property over there. Jerry Twinbrook? He says it's right on the water and he wants to sell. Can I get a look at it maybe? Sometime soon?"

"Twinbrook."

"Jerry Twinbrook. Gerald. Junior. I believe he's a junior."

"Hang on. Right with you."

While English waited he pictured Bob Edwards, a youthful man with perhaps his tie loosened and his shirtsleeves rolled up, dialing the police on another line.

"Hi. Mr. English."

"Lenny. Lenny."

"Lenny, yeah, listen. I'm afraid he's given you the wrong realtor. We rent him some office space, but we don't handle any property for him. Gerald Twinbrook, Jr.? I get that right?"

"Right." Speak. Tell me where it is. Tell me where the office is.

"Still with me?"

"Sure, but—you think he was pulling my leg? Office space."

"No, no, no, of course not. He's probably handling the sale through another realtor. Got us confused."

"Yeah," English said, his hands tingling. "That makes sense. Listen, can I get his office address from you? He doesn't have a phone there. I'll run down tomorrow and get it straightened out, and take a look at what he's selling."

"He doesn't have a phone in his office?"

"Not—not under his name, anyway."

"Gee," Bob Edwards said. "That's a long drive on a slim chance. What if he's not around?"

Goddamn it. Goddamn it. "I'm going to Boston anyway," English succeeded in telling him.

"Well then, stop off at the Thomas Building and see him. It's a converted Victorian just off Route 3 on your way into Marshfield. Got a big sign out front, little parking lot. Can't miss it."

"Good deal. Listen, you've been a big help."

"Sure I have. What a guy, huh? Give us a call if we can assist in any way. Will you do that?"

"Okay. Definitely. Yeah."

"If you pass the Amoco station on the road into Marshfield, you went too far."

"The Amoco. Thanks." Too far? He'd be passing an Amoco on the way out of town. "Thanks a million."

"Hey. What a guy."

On the outer door of WPRD's building someone had tacked a poster of a bound, silhouetted figure. Its caption read AS LONG AS AFRICA IS IN CHAINS YOU WILL NOT BE FREE.

As he read it, the probable truth of this idea lowered itself down immensely onto English's heart.

Suddenly he changed his reason for coming. He'd set out with the idea of quitting his job, but now he thought he'd just beg off working this afternoon. This world was no place to be unemployed in.

Inside, he was greeted solemnly by the program manager, a man named Haney, a small New Yorker with very dark skin and large, sentimental eyes. Haney stirred a cup of tea while he stood in English's way, and then he sucked loudly at the liquid's surface. Lately Haney's eyes had gotten tighter, and shiny. "I wanted to talk to you about that," he said when English told him he'd have to miss that afternoon's production date.

"I know you did. I've been missing a lot."

"Not a lot," Haney said. "Not a lot. But I wanted to talk to you about it."

"I was doing some secretarial work for Ray Sands," English said. "Did you know that? There are some things, some loose ends, some things to be cleared up."

"I understand." Haney sipped at his tea and began watching his desk, two meters across the room, as if something were happening there. "We'll struggle along for a time." But the struggle was going out of him. "I'm lost. I don't know where to begin, without Ray."

English would have thought that Sands had taken no hand in the management of this station; that his passing wouldn't have produced a ripple. He felt sorry for Haney. "I'll make it up to you. Sometime."

"As a matter of fact, now is just such a time. I'm about to engineer a show you'd be able to do much, much better. Will you give Alice a hand? Alice," Haney called, cradling his teacup as if it were a trophy for the type of managerial snooker he'd just accomplished, "Lenny's going to help, I think."

English turned around and found Alice Pratt standing behind him smiling a wide, sweet smile he couldn't quite have sworn was bogus. Alice was, to his way of thinking, a fat, discarded hippie, dragged down by two monstrous happy-face earrings.

Today Alice was interviewing Charles Porter, a young man to whom English thought the word "decent" would be well applied, the head perhaps of an infant family and a small business, a tenor in the choir—but Alice had invited this man onto her show because he was, it turned out, mixed up in the occult, and was supposedly a reader of invisible personal emanations he called "auras." In calm, assured tones, keeping his lips close to the microphone, Porter explained how the cones and rods in the average eyeball kept these things hidden from the sight of most of us, and blessed the good fate that had made his own eyes a little different. It was a live show, and English's job was to stay in the announcer's room with them—there was no separate engineer's booth—keeping track of program time and steadying the volume meter by dialing the "pots" up or down. He couldn't let go of his notion of Porter as papa to a wife and preschoolers, and English wondered how he liked eating breakfast with them and seeing them surrounded by colorful force fields like alien creatures while they drank apple juice in their pajamas. English noticed, and not for the first time, that Alice Pratt's dizzy overresponding irked him a lot, in particular because he couldn't decide if it was desperately false or only camped, as it were, on the borders of insincerity. As he wore earphones, they were talking right into his head, but English was busy enough that he didn't listen. He heard no words, only Alice's voice as it scratched at the edge of a plea, wanting what everyone wanted, whatever that was; listening to her, he wanted it himself suddenly, aching as if he'd downed a shot of fuel and chased it with a flame. What hid behind her smile wasn't bitchiness or malice but the trembling of the lost. This wasn't the way to be engineering right now, how unprofessional—I'm a mess, he thought. What is it we all want? Whatever it was, he wanted Leanna to bestow it on him, and he denied automatically and viciously the fact that he probably couldn't get it from her. Everything was so clear when it came through the earphones! Something was filtered out, some obscuring, personal static. It was his own presence. His reactions to people, their reactions in turn—all the fog of himself was lifted, leaving only the others.

After the show, he found himself standing out in front of the building with Porter, only because the two of them happened to be leaving at the same time.

"Okay," English said, zipping his jacket against the wind, "what do you see?"

"Your aura is green."

"I'm envious?"

"Green denotes empathy. In the case of auras anyway."

English thought, He reminds me of a dentist.

As if dealing in something embraced as universally as oral hygiene, Porter explained that English's greatest asset—and greatest defect—lay in his ability to feel what others felt. "It's a talent, a gift, but it can be a real hazard for you. It's easy to take it too far. You can end up suffering needlessly just because you can't stop suffering along with someone else."

"I hadn't noticed anything like that, to tell you the truth."

Charles Porter shrugged and smiled. "Then I'm wrong."

English was impressed by that. "And does every person get only one aura? Is there anything else you see?"

"There's a yellow, or golden, corona there. You have a creative streak—very dangerous when coupled with empathy. You can easily begin empathizing with situations you only imagine. Find yourself getting stirred around by things that aren't really—*real*."

Finding an affable, unapologetic citizen who believed this stuff was unnerving. English would have felt less uncomfortable if the man had tried to sell him something, or asked for a donation.

He pointed at the building door and at the poster that said AS LONG AS AFRICA IS IN CHAINS YOU WILL NOT BE FREE. "You mean I'm the person who feels like that poster."

"Or the opposite," Porter said. "The opposite danger is that in trying to protect yourself, you build up a calloused attitude. You cut yourself off from other people and from your true feelings. The thing to do," he said, "is to concentrate on seeing that golden light coming out of you, right from your heart. If you concentrate on the gold, you counteract the tendency to get too empathetic. The gold energizes your creativity."

"Excuse me, but this sounds like bullshit," English said, lighting a cigarette.

"Well, it's not stamped in bronze. I'm just an educated guesser, pretty much like everybody else. But I have the same tendency to empathize, and that's what I do, I try to visualize a golden light around me."

"I didn't mean to insult you."

"No, no."

"I'm sorry."

"No. Don't be." Porter smiled.

English blew his cigarette smoke sideways. Just the same, the cloud ended up in Porter's face. English waved it away, deciding to let that serve as a parting gesture. This whole business embarrassed him, and he walked off suddenly in search of Gerald Twinbrook.

The wind sang mindlessly along his VW's broken antenna as English passed over the Sagamore Bridge. This was the first time he'd left the Cape since the night he'd arrived.

To English it was ridiculous that anyone would go around imagining a golden light shining out of his chest. But he knew he'd probably start doing it. One of the things he liked least about his nature, and something the aura viewer had failed to touch on, was a way he had of falling instant prey to the power of suggestion. "I'll try anything twice," he'd sometimes joked, and the few people in his life who'd known him very well hadn't laughed.

He passed the Amoco station on Route 3 and turned around, having already missed the turnoff to Route 93, and also the left turn onto 3—every turn required of him, in fact.

The Thomas Building wasn't active today. The parking lot served only a small yellow bulldozer and a third-hand Ford with a flat tire, and now his own VW. A sign on the building's door said NO MONEY KEPT ON THESE PREMISES. A typewriter clicked faintly in an upper office, but the place felt empty, and despite its aging exterior, the inside of it smelled new, a hint of sawdust, a ghost of hammering. The walls and floor were thin and vibrated with his steps, while the staircase, evidently untouched by the remodeling that had broken the old house's spaces into offices, was solid. There weren't any lights on anywhere inside. The afternoon sun lit up the streaks and eddies of dirt on the window he climbed toward up the stairs.

On the second floor English found empty offices, their doors ajar, and one with TWINBROOK written across its wood with an indelible pen. The door was locked.

The confusion of wrong turns that had marked his route here now overwhelmed his mind—for some reason English hadn't thought of having to get in. He was no burglar. Yet certainly he lacked a key.

He'd been turning around and going back too much today, but he had to go back to his car for a screwdriver and climb with considerable self-consciousness back up the stairs to confront Twinbrook's door. He knew nothing of locks, but the door was flimsy and gave sideways easily when he pried between door and frame with the screwdriver. In the pauses of the typewriter upstairs, he held his breath. He might have pried the bolt from its housing in one try, but it took him a minute to work up that much boldness. It made a noise, just a squawk, coming open; he closed it silently behind him. The light switch did nothing, but soon he found a light, an overhead fluorescent that must have been provided by the tenant. Its cord hung down before the desk and lay across the floor in loops, a thick red extension cord that made English think of carpenters at work.

When he let loose the light chain, he located himself in a scattering of white papers. Stacks of books and typesheets covered the floor, spilling from Gerald Twinbrook's desk and chair: old wooden things from the era of steam heat and big iron radiators.

Sands had said it would be here, in this room, under a book; penciled in the margin of a letter, doodled absently on a pad—

a name, an address, a phone number: the answer. And English believed him. It only needed finding.

He judged it was around noon. No one had been here in months, and they wouldn't be coming back today. He had all the time he could use. Then why did he feel rushed? In a daze of reluctance he walked in small circles around the office, skimming the surface of all this data, glancing at the typesheets and file folders on the desk, reading the title of the top book on a pile of books beside the chair, failing to find significance or purpose in two dotted maps and a ragged list of names taped to the wall behind the desk.

The light hummed overhead. It made him nervous. He turned it off.

He sat in the wooden chair before the desk and lit a cigarette. There wasn't any ashtray around, however, and in fact not even a wastepaper basket—crumpled white sheets of typing paper, which English understood weakly he'd have to uncrumple and peruse, filled a corner like a drift of snowballs.

Catching the handle of a drawer with the toe of his shoe, he opened a space of visibility into which he peeked as he might have down a shaft of darkness, or under a shroud: more paper, more folders, more books, all stacked in a pile that stair-stepped into collapse at the back of the drawer, which he closed as soon as he'd fully opened it.

In the other double drawer he found Twinbrook's typewriter, an antique Royal table model that didn't need hiding to protect it from theft.

He checked the heating conduit along the office's baseboard and found it cold; but the room was sunny, and he took off his jacket.

On the floor beneath the window was Twinbrook's white telephone. English picked up the receiver, listened to the dial tone, and hung it up again. For a while he looked out the window at the trees beneath him, stubby evergreens addressed, almost dwarfed, by the great blade of a Caterpillar tractor beyond them, a looming brown shadow backed by the sun in a cleared lot of yellow dirt. High above the earth he'd scraped clean, the tractor's operator sat in the open cab, drinking from a thermos and looking at the trees in front of him.

English stood still while the typist in the upper office walked across the ceiling, shut the door overhead, and descended the stairs. When the door downstairs banged and the person was gone, English looked around the room at the mounds of papers and zigzagging columns of books with real irritation, as if the typist had intentionally left him here to do all this reading and thinking without anybody's comfort.

Now he stood behind the desk and examined Twinbrook's maps—two large ones, of New England and of metropolitan Boston, stuck full of red-, blue-, and yellow-headed pins and annotated with symbols he couldn't make out.

Suddenly English turned, gripped a stack of books and papers on the desk, arranged them before himself like a meal, and sat down.

At page 173 Twinbrook had left off reading a book by Stephen King, and marked his place with a shred of typing paper. He'd spilled coffee all over one called *Life After Life* by a man named Moody; the leaves were wrinkled and suddenly antique. A fresh-looking paperback copy of *Tarantula* by Bob Dylan appeared never to have been opened. There was a schedule of buses passing through Marshfield; nothing was marked or underlined. But signs and marks and annotations crowded the pages of *Encyclopedia of Card Tricks* by somebody named Hugard and another called *The Greatest Power on Earth*, which appeared to be about atomic weapons. There were in-house phone directories for several corporations, including IBM and AT&T, but none of the names in these directories was marked or underscored. It occurred to English now to shake out the copy of *Tarantula* in the hope a slip of paper, something bearing a name or a number, might float from among its pages.

At this point a plan for coping with the major part of this mess—the part that weighed the most anyway—came to him, and he went around the room stooped over, collecting stacks of books and leaving any other kind of paper to lie where it fell. He piled the desk with volumes and began shaking out the pages—a paperback *Tibetan Book of the Dead*, a dictionary, novels by Georges Simenon and Graham Greene, three James Bond books, a fat one called *The Fourth Way*, a Bible, another Bible, and then he ignored the titles—collecting every bookmark and looking at it.

On one he found four telephone numbers with out-of-state area codes. He pocketed it. Every other bookmark was a blank shred of typing paper.

Outside, the Caterpillar started up with a gigantic clearing of its throat, and English went to the window to watch it flounder, roaring, in the storm of dust it had raised. As the operator measured a sapling with its blade, it seemed to recover its mind; as it came against the tree, its bawling became steady and thoughtful for a few seconds, and then outraged as the rollers shrieked across the treads and the blade unstrung the plant from the ground. It was sweet to hear the noise.

Coming in through the glass window, the sun's mild warmth burned the air. English pulled his sweater over his head and sat down at the desk. For a moment he considered these questions: Twinbrook, are you missing or are you hiding? Have you left a clue or have you covered your tracks? He was chain-smoking, mashing his cigarettes out on the floor. Do you mind, Twinbrook? Come in and tell me to stop.

He began on the sheets of paper—hundreds, maybe thousands of them. Many were ballpoint sketches and doodles, some were handwritten lists of names, all of them brand names or the names of political groups or business corporations.

He found two carbon copies of such a list, neatly typed. The listed corporations included IBM, AT&T, all the big outfits English had ever heard of. There were about three dozen of them. The Daughters of the American Revolution, the John Birch Society, the Ku Klux Klan. There was a circle around "Truth Infantry."

English stood up, greatly excited. Circled! But had Twinbrook circled it, or had he, English? He was holding a pen in his hand. He put the page on the desk and drew a circle on it. The ink looked identical.

Twinbrook, is this a collection or something? What do you want with these names? I'm not going to read the typed stuff. I don't like reading.

By the time he'd separated the blanker, less intimidating handwritten sheets from those crowded with small print, the sun had passed by the window, and now he realized he'd have a harder time reading unless he turned on the overhead fluorescent.

In fact, most of the typed sheets weren't typed but photocopied articles from newspapers and magazines. Some of them described freeway accidents or the weather. Others showed beaming brides and grooms, looking, thanks to the copying process, like black-faced riverboat minstrels.

None of these reports seemed connected with any other. But the corporations turned up again. He found two lists of boards of directors, apparently copied from a magazine article. Twinbrook, Twinbrook, Twinbrook. Are you nuts?

English was out of cigarettes, his eyes felt dry and sleepy, and he'd decided, at what point he wasn't aware, not to turn on the overhead light for fear of attracting attention. He wasn't used to this kind of labor, this rowing through a sea of letters and words, and he'd satisfied himself already that he'd made a fair try at getting it done. But he stayed a little longer because, to tell the truth, he wanted to satisfy Ray Sands. Sands was dead, but English still felt his power to approve or disapprove. He was still working for Sands. He was carrying out Sands's instructions. After all, people didn't die instantly. Their images lingered, and they had to fade away before you could ignore them.

He carried a folder to the window for a little more light. Across the face of it Twinbrook had scrawled the name SKAGGS. English opened it and was shocked and irritated to read, in Twinbrook's handwriting:

> *Brain Death II*   *Veith, FJ*
> *Brain Death I*
> *JAMA*   *238 (15) : 1651–5*
> *10   OCT 77*
> *238 (16) :   1744–8*
> *17 OCT 77*
>
> *life after death:*
> *J   Nerv Ment Dis SEP 77*
> *(Stevensn) 165 (3)   152–70*

What he could read of these notes seemed to consist mainly of names and numbers and dates; but the dates were old, the names weren't full names, the numbers weren't phone numbers.

> *—1975 attitudes*
> ———
> *British physician*
> *—dead body*
> *—saving life*
> *death—heart lung death*
> *but DRS say should be brain*

Twinbrook, you sick bastard, what are you thinking? Are you aware you don't make any sense?

> *NYTimes*
> *call wwwwww what is guy's <u>name</u>?*
> *call people on panel*
> *—get address of wwwwww; where can I get*
> >   *copies?*
> *later, interview people by phone*

The folder held a thick photocopied article: "BRAIN DEATH: I. A Status Report of Medical and Ethical Considerations." English was terribly thirsty and wanted a smoke. There was a page evidently typed by Twinbrook:

> *what you are holding in your hands is a book about . . . etc.*
> *And I think it is always a book about the verge in*
> *conscoiiouslness, the splitting apart of the world, and the end*
> *of time.* ~~XXX~~ *I'm not a writer of essays. I*
> ~~XXXXXX~~ *write first of all because ———ETC.*
> *talk about the headless man or bodiless head in Brazil*
> *what a visitor to this country might think of as a pre-funeral*
> *ceremony: strangers who won't be invited to the funeral driving*
> *slowly in single file alongside an*
> *accident*

Yeah, I get it. People driving past an accident. I get that. Right, brain death, I get that.

I know more about you than your own mother.

> *How did panel operate?*
> *Was agreement the general rule?*
> *Did opposing views find compromise*

> *in final report? Or did*
> *some views go down to defeat*
> *while others formed basis for report*
> *findings?*
> *Who does all the work?*

Me. I do all the work. You go crazy, and I do all the work.
He must have been missing for years before anybody missed
him. English was frightened for this man.

Among the pages, most of them flecked with words in Twinbrook's tiny, nearly illegible hand, English found the photocopied columns of an old newspaper—*The New York Times*,
a heading revealed, of September 1, 1870; and others from
September 4 of the same year. They explained the name SKAGGS
on the folder's cover: in Bloomfield, Missouri, sometime in August of 1870, according to these articles, a man called John H.
Skaggs had been hanged for murder. His executioners had
marched him up to the front of the scaffold so that he wouldn't
have to look at the noose just at that moment, and asked him
if he wanted to talk to the crowd of people who'd come to
watch him die. The killer had obliged everyone with a long
speech. "I would like for you all to have some sympathy for
me," he told them; and, talking specifically to the young boys:
"In the first place avoid drinking of whiskey; and in the next
place avoid the love of money better than you do your God;
and in the next place whatever you do avoid lewd women. I
want every little boy that hears me to remember that until he
lies on his death-bed; then when he is on his death-bed he cannot
foller after these things, and never forget it whatever you do."
His sentimental sermon rushed down the column and the printed
words seemed to shrink on the paper. "I don't know but what
there is some here on this ground that looks upon me probably
as a tyrant, as an outrageous—a tremendous man, but then that

is not for you to judge, for you know not. I hope, therefore, that no lady nor no gentleman will look upon me with any contempt as disgraced in my name. I would be glad how well you may all do; I hope to meet you in the better world than this troublesome world is. This world is nothing but sinful— nothing else; one sin will lead to another. I hope this may be a warning to every one of you, that when you go home, and after you eat your supper and lie down in your bed I hope this may run through your hearts, not only one time, but as long as you live. I think that I know that it is a mighty horrible thing to be brought up right at death's door and stared in the face. There is none of you like me; you have no idea . . ." Maybe this incident was long past and everybody involved in it was dead, but English was filled with embarrassment. The guy should have spat on the onlookers.

English wondered how the townsfolk must have felt watching the finish of a person's life. Death wasn't such a stranger to them, probably. The people of Bloomfield in 1870 had probably, every one of them, strangled chickens with their bare hands and shortly afterward eaten them, and seen close relatives languish in their final illnesses at home, and one or two might even have had a loved one dying in an upstairs bedroom while they attended John Skaggs's execution. To watch a public hanging might have been a fascinating and exciting, probably a troubling, possibly even a terrifying and humbling experience. But it wouldn't have altered the shape of the soul of a Bloomfield resident.

English thought of those days, the mornings, afternoons, and evenings before the First World War, as a time when everything made sense. Everybody shared a philosophy of life as basic as the soil and as obvious as the sky. You couldn't go sixty or sixty-five down a turnpike and end your journey in a city of thunder and smoke. He envied the people of Bloomfield their assumptions, even though he couldn't have said, exactly, what their assumptions had been. He just knew that in those days the world had been founded on things everybody understood.

According to this article, however, there were two men present at this hanging who, while they also lived in the town of Bloomfield, had already found their footing in the twentieth century, this region of the blind where there was no telling the difference between up and down, wrong and right, between sex and love, men and women, even between the living and the dead. These were J. H. Jackson and Joseph F. MacDonald, doctors of medicine who were officiating at this ceremony. They carried with them galvanic batteries of a type generally used for feats of entertainment at carnivals. By the power of electricity they meant to revive John H. Skaggs after he was hanged.

English turned on Twinbrook's light and spread the article before him on the desk.

At the time the Sheriff cut the rope of the trap a violent shudder was manifested on his countenance; he leaped back and jumped down the steps at two bounds; subdued exclamations came from the crowd, the children screamed, and the women hid their faces in their handkerchiefs and sobbed as if their hearts would break.

A gang of deputies carried the murderer's body into a room in the courthouse and laid it out on a bench. The two doctors bared its chest and ran wires from the battery to the bone above the heart. When MacDonald turned the battery's crank, John Skaggs, though he was dead, flailed and moaned.

The sheriff and the reverend tried to stop them, but the doctors couldn't be distracted now. The sheriff took away their wires, and the doctors ran the current through their own bodies, placing a hand on the battery and a hand on the victim's chest. Was Skaggs still a perpetrator, English wondered, or was he now the victim?

*   *   *

It was getting cold in the room. He needed Leanna. In the space of two months he'd been broken out of a loneliness like ice, in which he'd felt nothing, and warmed in a way that charged every nerve and made two hours' solitude a torment.

The *Times* reporter closely followed the resuscitation attempt. At five past three the right leg moves; eight minutes later the left arm flails out at nothing, the mouth froths, and the face twitches; at three-twenty Skaggs's pupil responds to light, and the doctors draw some blood from his arm; ten minutes pass, and they turn him on his side and the reporter says he "now presents an appearance only to be described, perhaps, by the word slaughtered."

Leanna came back to his mind. She liked to put her head on his chest and listen to his heart. "How could one person ever hurt another after doing this?" she'd asked him the first time. "But we do."

By twenty after four the body of Skaggs is sweating and his feet are no longer cold; in five minutes his pulse is seventy-five. But he doesn't open his eyes or speak.

By nine o'clock the experiment is over. Skaggs is dead again.

The *collapsed* quality of Ray Sands's lifelessness came back to English's mind—the sense, as he'd stood and watched his dead employer, that every bone in the man's body had been ground down to powder.

When he got back to Leanna's, he could smell the camomile-scented steam rising from the hot tub before he rounded the stone steps onto her back patio. He heard someone laughing, and a splash. He wouldn't be joining her there. He hadn't been in the hot tub since the debauched night of Ray Sands's last coronary.

As he came around the building's corner onto the patio, he found her half out of the water, leaning over a woman he didn't recognize at first. They were kissing.

"Leanna?" he said.

She looked up at him. A casual greeting started from her, he could see it moving on her lips. But she couldn't quite pull it off. After a couple of seconds she said, "This is Marla."

English saluted mutely.

Leanna said, "Marla Baker."

Marla smiled. "Hi. How do you do?" she said.

Marla had gone under and come up, so that her hair was slicked back and her eyelashes glistened. She seemed very summery. English suddenly felt how warm it was today, and even a little humid.

"Well," he replied, "I'm feeling very weird."

"Lenny," Leanna said.

"Weird?" Marla said.

"Like—weird and kind of sick." He sat down on one of the iron lawn chairs. The seat was wet, and he stood back up.

"Lenny," Leanna said, standing up, too—naked, the water streaming off her—"maybe we should go inside a minute."

"I've got to get some air," English said.

"Okay," Leanna said after a long pause.

"I'll take a walk. I'll call you later or something. Nice meeting you," he said to Marla. "I remember you. I've seen you around."

The spot of wet on the seat of his pants bothered him as he walked down Bradford and then over to Commercial. And the warm and sweetened breath of the day bothered him, too. The springtime. Buds on the tips of rosebushes outside the town hall, buds like dewdrops shimmering on the shrubs, a frail green trembling in the tips of twigs. The demented crocuses were hauling themselves up out of the earth. He moved faster, trying to get away from the signs of this grisly miracle, looking in all the windows instead of at the world. There were merchants inside the shops now along Commercial, cleaning, painting, tearing loose the signboards of bankrupt businesses and raising up the bright names of new ones.

The trouble and ache of the last few minutes circled the center of his feeling and then dropped away. Later for that. Now was the time for other things—for the next thing—for figuring out what to do now, this instant. Oh this town, with its harbor glinting like a blowtorch at the end of every alley . . . He'd walked almost as far as Cutter Street, where Grace Sands might still be living. And where Ray Sands must have kept any material, any files, he may have had regarding Gerald Twinbrook.

English turned up Cutter. Right away he felt the strands of a certain kind of nauseated pity touching him. He didn't want to see Grace. On the other hand, he wanted those files. Maybe she wouldn't remember him. Or maybe she would reach out and strangle his heart, pleading for an explanation of absolutely everything.

Nobody home. His knock sounded the emptiness of the rooms behind the double doors. Standing tiptoe on the mushy lawn, he tapped on the windows and tried to peek in. The lace curtains seemed to have survived from obscurity, like the antique gown of a jilted bride. They were shut tight, without a crack to see through.

From the next-door neighbor, a young woman carrying a baby and walking barefoot and coatless across narrow Cutter, going tiptoe among the frigid rivulets of snowmelt, he got the latest. Grace Sands had moved to the old folks' home. "You know—Shirley Manor," she said. The baby, peeking out of its blue blanket, regarded him with a powerful serenity.

"Why are you barefoot?" English asked the woman.

"I'm just going from my mom's house back to my place," she explained with a little embarrassment. She pointed one at a time at two houses facing each other across the lane. The house she'd been making for was next door to the Sands residence.

"Who took Grace over there to Shirley Manor, I wonder," he said.

"It was the Bishop. Bishop Andrew," the woman said.

"Bishop Andrew?"

"Yeah, weird, huh? He comes over sometimes when he's on the Cape. He's a relative or something. The first time I saw him I was surprised. I didn't know he drove an El Camino," she said.

An El Camino? This irrelevancy irritated English unspeakably. He stood in the lane for a while after she'd left him, chewing viciously on the inside of his cheek.

When he was alone on the street again, he moved quickly, willing himself not to think about it, around the side of the house to the kitchen door. English hadn't been back here before. There was no yard to speak of, only a tall board fence three steps away from the glass-paneled back door. He broke a panel of the glass with his elbow, gouging a small tear in his jacket's leather sleeve. It didn't make much noise at all.

He took a deep breath, standing quietly by the door, and then surprised himself by bursting into tears. Something must be getting to me, he thought, yanking out his shirttail and wiping at his eyes. The sobs doubled him over and shook him as if dislodging a strange, heavy obstruction from his throat. When he stood up straight again his heart was lighter, though his head hurt and his eyes felt wounded. He reached his right hand carefully through the shattered panel, opened the door, and went through the kitchen and the airless living room to Ray Sands's work area.

English had a cigarette while he puttered around in his dead boss's studio, peering into the tripod camera's lens, repositioning the two tungsten lamps, and blowing smoke into the somber darkroom. In the office itself he found the file drawer open and empty. It stood to reason that Sands's executor would have been here, and maybe, thought English, there was cause to remove the files. But he couldn't help it, the numberless fingerprints of a conspiracy blazed brightly on all the objects around him now.

The telephone on Sands's desk was working. English dialed the numbers he'd found in Gerald Twinbrook's office, and had a couple of conversations. The first two were New York numbers, one no longer in service and the other belonging to an art gallery; but the person answering hadn't heard of any Gerald Twinbrook.

"So this isn't his gallery? He doesn't show paintings there?"

"I know my artists," the man said. "I don't know Gerald Twinbrook."

The third number belonged to the Notch Lodge in Franconia, New Hampshire. A recorded message told him the lodge was closed from October 10 until the first of June.

Franconia—the Truth Infantry—matters drifted together into secret shapes. His head said: What if this, what if that? What if it all ties together, what if somewhere a bad man sits making sense of it all, with my fate in his hands? This situation is adding up. I've got everything but the area code on this one. He picked up Ray Sands's felt-tipped pen with the idea of writing down all the facts of the case—the people, the places, the connections—Provincetown, Marshfield, Franconia; Ray Sands and Grace Sands; Marla and Carol and Leanna; Twinbrook and the Cape light and John Skaggs, the unholy nineteenth-century Midwestern Lazarus; Twinbrook and the big corporations and the Truth Infantry and God and Jesus and the Bishop . . . But the pen was dry and he decided in favor of letting these things boil inside him until they produced a driving steam. He turned over the few papers on the desktop, a couple of errand lists in Ray Sands's small, square hand, several bills with the payment vouchers torn away, and when he uncovered what he saw, for an instant, as a white card on which were penciled the words *Kill the Bishop*, but which he found under the lamp to be an envelope bearing, in Sands's print, the name

Leanna Sousa

it was like walking past a phone booth just at the moment someone says "Hello?"—that one word corkscrewing out of a whole life.

He put the envelope down and dialed the fourth telephone number, one in the 202 area. A woman answered and said, "Good afternoon, this is the White House."

"White House?"

"This is the White House. You've reached the telephone number of the President."

"The real President? I mean," English corrected himself, "the real phone number? Can I talk to him?"

"If you'll state your purpose," she said, "we'll connect you with a staff member who can help you."

English hung up on her.

He picked up the envelope bearing Leanna's name.

It wasn't addressed to Leanna, or to anybody. Her name ran across the upper left corner, just a notation. English held the envelope gently. He thought of steaming the flap loose or getting the thing X-rayed, and then he just tore it open with his thumb, remembering the owner of this communication was dead. The note was handwritten on yellow lined paper. He closed his eyes and willed himself to understand that it couldn't possibly be an instruction to him from God to kill the Bishop of his diocese. And it wasn't, he saw, from Sands to Leanna, which he'd also feared, but to Marla Baker from the lover who'd lost her that winter—from Carol.

Dear Marla,

This evening you called and before I recopy what I read to you on the phone I just want to say how important it is for me to express to you those thoughts. It's very frightening for me to put my feelings on the line, without that edge of "control" or the notion of the "observer" lurking in the wings. So . . .

Just spent an agonizing evening thinking and feeling about possibly everything under the sun—wanting to write down and clarify that confusion—the confusion of wanting you, really desiring you—a desire that runs very deep and continues to cut deeper—I say cut because this kind of opening is at once pleasurable and painful—I'm in a dilemma—for me, some very important things are happening between you and me— and I want for you to have all that you want for yourself—but I also have "wants"—at issue for me now is whether I'm able to continue being sexually involved with you while you are involved sexually with another woman again—with Leanna again, I almost couldn't write her name. —I know I've never felt the sexual and sensual highs I've experienced with you, but now I'm beginning to feel myself construct limits and barriers between you and me—in my mind and body. I realize that ideally this shouldn't be so—that I should be able to be totally and fully there with you—to leave myself open to the experience of your love and affection—regardless of who is sleeping with you tonight or any other night—and I've been

trying real hard to deal with that one in as open and rational a
way as I possibly can—but I know that for now that is
beyond me. I want you very much, I want to continue to grow
and nurture my love for you, to allow it to unfold, recognizing
our sexual selves as an essential part of that love's core—I
think you know I wouldn't ask for this unless I felt what was
happening now was pulling us apart—

I guess there isn't much more to say other than that you
embrace the above as an expression of some really deep feelings
that I felt compelled to share with you. It scares me when you
talk about being "fucked unconscious." That's definitely not the
Marla I know—let me know, please, how you're feeling and
what rages or anger you have for me. I hope what I've said
won't be resented—keep loving!!
    Loving you,

English put his head down on the desk. Why did everything
vibrate when he touched it?—strands of an indecipherable web,
connections that shouldn't be there. The coincidences of his life
assailed him. The walls of the world were soft; wherever he
bumped up against them he pushed through into inscrutable
chaos and naked meaning and Heaven and Hell. But there was
comfort in touching this letter. It gave him peace just holding
it in his hand. It brought to mind the lonely safety of those
nights he'd spent listening to Carol and Marla's conversations,
those nights when he, the only one awake in the world, had
known all about them and had forgiven them.

When he got outside, the sky had darkened. Within minutes
a stiff wind was blowing over the harbor. Now what? Was it
going to snow? Winter into spring into winter. Miss Leanna
had turned into Mister. Wafer and wine into body and blood.

And people dying—passing from life into meat. All these transformations. They were too much for him.

English stopped in at the Yardarm Tavern because they'd recently gotten a videotape player, and from all the way out in the street he could see film credits wandering up over the big screen. *Lawrence of Arabia.*

He sat down at the bar, and before anybody could get near him he said, "Nothing, thanks. Nothing. Nothing." A guy on drugs clutching a teddy bear to his chest pulled up a chair two feet from the screen and got in everybody's way, exclaiming about the music. His friend, an older man, said, "Daniel, I have a drink for you at the bar."

"The sound track is incredible! Unbelievable! I'm experiencing this!"

"Daniel," his friend said. "Please."

"Could you turn this *up*, please," the man cried out, passing his bear back and forth before the screen.

The older man led him out of the place by the hand. "I'm experiencing this!" the younger one repeated. His friend said, "Everybody's experiencing it. I'm very embarrassed."

English said, "Okay if I use the phone?"

The bartender snagged it and set it down in front of him with a negligent, easy grace. "Who cares?" he said.

English watched the movie, vaguely following the course of events in the life of this great hero. In a while, tiny figures lay slanted against the swirling yellows of a desert sandstorm. He thought it must look very much like the inside of his own mind.

He dialed the phone and when she answered didn't identify himself, just started right in. "I have various things to say to you."

"I'll have to cut this short," Leanna said. "I'm in the middle of washing my hair."

"You're not washing your hair."

"I'm washing my hair, Lenny."

"Let me hear the bubbles. Put your hair next to the phone. Let me hear the lather fizz."

"Don't be absurd."

"You're not really washing your hair," he said.

"I'm washing my hair, so now if you don't mind—"

"I do! Leanna, wait, I do mind— God, I wish I could look around on the other side of this jagged line, like they do in the comics."

"In the comics?"

"Well, they do that sometimes. I wouldn't, I wouldn't make something like that up, Leanna. Because I would never snow you. I would never lie to you."

"Are you just going to hassle me? Is this going to be that kind of call?"

"Okay. Okay. Okay. Sorry."

"That's okay."

"No. I mean, you know. I'm sorry." He sighed. "So how long has Marla been back in P-town, anyway?"

"Since April first."

"Right. And I'm the April fool, right?" He winced to hear her sigh. "How come I haven't seen her around?"

"You haven't seen anybody. You've been indoors for a month."

"Are you back together with her? Obviously you're back together with her. Why didn't you tell me?"

"It didn't come up."

"Jesus. It didn't come up? Come on. Why didn't you tell me?" She didn't say anything.

"We've been going together for *weeks* now," he pointed out.

"Is that what you call it? Going together?"

"Man, I don't get this," he said. "Please, don't back up on me like this!"

"Why don't you come over?"

"Why? So I can watch you two get it on in the hot tub?"

A silence. Then: "No. So I can dry my hair while you're on the way."

"Is she there?"

"No. Not—not when you get here."

"Christ. She's standing right there."

He hung up.

A crew-cut woman in dance tights and a big overcoat nodded off in the corner. There was celery sticking up out of her drink.

A muscle boy in a sleeveless sweatshirt laid his cheek down on the bar and gazed at English, his eyes misted with a barbiturate vagueness.

A small dapper gentleman two seats away knocked back a shot of something and exhaled an invisible sweet cloud. His smile broke in two and he quickly signaled for another.

In the midst of these chemically happy patrons, English tasted a sadness. Knew its idiot exile. He took nothing stronger than the free popcorn placed in salad bowls around the place, but he felt as if his own machine was running on the wildest concoction, the adrenaline and sorrow of a broken love.

He called her again within five minutes. "Is she there?"

"No. I'm alone now."

"How's your hair?"

"It's alone, too."

"Don't do that. Don't act like it's funny. Listen, listen, something's bothering me."

"Obviously."

"No, a question, one question, something's bothering me. The night I came in, in the morning, and your hair was all cut off. She did it, right?"

"No. I did it myself. I told you that."

"Okay. You're not lying?"

"She wasn't even in town then, Lenny."

"You're not lying?"

"Everything's right out in the open, isn't it? What is there to lie about? I'm seeing Marla, Marla's seeing me, we're going to try again."

"Try again. What do you mean 'try again'?"

"It's different now. Things were tense, we were tense, before. This stuff with her husband, all of that. Then she got involved with Carol, and then she got paranoid about this surveillance business. It was the circumstances. You don't know what it's like, feeling you're being followed around. We think we can . . . I don't know. We're willing to try again."

Anger started behind his eyes as he heard her talk about surveillance, about paranoia. "Look," he said, "you shouldn't be messing with your own sex. You and me, it's more natural. You and me—"

"For me, it's more natural to be a dyke," Leanna said.

"But you don't even make love!"

"We make love."

"But you can't, you don't, it isn't like you *fuck* her."

"Fucking isn't everything. With you and me, it really wasn't anything."

Though her words were direct, her tone was not unkind.

"But we just got to that part. Give me a chance. Now is when it starts to get good, don't you realize that?"

"You can have all the chances you want, Lenny. Nothing's changed."

"Nothing's what? Nothing's fucking changed? Are you back with her or not?"

"Yes."

"Then—"

"—but nothing's changed between you and me. I mean, not if you don't want it to."

"I want you all to myself."

"But now Marla's back in the picture."

"Are you saying you want to do a three-way?" A prurient thrill banished his anger for a second.

"No," Leanna said. "One-on-one with Marla, and one-on-one with you."

"What bullshit."

"We're free in this life," she said.

"What an absolute motherfucking fantasy."

"Why don't we figure out what we want and then make it work?"

"At least," he admitted, "you have the balls to ask for it." A sudden envy of her stung him, and he banged down the receiver.

He sat staring at the bartender, who opened a plastic bag and poured English's bowl full of free popcorn without looking at him.

Baby, we hated each other in another life, English declared inside himself as he left. Let that be the last word. Outside, the harbor was producing its effects, and again the weather was all different. Cancerous blossoms of fog undoing everything. Two blocks east he stopped at a wet pay phone and dialed Leanna's number, but she didn't answer.

English forgot completely, as soon as he woke in the darkness that night, that he'd been dreaming of tumbling in a coffin down a flight of stairs. But he certainly felt like somebody who'd just done something like that, queasy and rattled, his ears ringing. He thought he'd better write this down. He got out of bed and sat in his underwear with a big loose-leaf notebook and a disposable pen. Generally he carried this notebook around in his car's glove compartment. He'd meant to use it to keep track of all the cases he'd looked forward to solving here in this town, but the pages were white and unblemished. As if from outside the window, he looked at himself sitting in a blue chair stained with other people's drinks.

Holding the notebook in his lap, his ankle crossed over his knee, he started a letter to Leanna:

Many of the feelings I've been having lately, breaking down crying when alone, the sense of a cloud between me and God, the intuition that now, behind the cloud, is the time of faith—

But a shock of inspiration passed through him, and he turned to the next blank sheet and began a letter to his dead parents:

Dear Mom. Dear Dad.
I never knew how to talk to you. We made up a way of being together in the same room, and once we'd established that, we never deviated. Nothing ever got said. It was like some of the rote Masses I've been to. I know the priest isn't home, I know he's

He turned that page aside. It was all coming out now. He knew who he was. On the next sheet he started an open letter to the tattooed ghost that was stalking him, the dead GI in Vietnam, the one who'd been drafted in Lenny's place, sent overseas in Lenny's place, marched over swamps and shot at and killed instead of Lenny:

There are worlds, whole worlds too small to see, in these tears. Maybe one of them is at peace. I wish I could bring you there.

—Now he knew who he was writing to. It was the invisible one, the missing man, the ghost who could put real daylight into false landscapes; it was Twinbrook, Gerald Twinbrook, Jr.—

Resuscitation of a Hanged Man

If you like the fields we'd walk away from the road into the fields, or we'd go fishing, if that's what you like to do. The sun would set and we'd build a fire. The trees and rocks would shrink and their shadows would grow. People don't have eyes by the light of a fire. No, that's glib and pointless. It's all glib and pointless. In the worlds that live in these tears just as much as in the real world, I'd stare at you and have no idea who you were, for hours. One word after another would get choked in my heart. I wouldn't be able to ask your name. You wouldn't be able to see my face. After a while the fire would go out, you'd be lost in the dark, and I would cry these tears.

MAY—JUNE

It was more summer than spring now. Still, the evenings were cool, and the heavens at night had a wintry clarity that sometimes made him cry.

He was a citizen of a country north of Mexico that made no sense; he was an inmate of romance and a denizen of that terrainless geography, a lot more real than the geography on maps, that drifted down from these dark blue oceans to the Keys, passing over the Eastern megalopolis like a cloud over a desert but catching on the invisible peaks of Atlantic City and Cape May and Ocean City and the Southern beach resorts, a geography of heated sand and greased-back hair and surf glowing under a full moon. It was the off-season, but the off-season had no jurisdiction—the place was like a closed carnival—nothing counted but the thrilled ghosts.

It was no secret at the radio station that English was going nuts. Twice he appealed directly to Leanna over the airwaves, though he was aware she never listened to the radio. In the middle of reading the Arts Calendar he switched the mike off to scream and curse. He couldn't eat; he'd be ravenous and then suddenly nauseated after one bite of a sandwich. It got clear how a person could die for love just by going undernourished for too long. Also he was the victim of bizarre thoughts. He considered hiring a billboard or a hot-air balloon or a blimp and imagined depicting the extremity of his love in other ways, getting on TV somehow, perhaps by crawling on his hands and knees to the Vatican or impersonating the President. He wanted to do something melodramatic and endearing, but how could he be charming to somebody whose face he wanted to smash? He dreamed of shooting her—Didn't think I'd do it, did you, didn't know I loved you enough to kill you, no, baby, don't do it, yes, yes, I *have* to—he prayed, God save me from being angry, and he prayed, God help me track down an unregistered gun. Some helpful person left in his WPRD message slot a lapel button for him to wear that said *I'm a Mess*.

In less unreasonable moments he was disgusted with this mooning over Leanna. He couldn't understand why he hadn't just left town by now. He feared he might be living out some myth of seeking the goddess beyond the pale, entering the realm, being changed into one of its denizens, every footstep forward changing the shape of his soul, and every form of her dissolving as he approached.

He hadn't left town, but he'd left Bradford Street. Down by the water the rents had gone up as the landlords and shopowners readied their nets for another kind of fish. English had taken himself up the hill to a duplex next door to Shirley Manor, the old folks' home, which was situated, possibly with the ease of access in mind, just across the road from the town's biggest cemetery.

He hadn't liked it anyway, living in sight of the sea. He'd felt implicated somehow in the ruthlessness of its tides.

He liked the cemetery better. Although generally the light was kind to this place, sometimes giving to the grass and stones the hardy colors of a Surrey countryside, and making the markets blush sometimes in the sunset, it was not unknown for the fog to roll over the whole business swiftly, canceling everything, even the hope of anything, beyond the few nearest blurred grave-sites and the brown bones under them. English had no trouble feeling, really feeling, the presence of those whaling families with their arms straight down at their sides, only a bit more rigid in death than they'd been beforehand. He'd been reading *Reflections on the Psalms* lately, and he began to see in the defeated stoicism of these Pilgrim descendants the other side, the dark side, of the prissy smugness with which C. S. Lewis had been managing to nauseate him. For these people, as for Lewis, God had probably been an Englishman, but a less and less familiar one, passing beyond dotty eccentricity into madness and vomiting up whales and storms. On some nights English saw them trolling the fog for forgiveness and seeking for Jesus among the dewy stones. Little truths continually came into his mind. Whispers from the center of his heart. *All are martyred. Kill the Bishop.*

He knew that something big was going to happen, that he was at the slurring start of some grand opportunity or injury, like a person who's just lost control of the car on an empty street and entered the dreamy beginnings of an accident.

A rainy day calmed him, the tears of God dripping down the markers and trickling through the names of the dead. The next day was windy and sunny, and he stood around in the kitchen while his radio talked like a skull—a theological discussion on WPRD. He couldn't help listening to such things.

He walked into the living room, holding a cup of tea, to find Grace Sands standing just inside his home, and the open door shaking in the wind behind her.

Although she wore a pink robe and matching house slippers with fuzzy blue balls on the toes, she'd managed to get away from Shirley Manor with a tiny black pillbox hat and a veil sprinkled with black diamond shapes, from behind which she gazed with the cynical look of a mistreated child, saying, "The floors. The carpet. *Look*." She stooped over. "Use your eyes." Stooping must have hurt her back; her voice was full of pain. She stood up holding a piece of something between thumb and finger. "Wood!"

He didn't want this. He had things to do. Besides, he was waiting for this big thing, this opportunity to be snatched, this yes-no point dividing his wasted life from a future that was going to make sense. He wanted to wait in solitude.

"I don't know what to say," he admitted to her.

"Whatever happened to clean? Remember clean?"

"My vacuum cleaner's broken," he said. "I'm sorry."

"Broken," Grace said. "Vacuum cleaners were broken before they made the first one. You bend, that's how." She stooped over. "You pick up, that's what." She started picking bits of lint from the carpet. "Time passes," she said. Her face went dull with torment. She was eight feet into the living room. "It takes time. It takes effort." She stood up straight, wiped at her face and seemed alarmed to find it veiled. She flicked the lint from her hand and it fell to the carpet.

English set his tea down on the windowsill. Grace let out a long, shaking sigh.

"I'd better find whoever's supposed to be taking care of you," English told her. Grabbing the phone book, he leafed through, looking for the number of the nursing home. He was glad to have a chance to use the telephone. It was new in his life, and nobody ever called him except the station.

Grace wandered toward the back room while he dialed. "I'm about twenty yards down the road here," he told the receptionist when she answered. "Grace Sands is lost over here—do you know Grace?"

"Oh, my goodness. I'll send somebody right over. Which house?"

He told her and went back to steer Grace away from harm. She was standing in his bedroom looking down at his mussed sheets. The blankets had gotten onto the floor in the night.

"So this is the bed," Grace said sadly.

"I guess I'd have to agree, all right."

"The famous bed," Grace said.

"The what?"

She raised her gaze to him, lifting her veil carefully with both hands. "What?" she said. Then she lowered her veil.

English went to the living-room window and looked out. The cemetery and the world itself held still, burning in the sunlight. Then a young fellow with a beard came pushing a wheelchair up the walk, leaving the contraption by the door, where English now stood, looking at him.

"Grace here?" he asked.

English pointed inside.

Good health and good cheer emanated from the young man as he came inside saying, "Grace. We don't want you off the grounds. That's a rule."

His happiness seemed to make her suspicious. "My leg is broken." She lifted her veil with both hands and looked out the window.

"Then it's a good thing I have a wheelchair," the man said. When speaking, he looked only at English.

"I used to work for her husband," English said, "before he died."

"The Catholic cemetery in Hyannis is where they buried him," Grace said brightly.

"Grace: in the wheelchair," the man said, not unkindly.

She seemed in perfect possession of her mind as she told them, "They threw a shovel of dirt right down onto him with a"— she clapped her hands while looking for a word—"noise. Like that."

The man helped her by her elbow out the door, and then

together he and Grace lowered her bulk down into the seat of the wheelchair. "Where are we going?" English heard her asking in the sunlight as the man pushed her down the walk.

He heard somebody on the radio referring to God as "the infinite accent falling on the self." Infinite, yes. The accent—the stress—the falling, yes, English felt he felt that.

He thought, They'll all know me when it's over; and he thought, Who will find me when it's over?

He thought, You start to know these things. You make out just the shape of it, the incredible size, on the horizon.

Zealots. Martyrs. These guys are right. Nothing but faith makes it so.

In this state he walked out of the house, got in his Volkswagen, and took up the search for Gerald Twinbrook again, heading up the Cape toward the missing artist's abandoned office, going as fast as the car would go, which wasn't quite fast enough to get him even a warning ticket. It eased him tremendously to be doing something. He took the back roads through Truro, South Truro, Wellfleet, through the sparse shade of new leaves and the shadows of large hills. On the maps of the Cape these hills were named individually and called "islands," owing, perhaps, to the mapmakers' premonition—whose accuracy English trusted, if vaguely—of a great flood that would someday submerge almost everything.

When he reached Twinbrook's office, he found that somebody had been at work there. The door had been repaired. He broke it again.

Inside, too, the place had changed. The chair and wastebasket were stacked on the desk, the electrician's cord was coiled neatly between them, the knee-deep litter of papers and books had been arranged in two large stacks beside the chair. Someone had mopped the floor. The telephone was gone. A manila en-

velope was taped to the front of the desk: GERALD TWIN-
BROOK. Inside was a handwritten note lamenting Twinbrook's
disregard for previous letters and informing him that his property would be tossed or sold as soon as a new renter was found.
It wasn't signed.

Also in the envelope were a communication from a dry cleaners, which turned out to be a bill, and a letter from Blue Cross.
In all-caps, telegrammatic format, the letter asked Gerald Twinbrook to provide information about the amount paid for pre-
scription drugs following his emergency treatment on the second
of January.

Twinbrook had been missing since before Christmas, if English remembered right. This was the first evidence that he'd
been alive and functioning since then. And if he'd been treated,
if he was ill—he might be incapacitated somewhere, in a rest
home, for instance, with amnesia, or in a coma in a strange city,
with a tag reading JOHN DOE taped to his bedrail.

English's fingers trembled as he folded the letter and put it in
his pocket. He swore to himself that he wouldn't jump up and
run from the room, that he'd peruse these stacks of paper, that
he'd stay calm and analytical. On top of the nearest one was
the carbon copy of a letter Twinbrook had addressed to "The
Secret President of the United States." *Dear Sir or Madam*, he
raved, *Under the Freedom of Information Act I demand that
you comply with my request of August 13, which I have repeated
twice monthly since then. I am asking for all the records on the
corporations listed below. I will be satisfied with nothing less
than all the records in the world.*

English dropped the page onto the floor and walked immediately out of the office without looking back. It had suddenly
occurred to him where he might turn up some information about
Twinbrook's Blue Cross record. English wanted all the records
in the world on Twinbrook.

* * *

In the antiseptic corridors of the Cape Cod Hospital, English felt a soothing influence. He was an institutional man. He knew the hospitals, the cops, the universities. On a daily basis English had lived this scene, the waiting room with the glacier of afternoon light crashing mutely through the windows and the clerk yawning wide and the pregnant orderly knitting a small stocking. It was four-thirty. There was nothing much to do in the emergency room, because all the minor injuries and sudden headaches could be taken to family doctors' offices. Soon things would get lively, when the offices closed and the children, exhausted by an afternoon of play, would tend to fall from the trees or split each other's heads open with baseballs. Making their way home from the public parks, the children would be struck down by automobiles. At home their mothers would lay their thumbs bare to the bone while slicing up salads before supper, and then after supper they'd lacerate their wrists on broken wineglasses in the cloudy dishwater while Father, tinkering with the car, would be getting the bib of his overalls caught in the fan belt and destroying his manhood out in the garage . . .

"I'm off duty. I was just passing by," English said. "Do you remember me?"

The clerk glanced up.

"Detective English. You're Frank, right?"

"Oh. Hey. Hi," Frank said.

"I suddenly thought of stopping in and asking you about something. I wanted your help, maybe."

"Oh."

"Nothing urgent. It has to do with an old case."

Frank looked unsure. "Sure."

"I was wondering about insurance records, and suddenly I thought, Hey, Frank, at the hospital."

"That's me," Frank said.

"You deal a little with insurance records, don't you?"

"Sometimes. My job mainly consists of writing down the information necessary to have somebody billed. Anybody. Usually an insurance company."

"So, after a patient's been dealt with here, somebody sends a report to the insurance company, right?"

"Yeah, for some of the larger companies. Blue Cross, Travelers, State Farm. Not exactly a report," Frank said. "Just a series of code numbers."

"Who does that job?"

"The overnight clerk puts the codes and account numbers on file cards. Then a programmer puts all that in the computer and transmits it to the company."

"What do they do? The programmer, I mean, does the programmer just access—what do they access? Where do they put the information?"

"They access the insured's account number."

"Do they have access to all the data in that file?"

"Yeah. It's just a series of code numbers. I mean, you know, it goes back to the first of the year."

"Date of incident, hospital code, doctor code, injury or diagnosis code, that stuff, right?" English said.

The clerk showed signs of backing off. To an official person, English had long ago learned, a citizen gave four successive answers and then required an interlude. English examined the cover of a book, a psychiatric nursing text, lying on Frank's desk. In a minute he said, "Can I talk to you out here?"

Frank joined him by the water cooler in the waiting room. "Is this—a big crime thing you're working on, or something?"

"It's an unclosed case. You know—can't let it go. What I'm thinking, see—if I give you the account number, can you get the data on a Blue Cross subscriber and decode it for me?"

"Wow," Frank said, "I don't know, I wouldn't think the hospital—"

"A missing person," English said. "If I could track him down to a hospital somewhere, oh, man, what a wonderful thing, to find him and ease his family's worries— Give us a hand, huh?"

"Well, but Blue Cross. You could—"

"Yeah, we did. They're going to give us the information, but it just keeps getting snarled up in paperwork. This is the account number." English handed him the letter from Blue Cross. "Can you talk to the data clerk?"

"The programmer? Yeah. Okay," Frank said. "I can."

"Now? Take a break?"

Frank sighed uncomfortably.

"How long would it take? A few minutes?"

"I'll be back in a few minutes," Frank told the orderly.

The orderly was policing the waiting room now. She looked to be eight or nine months along, straightening slowly with a hand on her hip and standing that way a minute. She held a rolled-up copy of something like *Good Housekeeping*. She shook it at him like a warning finger. "I hate it when they tear the stuff out of our magazines."

Two janitors came down the hall, one with a mop and one with a running vacuum cleaner, talking under its noise:

"Hah?"

"Hah?"

"Hah?"

English went into Frank's cubicle and poured himself a cup of coffee. He picked up the psychiatric nursing text and started reading all about himself.

In a few minutes an obstetrician came downstairs from Ob-Gyn and wanted to show them the premature baby—no more than a foetus, at twenty weeks—he had just delivered.

The orderly paid him no mind. She was balancing her checkbook.

"This thing hasn't drawn a breath," he told English, "but the heart's still beating. Forty-eight minutes. That old heart's just ticking away." The obstetrician's hands and lips trembled, and tiny drops of blood flecked the front of his green surgical gown. His hair had been shellacked by sweat under his sterile cap, which he now used to wipe his nose. His eyes were large and morose, like a cow's. "I've been a practicing physician for eleven years," he said, staring at the foetus he was holding. It was in a plastic ice-cream cup.

Frank came in. He was holding the printout.

The obstetrician put the foetus down on the counter in front of him. "Dessert?" he said.

Frank peered into the cup as over the edge of a cliff.

"Is it alive?" English asked him.

"Are you kidding?" the obstetrician said. "Would you call it living if you looked like that?"

"But you said the heart was still beating."

"Well, you know, the heart's a strange muscle. You can keep it going practically forever with a little electricity."

The orderly got up and left.

"Where did you get those shoes, man?" English asked the doctor suddenly.

"These are golfing shoes," the doctor said. "I got them at a pro shop. I'm just waiting for this thing to die, okay?"

Frank went over and sat down on the orderly's stool. "Here you go," he said, handing English the printout.

English studied it but didn't know how to read such a thing.

"What is it now," the obstetrician said, looking at the clock and sobbing and wiping the snot from his nose with his green surgical cap, "about fifty-three minutes?"

"It's dead," English told him.

"How do you know from way over there?" the doctor said. But he knew, too.

Frank crossed his arms over his chest and looked at English. "The codes mean this person had a skin rash, sudden onset.

The diagnosis code is for Chinese Restaurant Angioedema. Treated with Benadryl and released. Littleton Hospital, Littleton, New Hampshire."

"Where's Littleton, New Hampshire?"

"I wouldn't know. Somewhere in New Hampshire, obviously."

The obstetrician stood up tall and opened his arms out wide. "All I can tell you is, I'm going to go the distance, and the sons of bitches can fight over my footprints."

"Everybody's tired," Frank agreed.

"Chinese Restaurant Angioedema," English said.

"It's an allergic reaction to that meat tenderizer," Frank said, "that flavoring agent." He slumped forward as a sigh went out of him, and ended with his elbows on his knees and his chin in his hands. "MSG," he said sadly. "Chinese restaurants use a lot of that stuff."

On his way out of the building English used a pay phone to call the hospital in Littleton. He identified himself as a detective, and explained he was looking for a missing person who might have been a patient there. "Are you near Franconia, by any chance?"

"About ten miles, yessir," the admissions clerk said.

"Well, that adds up, that adds up," English said. "It all adds up, and it's been adding up and adding up."

"Pardon me?"

"His name was Gerald Twinbrook, came in on January 2. I need to know the address he gave when he was treated. His local, his Franconia address. Goddamn, I knew he was in Franconia," English said.

"But wait a minute," the clerk said, "I can't give that information out over the phone."

"Can you look that up for me, please? Immediately."

"What department did you say you worked for again? What was your department and badge number?"

"Aaah, fuck you," English said, hanging up.

He considered calling the Notch Lodge in Franconia, whose number he'd dialed so many times he'd memorized it inadvertently. But he'd always gotten the same recorded insistence that the lodge wouldn't open till June 1; he didn't need to hear it again. He'd made up his mind to see them all personally up there anyway one of these days. Maybe, in fact, tomorrow.

People seemed to be staying at Leanna's hotel now; English saw lights in a couple of cabins as he cruised to a stop out in the street. Leanna's living-room window, too, was bright. He often stopped here and looked up at her windows.

He reached for the key to turn on the ignition, but the car was still running. He turned it off.

Now was the time. Time to clear the air, to ease his mind about a few things, maybe—he saw in one lighted cabin a young woman with a bucket and a mop—maybe patch things up.

He rang the front doorbell and Leanna raised the window above him. "Is it you?" she said.

"I guess so," he said.

"Are you going to sing to me?"

It seemed to imply he shouldn't invite himself in. He turned and looked down the drive, between the two rows of cabins, at his little car. "I think I'm heading off to New Hampshire tomorrow."

"Are you moving?"

"No."

"Oh," she said.

"You want to go for a drive? The night's beautiful."

"Sure, okay," she said. "I'm glad you finally came by."

* * *

They drove to Herring Cove, a beach on the Cape's east side, and sat in his car looking out over the Atlantic in the general direction of France. He liked being next to her; he felt all the possibilities returning when he touched her cheek with his finger. He felt the Atlantic tide going out, washing the hair of souls. "Would you mind if we spent some time together tonight?" he said.

"We're doing the last-minute cleanup till all hours," she said. "We always open the first weekend in June. A lot of folks come up for the Blessing of the Fleet."

"Is that a major festival?"

"Not really. But it's fun if you have a boat."

"I'll get one," English said.

"Really?"

"No," he said, surprised she'd taken him at all seriously. "I'm just bullshitting."

"Are you bullshitting about wanting to see me tonight?"

"Definitely not."

"I wouldn't mind seeing you," she said.

"What if I come over later?"

"Sure. Real late. After midnight, like 2 a.m. maybe."

She took his hand, and they sat in the car kissing for a while, until the clouds thinned out and the sea took on a slanting strangeness under the moon, and in a spirit of reconciliation, English tried to explain himself. "Last March," he began, "I got kidnapped." She was quiet while he told her about Gerald Twinbrook, about the look of Twinbrook's paintings, the light he laid on the canvas, the unidentified mania that had taken him away missing. English told her about the men who'd come to his room and pistol-whipped him in the middle of the night, and he mentioned Ray Sands's friendship with Bishop Andrew in a way that he felt sure communicated the suspicious nature of that relationship. But a sadness grew in him as he realized that there was a thin, obscene sediment between his tongue and the truth. He wasn't telling her that Ray Sands had been an investigator, that he'd sent English to look for Gerald Twinbrook in the capacity of a hired detective—that he, English, had eavesdropped on Leanna and Marla Baker's conversations, that he himself was the person who'd frightened Marla out of town. Talking around the facts made him feel deaf after a while. He stopped speaking and looked out at an ocean that seemed incapable of sound, though all around them the surf acted. Nothing was clean under the spiritless hygiene of the moon. "Look," he finished as he'd started, "I got kidnapped."

"Hm" was all Leanna said.

Immediately he felt like defending all this, felt like coming right out and saying what he suspected, although he hadn't even come right out yet and said it to himself. Many times these last few days he'd told himself, This isn't a hunch, it's a psychotic delusion. Don't tell anyone. Don't tell anyone because—Joan of Arc, Simone Weil, they spoke of their delusions and were believed. And then? . . . martyred. It was big. It felt very big to him. "These guys were part of this Truth Infantry. Do you see what I'm saying?"

"Those men aren't part of a conspiracy. They probably really thought you stole some stuff," Leanna said.

"But the guy, their boss, he had a professional air about him."

"He was a nut, Lenny. A bizarre man in a bizarre hat doing strange stuff on chemicals. Same with his friends. They're just too stupid-sounding for anybody to trust them in any kind of *commando* organization, or whatever you think it is. Which it probably isn't. And Ray Sands wasn't a fascist guerrilla. Everybody knew Ray Sands, more or less."

"Less, I think. Much less," English insisted.

"Lenny, Lenny," she said, "Lenny."

Her tone irritated him now. "Don't you see what happened? These guys kidnapped Gerald Twinbrook. Nobody would know about it if he hadn't needed medical treatment at the nearest hospital to their headquarters in Franconia. Probably," he said, "they still have the guy."

"And what was it you said he needed treatment for?"

"Chinese Restaurant Angioedema," English said.

She blew a fart of laughter through pursed lips.

"Damn," English said, "sometimes you have no grace. None. You fry my blood."

"You're kind of funny, is all. I'm sorry," she said, still laughing.

His chief hope had been that she'd debunk his ideas. He was surprised to find that now he wanted to defend them at all costs.

"He's still there! They have him. And Ray Sands ordered it."

"Why?"

"He doesn't know why. He was following orders."

"Orders? From who?"

"There's a web—a nest, man, with tentacles reaching out of it—and I swear to you, at the center of it is Andrew, our Bishop."

"Wo, wo, wo," she said. "You're scaring me."

"It *is* scary."

"Not *it*. You. You're going beyond all sense. Really. Please," she begged, "don't think that kind of stuff."

"I'm just trying to go with what I feel," he said. "Follow out my instincts."

"Yeah, and next thing you know, you'll turn into an animal and they'll lock you up." She began doodling geometrical figures on the fogged front window with her finger.

"Animals don't make mistakes with their lives," English told her, and began trying his hand at a few designs on the window himself. A hexagon, a cube; here comes a parallelogram. She did, he thought, seem a little frightened.

"It isn't like you think it is," she said.

"But everything is like we think it is, don't you get it? Out of the million little things happening on this beach, you can only be aware of seven things at once, seven things at any given time. I heard that on a tape."

"A tape."

"Yeah, a tape, a cassette series on salesmanship."

"I can't believe you were ever a salesman," she said.

"If I can only pick out seven things to be aware of, then I'm selecting just a tiny sliver of reality as my experience. We never really get the whole picture. Not even a microscopic part of it."

"So? So what? We have to go on it anyway."

"That's what I'm saying. Our delusions are just as likely to be real as our most careful scientific observations. And we have to go on them."

"You're defending a delusion, and calling it just that," she said. "Are you aware of that?" She started laughing. "Is that one of the seven things you choose to be aware of?"

"The Bishop is behind all this," he said in order to shut her up.

But she only laughed again, in a different manner. "Well anyway, I've got to go supervise the cleanup," she said.

"I wrote you a note. The day I came over and Marla was there, that night I—" He broke off, searching in the glove compartment for his notebook. "Here it is, listen. 'Dear Leanna. Many of the feelings I've been having lately, breaking down crying when alone, the sense of a cloud between me and God, the intuition that now, behind the cloud, is the time of faith . . .' "

"Go on," she said.

"That's all. But I mean—"

"Lenny. I asked you before not to go off following your faith too far." She gripped his arm tightly with both hands. He liked it. "Just drop all this, okay? Don't think about it anymore. Stay with us. Stay with me."

"I want to see you tonight," he said.

"Okay," she said.

"I want to sleep with you."

"We're going to," she said.

"I feel like I'm willing to try. I mean, with you."

"I'm glad."

"Even, you know, with Marla in the picture and all."

"I'm glad," she said.

English drove home and got his jacket and then walked, shivering, through the Provincetown night. People were saying that a cold spring meant an early heat wave in summer. Off the hill and nearer the water it was windless, and warm in a way that was accentuated by the many newly opened restaurants spilling their light into the street. There were plenty of people in town, with the bulk of them to come in the next two days to enjoy the first weekend of the season, the bargain gift shopping and the annual Blessing of the Fleet, when fishermen and pleasure boaters would glide past the town wharf under the slowly waving scepter of some clergyman or other. It was almost eleven now. Couples walked home from late dinners. Two women in high heels sounded just like a horse clip-clopping by. From down an alley came the sorrows of a trumpet letting out soft jazz. A man passed him walking an invisible dog—a novelty item, a stiffened leash and collar that bobbed along ahead of him, empty. English crossed the street to avoid a gang of meaty lesbians and screaming queens who bore down on him with their arms locked around each other's shoulders, singing, "Faggots and fairies and dykes, oh my! Faggots and fairies and dykes, oh my!" He liked the look of things. The town was getting a woozy, criminal feeling that rather matched his own.

He went into a basement tavern on Commercial. He remembered drinking here with Berryman and Smith, the overanxious Portuguese disc jockey. He didn't much care for basements, but he thought it might be a place the tourists hadn't yet located and filled.

He heard Phil, the cabdriver, speaking loudly inside before he was halfway down the stairs. The jukebox was playing "Misty Blue."

Phil sat at the bar between a thin gay man with the arching posture of a heavy-headed blossom and Nguyen Minh, the Vietnamese factory worker. Somebody was laughing at the words of a blond and cute but quite butch-voiced transvestite whom English had noticed on the streets several times this winter. English couldn't hear what she was saying.

Phil was telling Nguyen Minh: "And I asked myself: The way you are now, would your eight-year-old self approve of you? Would your eight-year-old self—that totally innocent child, with those ideals that are real, man, and human—would he approve?"

The tall thin man got up and headed out the door.

"No fucking way. I was *betraying* that kid," Phil said, "my childhood self. I'm talking about the real feeling of like if you stuck a bayonet in your buddy's back, not just ripping off a friend or something like that, but *killing, death*. You know what I'm saying, man?" Phil's face was crushed under the pressure of his pain. "I don't think you know the kind of treachery I'm talking about."

"Whatever's on tap," English said, and the bartender drew him a glass of beer.

Phil's troubled scrutiny had floated over and snagged on the cross-dresser. "You never tasted that kind of treachery, man."

The cross-dresser smiled and shrugged. Her eyes were very red.

"But then, and then it was like," Phil said, holding his hand out before him, gazing cross-eyed into his open palm as if this memory rested right there in it, "the ghost of John Lennon appeared to me. And he said, Fuck that, *he* can't judge you, because an eight-year-old doesn't have the knowledge, man.

Those ideals of yesterday, even everything you believed two hours ago, man—fuck that. We don't need to apologize to our past selves. *They* were the ones who turned into *us*. *We* are just who we *are*. You know?" he asked the cross-dresser.

She sat in splendid isolation, putting her very red lips around the cherry from her Manhattan.

"Mister Hey There," Phil said, noticing English. "What the fuck. Right?"

"Hi," English said.

"How's progress?"

English raised his glass and shrugged.

"A little better every minute, huh?"

"You got it," English said.

"No, but—do you get my drift? Hey, brother, one thing: I remember I said a couple of things about our mutual friend. Ell Ess would be the initials. May she remain nameless."

"Nameless, okay."

"I hear you're still going with her."

"Going with who?" the transvestite said.

"Somebody nameless," said English.

"So I'm sorry if I stepped on anybody's toes," Phil said.

"Aah," English said. "It's nothing, man."

"I hardly even know her, except we grew up in the same town, for whatever that's worth, okay? She's a good person," Phil said. "She's a good person." He flexed his hands. "She's a good person, but she's mentally ill. I don't know."

Nguyen Minh wiped his mouth with the palm of his hand and entered the conversation. "I'm very quite drunk now," he said to Phil.

"We were there, man," Phil reminded him. "You in the air and me on the ground. We kicked their asses."

Nguyen lifted his glass to the cross-dresser. "I am a gook," he said.

English toasted him with a double Scotch rocks, the first

swallow of which changed his smile because it went down like poison. "What's your name?" he asked the blond-wigged man.

"Tanny," the transvestite said, and started singing "Sad-Eyed Lady of the Lowlands" in a taught, professional baritone.

"MA-AH-AY WARE! HOUSE! EYES," Phil screeched, joining in, "MY ARAY-BEEYUN DRUMS. SHOULD I LEAVE THEM BY YO GATE?"

He broke off, letting Tanny sing, "Or, sad-eyed lady, should I wait?" all by herself.

Sitting here with the tavern glow shining softly on the blond bar, the light touching the self-described gook's somewhat greasy cheeks in a way he could never touch back, filling the glasses with something nobody could drink, English felt his heart tearing on loneliness like a diamond. "I want to apologize to you both," he said, "for dodging the draft." He drank down his drink. "I could have gone in. My asthma wasn't that bad."

Phil only stared at him. Nguyen smiled as if aping a photo of a smiling man.

"Okay," English said, "there."

"Anything else?" Phil asked.

"Yes," English said. "I may need a gun."

"They're everywhere, everywhere, everywhere," Phil assured him.

"Ah. The violence," Nguyen said, shaking his head.

"It's not that," English said.

"Yes, it is," Nguyen said.

Phil raised his glass. "To the ghost of John Lennon, dead these several months."

Something lurking in English's mind now stepped into the light, the shadow became a shade—not by any means the ghost of a dead rock idol, but a question to haunt him: the mystical message Phil had been describing, the greetings from John Lennon, what if a person heeded all such inner rebop, would he be damned or saved? How quickly would a person's life progress along its lines if he followed every impulse as if it started from God? How much more quickly would he be healed? Or how much faster destroyed? Saints had done that. Also mass killers, and wreakers of a more secret mayhem, witches and cultists and vampires and so on. I'm your God, come here. But you're standing in a storm, God. Yes, and I'm calling you to come here. But how do I know you're God? Because I'm all that's in front of you, and all that was behind you is gone: choose the storm or you get nothing.

English saw himself standing up in a movie theater with a grenade, crying, God told me to do this. Simone Weil wasting down into death on orders from her conscience in God, extinguishing, for herself, the whole world. Deranged men climbing onto tall structures to snipe down people they've never met, at God's behest. Headlines: MOM ROASTS BABY TO DRIVE OUT DEMONS.

Right and left of him he heard the drinks swirling in their glasses. The bartender's rag was dropped just this way on the metal sink with its corner lapping into the water. That was all he knew.

If he gave up all the hearsay, the whispers of the past and the hints from the future, he didn't know anything beyond the crossdresser clearing her throat deeply and Nguyen Minh squeaking his hand in the little pool of sweat under his cold drink. But he didn't know for certain even that it was cold. "I'm going to put my finger in your drink," he said. Nguyen watched him do it. "It's cold," he told Nguyen. "That's good."

"It's good," Minh said, "but you shouldn't put your finger."

Phil belched loudly without any consciousness in his red eyes.

English said to Tanny without shame, "I find myself thinking of you as a woman."

"I'm more man than you'll ever be," Tanny said. "And more woman than you'll ever have."

By the time the bar closed it was raining outside and it was cold. Phil and Nguyen Minh and English climbed the hill to forage for breakfast in English's kitchen. "What's this?" Phil demanded of English, who set three bowls on the chipped Formica table. "What are you, a vegetarian?"

"It's cereal. I don't have enough chairs. Eat standing up," English said. He poured bran flakes into his bowl. "How about handing me the milk," he said to Minh, pointing at the refrigerator.

"Hey, we're not cows, man. We eat meat," Phil said.

"Maybe Nguyen eats cereal," English said.

"He's not a cow. He's a man."

"And Nguyen. What does Nguyen say?"

"I like eggs and bacon," Nguyen said shyly. "It's good."

"We fought a war, motherfucker. We eat meat," Phil repeated.

"It's very cold inside your house," Nguyen pointed out.

They had to drive in English's car to Orleans, twenty-six miles away, to find an all-night restaurant that would serve them warriors' fare, which English, the draft dodger, also liked better than cold cereal. But by the time the three of them were facing one another around a table, spilling their water, dropping their spoons on the floor, losing their napkins in the process of retrieving their spoons, English felt lousy and wished he'd stayed home and gone to bed. He seemed to be drifting in and out of the universe, meeting with fuzzy dreams and then arriving back at the table to realize he'd already ordered, while Phil was just finishing: ". . . and some OJ."

"What?"

"Uh," he said, "orange juice?"

The waitress nodded.

English rapped his fork on the table for Phil's attention. "Aren't you married? Don't you have a family? Where's your home?"

"Everybody's happier if I don't show up there all the time," Phil said.

Evidently they'd all three ordered the breakfast special. Nguyen didn't say a word the whole time they ate. There were pancakes, sausages, and two eggs each. For a while English didn't talk either, and didn't even eat, but Phil held forth incoherently—and still, inside of three minutes, his fork was ringing against the china and then he was shoving his empty plate aside. "Do you want my breakfast?" English asked Phil.

"I just ate. I'm telling you something. Do me the favor of listening. Hey, hey, hey." He slapped the tabletop, jutting his chin.

"I'm listening," English said. "Fuck it, we're in session."

"Well, man, you were like hanging *out* with her for weeks, man, right?"

"Right. Okay."

"And she was trying to get a taste of regular life and you weren't giving it to her. I mean, I don't know all the details, she didn't say too much."

"Say too much? Who?"

"I mean, she wasn't putting you down behind your back. Definitely not, okay?"

"Who? Definitely who?"

"I'm trying to explain this to you. Okay?"

"Explain about who?"

"Her. And me. The dyke, your girlfriend, or whatever."

"Her and you? Do you even know her?"

"Since the first grade. I mean, I don't *know* her. This wasn't a hugely personal thing. It was one night, about an hour. Haven't spoken to her since."

"What are you saying?"

"And I really didn't know you at all, brother. I mean, I knew you a lot less than I've gotten to know you the last few hours."

Somehow this disclaimer put everything into place. English's hands suddenly felt numb. "What happened?" he said.

Phil looked at Nguyen as if he expected his comrade to take over the telling. Nguyen looked back and forth between his companions. Then he sipped his coffee.

Phil said, "What happened was, I met her coming out of her aerobics class, and she started talking to me, and she just picked me up. We went over to her hot tub, and then . . . that was that. We did the deed. Then I left."

English stared at him. He tried a little of his orange juice.

"That dance center is just two blocks from her house. You know, the Martial Arts Center. It was just—a short walk," Phil said. He shrugged with embarrassment.

English felt as if this orange juice were something he'd just vomited up. There was no chance of drinking this stuff. A short walk? "I know it is," he said. He shoved his OJ over in front of Phil. "Here, goddamnit."

"Listen. Don't get me wrong."

"Yeah?"

"Well, hey. Yeah."

"Don't get you wrong what?"

"What."

"Don't get you wrong *what*? You didn't say anything."

"Well, I mean, I fucked her."

"We know that. We know that. We know that."

"That's been well established, you're saying."

"*Yeah*."

"Okay, so you're saying—what?"

"I'm saying I'm pissed off. I'm completely pissed off, man."

Phil winced and made half a gesture with his hand.

"What."

"Maybe—I don't know—" Phil said.

"Fuck."

"Fuck is right. Fuck it."

"Fucking-A."

"Okay. Fuck you, then."

"Fuck *you*, you mean."

Phil got up and left the diner. What English felt good about was that he knew Phil would go on in his anger, would hitchhike back to Provincetown in the chilly rain without a jacket, suffering every step of the way in his pride. And English, in his pride, would pass him by on the road and for that would suffer guilt. English paid for everybody's meal, including Nguyen's.

He could see that Leanna had been up all night, too, cleaning rooms and taking care of paperwork. She was sitting at her desk in the living room, fiddling with a pencil and drinking from a bottle of beer. He just opened the door without knocking. She didn't mind.

"Hi, baby," she said, and turned toward him.

The pain he was feeling was sexy. She really was a beautiful woman.

Now wasn't yet the time. He needed to touch her first. He wanted her to feel the anger inhabiting his skin.

She kissed him, clutching him around the neck. The bottle in her hand rubbed against his ear. He liked the taste of beer on her tongue.

"Make love to me," she said.

And so he held her in his arms. She took hold of his shirt at the back, pulling on it, and he let his arms fall from her while she removed his shirt for him and unbuttoned his jeans but did not touch inside his fly. They lay down and floated on her water bed. He kissed her seriously and deeply. He kissed her breasts and then her stomach and thighs all over, and then between her legs: saliva on the crotch of her sleazy little panties. Leanna started breathing rapidly. He removed her panties and kissed her vagina for a long time. She spread her legs wide apart, legs thin and unshaved and somewhat muscular and lovely, as he put his tongue far inside her, and she liked it a lot. But what good was any of this? An ancient discouragement welled up in his chest, the feeling of a loveless moment. She had lots of hair on her legs. He felt his isolation, his inability to connect—it was stronger, essential, cosmic. Right. It was now. "I'll tell you what I feel like, kissing you," he said to her. "I feel like somebody's writing swear words on my balls."

Yes, now was the time. He sat up and lit a cigarette, wiping his mouth first with the pillowcase. "What you need is a goddamn operation," he said. "What you need is to get your head on first so you can learn to fuck."

Leanna sat up, too. She looked at him, opened her mouth, couldn't speak. She regained herself quickly, her scattered forces recollecting in her eyes. Then she didn't have to speak.

"You think I'm a goddamn lunatic?"

"Yeah," she said.

"What about you? What about your attitude, what about being a lesbo one day and a regular person another day, and—shit," he said, running out of words. "It's all a bunch of shit. —Wait a minute," he said as she started to say something, "*wait a minute*. What about it, the way you treat people you supposedly love?"

She was quiet now. He felt her trying to calm him by her silence.

He went ahead more slowly. "And what about Phil?"

"Phil," she said.

"Yeah. Scuzzy local fucker? Drives a cab? Kind of spent the night with you?"

"Phil?"

"Yeah."

"What about him?"

"Excuse me. Isn't that the question I just asked?"

"Well, I met him at the Martial Arts Center. Outside, coming from aerobics."

"It doesn't take all night to meet somebody. Meeting is like a short thing, right?"

"Lenny—"

"So it wasn't meet. It was more like you spent the night, huh? Got laid? Or eaten out, or whatever the fuck, if you tried to make him into a dyke. Fuck you. Dyke cunt."

In a gesture he found both graceless and heartbreaking, she took a long pull off her beer and exhaled with a gasp. "I feel all right about it."

"Hey, shit, I don't give a fuck, if you want to know the truth."

"Okay, then. I'm not going to pretend I feel guilty."

She got up off the water bed. He watched it quiver and grow calm, thinking, We did, we hated each other in another life.

"Who do you think was following Marla all last winter?"

Leanna was putting a leg into her panties and didn't answer.

"Marla Baker, your little bisexual honey. Do you know that Ray Sands was a detective?"

"Ray Sands?" she said.

"And do you realize I was his assistant?" He leaned right down in her face. "Who do you think was listening while you guys cried in her bedroom all night? Guess who." The anger tasted good in his throat. "I'm the eavesdropper. It was me."

Leanna surprised him by shoving him backward, quite hard. He had to put his hand behind him to keep from hitting the wall. He was embarrassed.

"You're not eavesdropping anymore. You're right in the middle. Burglar," she said, and started to cry. She moved, practically lunged, to her desk. "Burglar, burglar!"

She pulled an enormous revolver from the drawer and pointed it at him, using both her hands to lift it.

"Oh," he said. "Huh."

"Goddamn right," she said.

"Are you," he said, and stopped. "You're kidding, right?"

"It's my old Magnum .44," she told him. "Eddie lent it back to me."

When he stayed speechless, she said, "Eddie, the cop. You met him."

"Eddie," he said, "the cop. Did you fuck Eddie, too?"

"What?" She shook the gun in his face with such vigor his mouth dried instantly. "Did I what? Did I fuck him?"

"I'm sorry," he said. "I'm dead, right?"

"You're an infant, you're a psychotic baby."

"I'm sorry. I'm sorry."

"Your libido is like a tiny child's."

She put the gun back down on the desk.

English shuddered down the length of him, like a wet dog. "I oughta pick that up and shoot your face off."

"It isn't loaded," she said.

"So what? You could've killed me with it anyway. I could die of fright."

"Get out of here," she said.

"No."

She lifted the receiver off the phone and smiled at him in an almost truly friendly way. "I'm gonna have you locked up, Lenny," she said. She dialed once. "The police, please," she told the operator. "It's urgent, no kidding." She waited with the receiver at her ear.

"So," she said to him, "you were the one. The spy."

He made for the door. "I just wanted to find out what you'd say about my theories. Then I go with the opposite, because you're a liar."

Suddenly she looked hurt. Or was it pity in her eyes? "Get out of here," she said.

He slammed the door behind him and stood at the top of her stairs, putting on his shirt. "I know what you did," he shouted in the empty stairwell. "I know what they did. And I know what I'm doing."

In ten minutes he stood in front of the bank, having withdrawn all his money, less than eighty dollars. A slow-eyed dyke with a cigarette hanging out of her mouth drove past. A cloud followed her, and rain fell down all over the street. The raindrops were big this year.

English headed north, driving recklessly. The Cape highway was crowded with cars, most of them coming toward him. The boards had been pried off the roadside drive-thrus, and the crowds loitered around them eating frozen custard in the rain. English felt sorry for them, their small lives made cheap, their cheap lives made sad, by the failures of the weather.

Well north of Boston he stopped at Jerry's Seafood Diner to get something to eat. It was just a little joint, next to another one called the Alaska Bar, in the emptiness between two towns on Route 1. Maybe he was in New Hampshire by now, he didn't know.

He was parked and standing outside the car before he realized the neon sign above Jerry's was cold. Their dinner hour, according to the notice by the door, began in forty-five minutes or so.

Right now it was that time of the day known as Happy Hour. English went into the Alaska Bar.

When he opened the door, they all swung their heads up as the afternoon light cut into their dreams.

"Oh, just the thought of you," the jukebox was singing, "turns my heart misty blue."

Everyone was quiet.

"It's been such a long, long time," it sang, "but still, just the thought of you."

Including English, there were four of them drinking in the Alaska Bar, all men. The middle-aged woman mixing the drinks was called Madeline. The bottles of liquor hung upside down behind the bar within Madeline's reach, with metal teats on them that automatically delivered a shot and an eighth. Scenes of Alaska in old frames were nailed up around the mirror. People had been blowing cigarette smoke onto them for years. The glass was so tarnished they could hardly be deciphered. Madeline hummed along with the jukebox. To English it was amazing how a song will take a whole confused epoch in your life, and fashion it into something sharp and elegant with which to pierce your neck.

"Is there anybody in this bar who actually has anything to do with Alaska?" he asked eventually.

"The owner," Madeline said.

"Is he from there, or is he going there?"

"Kind of both. He visits back and forth," she said.

A man two seats down said, "I went to Alaska once. I wouldn't go back."

"I've been there. I used to live in Seattle," another of the four of them said.

"Ralph worked for Boeing in Seattle for twenty years, and they fucked you in the ass, didn't they, Ralph?" his companion, the fourth man, said.

Ralph said, "When they canned thousands of us, there was a joke—Last one leaving Seattle, please turn out the lights."

"I'm in computers," the man two seats down said. "I've only lived here about ten months."

"Excuse me?" Ralph's friend said. "You're kind of far away, I didn't hear."

They all moved over to a table, the four of them, and continued talking about Seattle and Boeing and anything at all. They took turns buying rounds. English skipped his turn. He drank only coffee.

Ralph didn't seem bitter about having put in two decades at Boeing before the big layoff. "I sell boats now," he said.

"Can you get by all right doing that?" English asked.

"It's touch and go. Feast or famine. My kids are gone now. My wife works."

"But you can really score—when you score—right?"

"My second wife," Ralph corrected himself, taking a drink from Madeline's tray before she could even set it down. "I lost my first wife right after Boeing cut back."

"Better bring another round almost right away," the man in computers suggested to Madeline.

"I just went crazy," Ralph said of that other time.

Madeline said to Ralph, "I heard about that."

But her manner of saying it was like this: She paused, looked at him, laid down her bar rag gently on the tray, and said I *heard* about that, as if she'd always wanted to get the whole story. But Ralph didn't seem to want to tell it.

The man who worked in computers revealed that his name was Elvis. "I was born in '42," he said. "I wasn't named after Elvis Presley. My folks just picked it out of the air."

"That must've been kind of strange, having a name like that in the fifties."

"Other kids looked up to me," he said. "It gave me a whole kind of mystique. I was sad when he faded out. But I was never too big on his sound, to tell you the truth."

Elvis described something that had been going on at his office for a while, a series of events that had resulted in one of the other workers getting fired for sex discrimination. "Or rather it was sexual harassment, is the proper term," he said.

"This guy was unbelievable," Elvis went on. "He's married,

got three kids, or maybe four, I don't know, and he just kind
of started in on this woman who works right at the next desk.
But she was like lower down on the scale—not working under
him, but he had rank on her. She was just a secretary, more or
less, and he was management. One day he puts this Personals
ad on her desk. You know *The Midnite Shopper?*"

"What a stupid rag."

"Yeah, it is. And especially the ads, the Personals. Did you
ever read those?"

None of them admitted to such a vice.

"Well, after this started happening, we all started reading
The Midnite Shopper at the office. Those ads are pretty straight
out. They're all about sex. Well, this guy, Remarque—he's
Canadian—he circled one of the ads, and put it on her desk
with a note on the office memo paper—a memo right? He says,
Dear Louise, why don't you answer this ad?"

"So did she?"

"Fuck no. He answered it for her."

"Yeah? Jesus."

"But not exactly, not really—because *he* was the guy who
took out the ad in the first place."

"What did it say?"

"It said like: 'I like them bouncy. Soft. Heavy. If you're a
female between thirty-five and forty, over 150 pounds, brown
hair, reply to Box So-and-so.' She fit the description—she's over
one-fifty for sure. In fact, I'd say she's more like over two
hundred pounds."

"Two hundred?" Ralph's companion said.

"*Over* two hundred. Anyway, Remarque, he just answered
her like he would've if she *had* answered his ad. He writes her
this long letter, saying he admired the photo she sent him, let's
get away for a weekend in two weeks, please phone me at this
number—it's the guy's *work* number. I mean, the phone is right

on the desk next to *hers*. This guy really made a geek out of himself."

Madeline, coming to the table with drinks, had been overhearing them. "He made it pretty obvious," she said, "using his office phone number and everything."

"Sure," Elvis said. "But it was even more obvious than that. It didn't start there, with the advertisement. It was like an ongoing thing. First of all, before any of this other jazz, he was always making remarks to her. Real quiet, so nobody could hear. But you could stand across the room and get the idea just by looking at how close he was standing. He'd be trembling. You could see it. I mean, he was overboard. He kept changing his image. First he started—he wore these like checkered, sort of plaid pants, really loud clothing for an office. And he'd look down at his pants every so often, and then he'd look over to see if she was noticing his new look. The whole office, we just observed this stuff as it was happening, day after day. I mean, it was *all that was happening*. He dyed his hair three or four times, different colors. That's not an exaggeration. He wore a wig one time, too, like a Beatles haircut. I wonder what his wife must've thought . . ."

Elvis paused. He pinched the last quarter inch of his cigarette tightly, and sucked on it so hard it squeaked.

Ralph, meanwhile, turned his drink around and around on the table, as if the other side of it was going to show him something different.

They waited for the rest.

According to Elvis, what happened was that the woman, Louise, showed the letter to two or three of her girl friends in the department. The letter wasn't signed, but they all had a fair idea who'd sent it, and within days it was being quoted, and even photocopied and sent, all around the company. On the advice of her friends, Louise sent the original to the personnel office, who forwarded it to people even higher up and more central in the corporation.

In a couple of weeks, a team of investigators came through the office doors. They were three men. In front of everyone they walked straight over to the Canadian's desk and showed him the letter.

"We need your assistance in this matter," one of them said.

"All right," he said.

"Did you write this letter?"

The man refused to speak. He looked over at Louise, who was sitting as usual at the desk right next to his.

"Is this your letter? Did you send this?" another asked him.

He said, "Why don't you just have Louise ask me?"

"Because," the investigator said, "we're the ones asking you."

"Maybe Louise should ask me," the man said. He put his hands together on the desk and stared down at them. "His face," according to Elvis, "was as red as blood."

"It's a simple matter to trace this letter," the investigator said. "You can make things easy by telling us you wrote it, if in fact you did."

The man, his face red as blood, wouldn't look anywhere but at his hands gripping each other before him on his desk.

"Tell Louise to ask me," he suggested.

All the investigators looked at Louise. Everyone else in the place did, too.

She was wiping at her eyes and sniffling. She finally said to him, "Well?"

Silence.

She said, "Did you write this letter to me?"

He said, "Yes. I did."

Nobody in the office said a word.

And here in the Alaska Bar they were also silent. From the one narrow window the daylight was draining away. Jerry's

Diner was open, its red electric sign applying to the evergreens a taint so subtle, so tantalizing, that English ached to drink it.

Elvis drained his double and chewed up an ice cube, saying, "So—he's losing his job. Lost it already. He cleaned out his desk yesterday, and it was just sitting there empty all day today.

"And the thing is that it was just crazy! It was absurd! I mean, this woman is kind of a . . . *pig*—I'm sorry, but I have to say it. She's fat, she's married, she's homely as hell. There's *nothing there*. He wrecked his whole career, probably completely shredded his marriage. And she's just, I mean this woman is just . . ." He lifted his hands helplessly. Words wouldn't come.

"Jesus!" A couple of the others laughed.

As for Ralph, English noticed he wasn't laughing. Ralph was staring at the three of them with loud, blind eyes, smoothing his mustache with a finger.

When Happy Hour was over, English stepped out into the blue dark, and wouldn't you know he'd be coming down the road at that moment?

English had seen him dead by the side of the street. He'd seen him lighting a cigarette at the bottom of an alley, zipping himself up in a urinal, passing out and going down and being trampled at a riot.

It was the guy, the geek, the one who'd dressed in loud checkered pants and worn a wig to work and made a fool of himself and lost everything.

He was bent over nearly double and dragging his shadow behind him. It scraped enormously over the road, turning a deep furrow in his life. He got closer and closer. Then he was right on top of English, he was going to crush English to death. And suddenly English couldn't find him anywhere.

He slept in the car by the side of the road and woke up he didn't know when. The world was dark and moonless. The night was upside down. He turned on his headlights and engaged the engine, and a series of images began dissolving toward him, faded white lines snaking down the window in a frame of evergreen boughs. Far ahead one other light bobbed slowly on the waters of the darkness. Then the light grew into a symbol, the symbol into a word, and the word was MARY, blinking in the window of a diner. The counter stretched across the window, and a woman stood behind the counter brushing a rag across the surface with one long, sorrowful gesture. English wasn't hungry, but he went inside anyway. He didn't know where he was.

Inside, the neon sign—the word MARY with its apostrophe and s extinguished—buzzed loudly.

"Good morning," English said.

"Can I get you some coffee?" the woman said. Her uniform was sky-blue. Her hair was as short as a boy's, and she was thin, no less so than a carnival freak. Her skin, stretched over tendons and bones, had the delicacy of rice paper. It looked as if all you had to do was apply a lighted match to make her ready for the grave. She gave him coffee though he hadn't answered her. She laid a menu on the counter.

"I was going to Franconia, on 93," he said, "but I think maybe I'm all turned around."

"You're on Route 1," she said.

"I've been going north."

She shook her head slowly. "Go south."

"It feels wrong to turn around now," he said.

"It's the only way I know of. You'll never get where you're going by just going on and on north. You'll never get there."

She was leaning on the counter with both hands. It was all he could do to keep from touching those hands, those fingers of an ivory sadness, outspread on either side of his heavy white mug.

"Simone," he said.

He believed he'd never seen anyone stand so still. He had to cover his face with his hands to keep his eyes from beholding her.

"Franconia, you said, didn't you? Simone . . . I can't tell you. I don't know." She laid one finger on the menu and moved it toward him an inch. "Eat."

He reached Franconia well before noon. It was just a string of motels, a big white church, and a field of wet yellow grass in a valley a little way off Interstate 93. The clouds moved behind the white steeple. He'd seen that very thing in a lot of movies. It made him dizzy when it happened in the movies and it made him dizzy now.

He stopped the car and rubbed his eyes.

Before he did anything further he was going to collect himself. He went into the large white church, Our Lady of the Snows, overlooking the yellow field. It was unreasonably dark inside, and he just sat for a few minutes amid the stale whiff of censers and the little musk of the ranks of votive candles, his arms wrapped around himself, until he had to admit that it was just no use—he was only sitting here hugging himself in still another of his faith's innumerable churches named for saints and ladies. As his eyes adjusted to the dimness he began to feel dominated by the blank stares of the plaster martyrs. Our Lady was no longer a nurturing mother but an enchantress—a shimmering goddess—no more a present comfort but a tantalizing absence. What ark would he sail, what chariot, with what wings, how could he reach her?

No use. Cold silence for his morning prayer.

He found the Notch Lodge at the far end of town—five cabins surrounded by a carpet of pine needles, right on the main road. It was still closed, and English couldn't tell which cabin served as office, but a man chopping wood beside the house next door, an immense, hairy person in overalls, called to him, "Can I help you out, there?"

English approached him carefully; meanwhile, the man sundered a huge round into seven pieces of firewood with six blows of his maul. The sound of it echoed off the mountain about a half a mile across the field. After each swing he said *uh*, or *shit*, or mother*fuck*er.

"I wanted to talk to whoever runs the motel there. Do you know them?"

"Sure," the big man said. "Mrs. Vance runs it." He split the last of the round: *Bitch*.

"Do you know her?"

"Yeah. I'm Mr. Vance."

"Oh," English said. "How do you do?"

"Well, I do great. But I don't do much. I have nothing to do with the motel. I mostly chop wood."

He demonstrated by shattering another round, causing English to step backward in alarm. "I'm an investigator," English told him, nearly pleading. "Leonard English. It's a missing-persons case."

"Nobody missing around here, I wouldn't guess." Breathing heavily, Vance wiped a forearm across his face and set his maul aside.

"I guess a lot of people come and go. Lot of tourists and so on around here."

"In the summer, yeah. The skiers go over by North Conway in the winter."

"What about people who aren't exactly tourists? Other groups, like."

"Other groups," Vance said.

"Well, have you ever heard of the Truth Infantry? It's supposed to be kind of a secret paramilitary group," English said, embarrassed by his own lack of tact, "located somewhere around here."

Resuscitation of a Hanged Man

"What's secret about the Truth Infantry? I'm a member myself."

"Oh," English said, finding no other words.

"We just get together in the summer and shoot at targets, mostly."

Vance sighted down the length of an invisible weapon.

"I'd been given the idea," English said, "that it was much more serious."

"We have barbecues and get seriously wasted."

"That it was sort of a radical underground thing," English insisted.

"We don't drink and shoot," Vance assured him. "We shoot in the morning, then we drink."

"That's fine, that's a sensible way to approach," English said dizzily, "the whole endeavor."

"Folks who have a little Vietnam in our background."

"Yes. Right."

"We need the fellowship. It's kind of healing."

"Right. Right." English sighed. Had he been brought here as some kind of practical joke? I played it on myself, he thought. "And what about a headquarters. Do you have a building or something?"

"We use this old forestry camp up the mountain. As long as we police it up afterward, everybody's happy."

"And there's nothing secret about it."

"You knew about it, didn't you? If it was secret, would you know about it?"

On the left was a massive pile of what appeared to be birch rounds. To the right was a pile of split birch, its meat green and wet, and between the two piles stood the woodcutter Vance with his several heavy tools and the unattainable simplicity of his task. "I suppose I better tell you the investigator I work for is a friend of yours," English said at last, "Ray Sands. You knew he was dead, I guess."

"If he *was* dead," Vance said, "then he's probably still dead to this day. I've got a lot of friends like that, and it works out to an identifiable cosmic rule: once dead, always dead—but I gotta tell you, English, I don't feel trusting toward a person who has as many nervous gestures as you, shifting around and whapping on your pockets like a fucking mechanical man. Could you stop that shit?"

"I was just looking for a cigarette, I think," English said, but he wasn't completely sure.

"—Many dead friends, I was saying, but no dead friends named Ray Sands."

"Ray Sands, Sands—Raymond Sands of Provincetown. The head of the Truth Infantry."

"We have a guy who puts together a newsletter once a year and sends it out. There's no leader. No Ray Sands. You and I have no common acquaintances."

English looked out over the field toward the wall of the mountain. A sense of his own idiocy dominated the area behind his eyebrows, and started to grow rapidly into a headache.

"Is Mrs. Vance around?"

"She's in St. Johnsbury trying to hire some maids. The local girls all want to work in restaurants in the summer."

"The man I'm looking for had the motel's phone number in his office. He might have called here or stayed here. Do you ever have winter guests?"

Vance shook his head. "Summers only. The only guy who stayed here this winter was a friend of mine, this guy who's an artist," Vance said.

"An artist. Not Gerald Twinbrook?"

"Yeah. Jerry Twinbrook."

English's blood sang so loud he couldn't hear his own voice saying, "We do have a common acquaintance." His excitement nearly blinded him. "He's friend of yours?"

Vance seemed uncertain of the fact now. "I know Twinbrook,

yeah. He's one of the guys. He was up last summer for drill, and he came up last December—I don't know, right around Christmas, or earlier, the beginning of the month. I don't remember."

"He's in the Truth Infantry? Is that what you're telling me?"

"As far as I know," Vance said. "Listen, you know what? Should I be talking to you?"

"I thought you said there was nothing secret about it."

"What's your purpose here? Is he in a lawsuit or something?"

"His parents miss him."

"And that's the extent of it," Vance said.

"He's gone missing," English said.

"Well, he cleared out of here last January, man, and I never knew him very well. He was just up about two weeks in the summer, and a couple weeks last winter."

"Where'd he go? Did he say?"

"I never even talked to him once," Vance said. "I wasn't really his friend."

"Come on. He's not in trouble. Nobody's in any trouble," English assured him desperately.

"I just knew him, he knew I had this place, he gave us a call, he came up and hung around and kept to himself. Hiking and such."

"In the winter?"

"I told him not to do that," Vance said.

"Where did he go when he went hiking?"

"Man, I don't know. He wanted to go up to the summer camp, but I talked him out of that bullshit. The snow is four feet deep by New Year's. You'd have to be insane to go a hundred yards up one of those trails. He must've just walked the roads."

"Well, he was a little strange, wasn't he?"

"You know who's strange, man, is you. Your eyeballs are

sort of quivering, and I don't like the way you keep chewing on your tongue, or whatever you're doing."

"I gotta get some rest," English said.

"Get lots and lots" was Vance's counsel.

"But, you know—Twinbrook," English prompted him.

"No idea. None. One day he was just gone. He took all his stuff."

"But if he went into the woods," English said, "he could still be up there, lost."

"He'd be a hell of a lot more than lost by now," Vance pointed out. "But I think he would've left something in his room, don't you? A toothbrush, couple of dirty socks—he didn't leave a thing. No, he split town."

"He took his car and all," English said.

"He didn't have a car. Just a knapsack and sketch pad and such. He probably took the bus out of town."

"If I want to go up to the forestry camp, what do I do?"

"Don't," Vance said. "The road's a mess. It's officially open, but nobody goes on it till well after the spring breakup."

"I've got to get up that mountain," English said.

Vance disagreed. "If there's anybody up there, he's a corpse subject to our simple cosmic law of deadness, which states that he's going to just keep on getting deader. You're not in a hurry."

"Is it right on the road? The camp?"

"Look, figure it out," Vance told him now. "I advise one person not to go up there, awhile later you turn up and say he's missing. Now I tell you to wait till the road's passable—can I expect somebody to show up in a couple weeks looking for you, too?"

"I see," English said. "That's a threat, isn't it?"

Vance closed his eyes and shook his head, regretting English's folly. "Take a break, dude. You're very wired."

"Which road?"

"Number 18, straight out here eleven miles; take a left and then straight up that motherfucking mountain. Very muddy, very slushy. You'd need a boat this time of year."

But English found his transportation just across the street, parked almost next to his Volkswagen, within earshot of Vance's thunderous labors.

As English walked across the parking lot, a man in a softball uniform accosted him, saying, "If you park your car here for very long, somebody's liable to buy it. This isn't a parking lot. It's a used-car dealership." The man was carrying a fur-collared suede coat on a hanger, draped with a dry cleaners' plastic bag. He touched English's shoulder and then gripped English's hand. "I'm Howardsen: owner, salesman, et cetera."

"Sorry," English said.

"No, you didn't see the sign."

"I still don't," English said.

"It's being painted. Vandals changed the other one from SPUD AUTOS to PUD AUTOS. The new sign's just going to say AUTOS, real large."

"Oh well," English said, meaning to sound unhappy for the man, though he couldn't have cared less.

"I know who it was. They're good boys. You couldn't expect them to resist that kind of a lure, though, could you?"

"Who were they," English said, diving through the meagerest opening, "guys in the Truth Infantry or something?"

"Truth what? No, they were from the high school, I'd guess."

"No," English said, "I just said that because I was talking to Vance over there about his group, the Truth Infantry. They meet up on road 18 in the summer, I guess, huh?"

"Oh, that bunch, yeah, they train up there or conduct exercises or some such fuck-all. Nobody ever got hurt, I don't believe."

"I was thinking of taking a drive up road 18, is how the subject came up."

"Which one is that, now?" Howardsen gazed off in either direction as if the world were a map.

"Up here about eleven miles?"

"Oh, Jesus God, you'd need a four-wheel drive."

"Is it real muddy?"

"Nope, that's on the north side of things. Up another couple thousand feet there'd be more snow than mud."

"Oh."

"But plenty of mud before that."

"It's very important that I make the trip."

"And you'd need a gun. For the Sasquatch."

"A gun?"

"Kidding. Kidding. Kidding," the man said. "I'm just kidding you."

"I'll rent a jeep." English had a thought now. "How about that car right there? Would you want to buy that car?" He pointed to his Volkswagen.

"I'd buy anything, if the price was right. I've bought more horrible things than that. And sold them again."

"What do you mean, horrible? It gets me everywhere."

Howardsen let English hold his suede coat while he walked a circle around the vehicle in a kind of half crouch. He took back the coat and stood still and regarded the car for another few seconds, managing to seem both meditative and astonished. Then he spoke: "I mean, starting from the ground up, the tires have about four hundred miles of tread left. If that. These old VWs, the heater's not powerful enough for our winters. That's okay, I'll sell it in the summer." He stepped to the rear to raise the hood on English's horrible engine. "These things start to run kind of dirty after a while. You get a kind of chugging action, sort of? Quits chugging after you get her on the open highway for a while? That's the valves burning off the crud after you get the rpms up. Crud collects," he said, "driving at low rpms around town. If you're hysterically desperate for cash, like two hundred and fifty dollars, I could give you that much." He dropped the hood. "Hood don't fall right," he said, shutting it a second time. "Did you have a little wreck maybe?" One last time he lifted and dropped the bonnet, letting that put a period to the sad catalogue.

"I'm kind of insulted."

"But fairly desperate."

"Three-fifty?" English said.

Howardsen plucked a roll of money from under his baseball cap and peeled off three one-hundred-dollar bills. "I have some papers for you to sign," he said. "Also, I've got a four-wheel drive you can rent."

As English was driving out of the place in an open jeep, he stopped and called Howardsen over to try, one last time, to get the man to let him keep a little of his money. "You could live without one of those hundreds, I'd think."

"What would you spend it on in the woods?" Howardsen asked. "It's better all around if I keep it till we have the jeep back. If you had a major credit card it'd be another matter."

English saluted and engaged the clutch, and as he did so Howardsen raised a warning finger: "Beware the Sasquatch."

English now recognized this man as a messenger.

"You'll know the Sasquatch. He looks kind of like Señor Mister Vance over there across the street, who you were talking to."

A sour feeling of dread stroked English under his throat. "Are you saying," English asked, "that he might follow me out there?"

The man winced. "You're lacking a sense of humor," he told English. "Maybe I shouldn't kid with you."

"Should I be taking a weapon?" English asked carefully.

"There's nothing in season now," Howardsen said, and looked so uncomfortable that English realized, a little too late, that he'd made a sort of crazy mistake. He didn't know what to do, other than gun the engine and drive off before the man could ask for his jeep back.

Road 18 crossed a railway track, travelled for a few miles alongside it, and then headed up the mountain in a series of narrow switchbacks, crossing a small creek repeatedly. The road wasn't icy here, but English heard what he thought must be ice thumping, sometimes splashing down into the creek, the water wearing its groove over eons while people built their churches and laid out their railroads in a geological eye blink. For a while the dread dissolved, the feeling that he was launched on a fatal errand left him, and he forgot he was here without any good reason but with complete certainty. It was nice to be out in the country in May, when the rivers were young.

His machine shimmied somewhat in the particularly muddy patches, but even in the steepest places its climb was happy and relentless, and wherever the road forded the creek English plowed into it without bothering the brakes and charged across like Moses, turning great furrows of water on either side of him. He was elated. Whenever the road switched back south in its upward zigzag, the roof of trees opened up and he glimpsed, high above him, a promontory with a slender falls coming down over it like a white cowlick. This gnarled outcropping seemed to form the head of a cliff that had pushed up out of prehistory to block the region from the southern sun; ten miles up the road English came into its shadow.

Here the thaw was late, the mud of the road was firm, and he crossed inexplicable stretches of pure winter, with the lane and the evergreens immersed in a silent whiteness.

The jeep's big tires travelled the snows without any trouble, but when they found slush beneath them they seemed to forget completely the purpose of their manufacture, and English's ride began behaving less like an all-terrain vehicle than like a merry-go-round. He was, he had to admit, spinning out of control and leaving the road.

Now he was stopped, facing the direction from which he'd come and tilted leftward to such a degree he had the sickly suspicion that at least two of his wheels might not be on the ground. He put the thing in reverse, engaging also a certain mechanism of the mind by which he found it possible to pretend that he couldn't by any means have got himself stuck in a rut miles and miles from any human place and at the same time to spin the tires and rock the car and whip the steering from side to side, installing the jeep permanently right where it was. He got out and put his back against the grille and his feet against a tree and pushed until satisfied he was dealing with an inert mass. He turned his back on it and took to the road again. He had to walk, and his shoes, while fine for walking, were no good in the snow; but his elation remained. He was happy to see the empowering things of man flounder sideways into their natural uselessness.

He walked carefully at the margin of the road, seeking the crustier surfaces and only occasionally plunging himself to the knees in old snow that was more like crushed ice. In many places the thaw was complete, and he trudged through mud. The slope gentled. The bluff and the long waterfall down the face of it now took up a good part of the sky. He expected to hit the wall of the cliff somewhere up ahead. The temperature was more than bearable, and in fact in his leather jacket he was far too warm. There was no question however of laying it aside, of shedding his image, his crest, his coat of arms. Even Joan of Arc had had her breastplate, anyway she did in the paintings he'd seen of her, and Simone Weil—who knew what she had, beyond her silly delusions. But isn't it a question of following it out anyway? Isn't that where faith comes in? Didn't Joan of Arc admit the voice of God was in her imagination? Isn't it a matter of faith marching after the delusion? Isn't that what the saints are proving?

He'd come to a gate and a sign. He couldn't have walked much more than a mile.

The Forest Service sign informed him that the structures in the encampment were considered antique. Tampering and destruction were barred by federal law and would be punished.

The campground lay beyond the gate—which kept out only vehicles; a footpath went around it—in a large hollow wide enough to be called a meadow. The sun apparently never got to it, and most of the winter's snow lay around in big patches. Among the antique structures referred to by the sign there was, of all things, an antique feedlot—for what kind of livestock he couldn't imagine. Maybe farmers had once driven their sheep up here for the summer grasses. There were half a dozen one-room cabins painted white. To English they didn't look so old. One after another he found them locked and undisturbed. From the roof of one a sheet of snow had slid halfway off, curving down but not breaking, lengthening the eave by nearly three feet, and then melting irregularly like paraffin.

Next to that cabin was a large outhouse of sorts, its door open and the hinges sprung not by an animal or by a person, but only by the snows that had drifted into the cracks and hardened, expanded, and been added to by further drifting.

Gerald Twinbrook hadn't broken this door open, but he'd entered here. His knapsack and sketch pad and sleeping bag lay on the floor, candy wrappers scattered around them.

English sat down on the concrete floor, on the sleeping bag, and took a look at what he was sure must be Gerald Twinbrook's last sketches.

The top sketch was a landscape, a study of the outcropping English had seen from farther down the road. He'd seen it from farther down, but it lay above the encampment somewhere. He turned the pages over. The next sketch was one of a gallows. Another of the outcropping, another of a gallows fixed to the outcropping. He knew the style, the stovepipe broken-necked figure hanging from its noose. With a few strokes Twinbrook had managed to give the hanging man a certain heft, an inertia implying movement.

Touching these pages, English's hands were as steady as the artist's must have been. All anxiety had left him. He was happy.

There was a sketch of the encampment itself, with a trail of animal tracks leading across the snow. And a sketch of a man laid out with a noose around his neck. He read Twinbrook's note beneath it: *Now we are allowed to take the dead man / and strike him with lightning of our own making / and bring him back to life.*

Anything was possible, anything. English looked to the sky for lightning. Three large grey clouds in what he believed was the east; nothing more.

He decided to climb up around behind the distant outcropping and overlook the entire scene. He wished he had binoculars.

The road led nearly to the cliff, and then sidled right; English took a game trail left, a very steep one that eventually curved back right, not quite so steeply, and aimed straight at the head of the falls.

In ten minutes he was higher than the outcropping and somewhat behind it, looking down at the waterfall. The embankment leading down to the edge of the cliff was much steeper than it looked, and there wasn't any path down that way. He left the path, sat on the earth, and let himself down the bank just a little at a time. But he wasn't liking this. Even twenty meters from the ledge he felt nothing protecting him from the drop.

He thought he might make it hand over hand, hanging on to shrubs and tiny trees, until he got close enough to see almost everything below, but he didn't need to go even five more meters to be quite sure he'd made a mistake. His courage gave out and he froze, breathing too fast, his heart working in him like a toy. The cold mist from the falls wet his face. All the life in him seemed to have congealed beneath his throat, and he was completely without strength in his hands, arms, and legs. On top of everything, the outstretched vista lent a kind of infinitude to his vertigo, and now he panicked, certain that he'd be stuck right here until he died of exposure or slipped away, still completely paralyzed, over the edge and joined the waterfall. But he was relieved to discover that whatever else happened in his life, his hands were not going to let go of the sapling evergreen they'd attached themselves to like the talons of a hawk. And from the height of hawks he looked down the Franconia Notch out into the New Hampshire lowlands while the spirit leaked back into his extremities.

Well below but closer to him, on what might have been a trail leading out of the encampment's perimeter, he caught sight of a patch of earth with a blue tint to it unlike the surrounding patches. The area he was looking at lay outside the shade of the mountain, and the green of the pines made it hard to say —he might be looking at a freshly fallen bough, more green than blue. From this distance, some several hundred meters, nothing about it was definite, and in fact the spot of blueness disappeared as he stared at it. He let go of his branch with one hand, as carefully as if he were releasing half his hold on life, and reached behind him toward another very fragile-seeming frond, starting the climb back up to the trail he'd come by.

Going down he felt no safety in the level of the path. As long as the ledge was below him, he felt sure he was about to go over it. On the wide level of the Forestry encampment his feet were firm, yet the meadow itself seemed to drift slightly, ready to submerge in a general precariousness.

There was indeed a trail out of the encampment, but he couldn't say whether it led to the thing that had caught his eye. He moved down the path for a long time, in many places pushing sideways between the brittle shrubs, but he thought he must not be getting very far. The trail led onto a ridge that widened considerably, until he was well out of the mountain's shadow. Apparently this ridge didn't get much more daylight than the encampment, however, because the woods, and particularly the trail, were patched with snow.

Ahead was the bit of blue that had drawn him to this place —clothing; a man's parka, in fact. The man was still wearing it.

English was dazzled by the golden light coming out of himself as he approached the body. It was the afternoon sun following him down the path. The woods were rotten and wet, like a wound reopened. Patches of old snow were pink in this light, deep blue where shaded. The thaw trickled and dripped nearby, and in the distances it cascaded, echoing.

A frozen man English took to be Jerry Twinbrook lay under a thick limb beneath a sugar pine. It looked as if maybe he'd been strolling along and the branch had broken off and hit him over the head. But his neck was leashed to the branch by a yellow nylon rope that bit deeply into the flesh. The flesh, English couldn't help reminding himself, that God had made him out of. The branch must have held for a long time and then broken off when a bad freeze had made it particularly brittle. The snow had come and covered Twinbrook up, and then it had melted away. His eyes were gone, and the black sightless sockets made him seem impossibly alienated from his surroundings. He looked like a victim wasted by some horrible addiction that had finally blessed him with this death. Birds had eaten the eyes. It happened to everything that died in the woods. English went over these points as if explaining them to someone else. He took a deep breath. The air flooded him. The life's blood gurgled in his fingertips. Suddenly his eyes burned, he felt sexy, and he wanted to take off his clothes and dance around, fondling himself and screaming. In a while he did exactly that; he tossed aside his garments, even his shoes and socks, and for a few minutes, until he got too cold, he pirouetted whitely through the woods, like the naked soul of Gerald Twinbrook liberated from the corpse.

English took a Yankee Flyer out of Franconia. As the coach of this obscure bus line dropped down into towns he'd never see but this one glimpse of, his vision dipped into his fatigue, dredging up brief dreams. Nobody sat down in the adjacent seat, not because he was obviously the kind of person nobody would sit beside on a bus, a person who'd slept in a chair and spent most of his money getting a jeep towed down a mountain, but because that seat was occupied by Gerald Twinbrook's essence, or ghost.

English was in the back with the smokers, in this case a young lady of the hippie-gypsy type and a Georgia boy from an air base farther north; also a bony lad who asked English where he was from and then said, "They read you pretty good in Massachusetts?"

"I don't exactly place your meaning," English said.

"They read you deeply there, huh?"

Pretty soon the others were passing a pint bottle and singing "Ain't No Mountain High Enough," acquiring the luminousness of sleazy angels as the pink dawn struck their faces. The coincidence was appalling to English, but by now he was resigned to the fact that God was on him like a harpy, and was riding him toward his destiny, and wasn't bothering anymore to veil the workings of His terrible hands. The light of midmorning woke him and he got a clear look at Gerald Twinbrook, who lounged beside him with an innocent irony glowing out from deep in his excavated eyes. Across the aisle the gypsy girl and the Georgia boy were locked statuesquely in a drunken kiss.

English had acquired a wonderful new sensitivity that disintegrated walls. As the sun rose over the little towns, he heard the chiropractors crying out. He heard the bankers' feet searching for their slippers, the schoolteachers cursing in their bathrooms. Meanwhile the Georgian had his hand up under the skirt of his new friend. "When did you get out of the Air Force?" she asked him. "The second I went AWOL. I turned Communist," he said. "I was gonna *say* I bet you're political," she said, and he told her before he kissed her again, "I'm a Trotskyite. I'm gone take to the hills till I overthrow the government."

The rain had stopped and it was sunny and hot, but it was very wet. Two beautiful, almost silver aluminum tank trucks ahead created a tunnel of plunging evergreens, the dirty mist of standing rainwater exploding behind them, nature stirred by their passage in a way that made it seem man is very powerful indeed.

English showed Jerry Twinbrook one of the drawings from Twinbrook's own sketch pad.

"Okay, your fish is definitely a fish, right—"

"Yeah—"

"Not a very good fish—"

"No—"

"—but it's definitely a fish. But what is that behind it? Is that a radio, is that a ghost—"

"It's a clock—"

"—is that a ghost of a radio?"

"It's a clock with a cup on it. What do you know? You don't know anything about paintings—"

"I know something about clocks—"

"—not a fucking thing about paintings—"

"I know about clocks—"

"You know what you *like*, you—"

"I can recognize a clock, and I look at that and I see a ghost of a *radio*, because you're afraid of the clock the way it really is. That's what it's all about, isn't it—"

"You're the one who's afraid of time."

"—it's all about fear."

" 'Fear' or 'feet'?"

"Come on! Don't back off on me, man, tell me the truth—you're blurring these things. The reason you don't paint them the way it really looks is because you're *afraid* of it the way it really looks."

Twinbrook said, "Yeah. I think this is the way they really look, though. Don't you know the lessons of love? Nothing is what you see."

"Nothing is what I see," English said.

"As long as one slave walks the earth, you cannot be free. As long as one prisoner remains, you yourself are in chains. That's what Jesus was saying—when you visited the imprisoned, when you ministered to the dying, you did it to me. He's one of them, until the last is free. And so are you. So am I."

"That's what Simone Weil was doing? Starving with the starved?"

"And Christ on the cross with the thieves, and St. Paul languishing in jail."

"What about Joan of Arc?"

"Joan of Arc," Twinbrook said, "was a self-signifying slut."

The others around him had found their stops and cleared out by now. The bus driver must have realized that English was talking to himself, because at the next stop he came back to interrupt.

"I'm perfectly okay," English said.

"Are you aware you're raving out loud so everybody can hear?"

"It's okay. I'm cultivating it."

"You're cultivating it?"

"I'm letting it happen. I'm in control. It's cool."

"I hope it is. I hope it is."

"I'm learning things," English told him.

"Not so loud, huh? Okay?"

"Okay."

"Okeydokey?"

"Okeydokey, all reet, and ten four," English promised.

He had to change buses in Boston. While he was waiting in the Boston depot, he called the highway patrol and instructed them anonymously how to find Jerry Twinbrook's corpse. Then he got on the bus heading down the Cape to Provincetown.

Twinbrook wasn't on this bus. English looked everywhere, but he was gone. That was par, it seemed to English—everybody was backing off on him, even the people who weren't exactly real.

It took half an hour to get across the Sagamore Bridge. The Cape highway was completely choked with the season's arrivals. Two hours later, after the stop in Hyannis, the bus swung around a hitchhiker chasing a stopped car and crawled past a rest area where a team of exhausted bicyclists had draped themselves on the picnic tables. They'd all reached the lower Cape, where the four-lane road narrowed down to two, and where a white sign by the road beseeched those who passed

DO NOT

DRIVE IN

BREAKDOWN

LANE

and where English was thinking about the woods again, and about Gerald Twinbrook laid out at the end of his own road.

That strange naked moment, he thought. That is my slot, my path. Not Success, not Romance. Nothing easy or even anything that can be understood. I saw the goddess: dead, and in the form of a man with his eyes pecked out.

Many of the feelings I've been having lately, breaking down crying when alone, the sense of a cloud between me and God, the intuition that now, behind the cloud, is the time of faith—

these could be a madman's feelings, a maniac's—

He stood in Leanna's living room–bedroom, bent over her desk, adding to his note. He was going to finish this thing, he had something to say. But he didn't like the way he smelled—he was rank with bus station grime and the sweat of fear and pilgrimages. He had a dizzying impulse to slash her water bed with a knife and bathe in the flood. Also, it wasn't right that his words turned from blue to black after the opening thought.

I'm going through some unspecified change—

I've never really known where to find the slot marked LOVE—or at least ROMANCE—it's not there for me, I realize.

You'd say everything was just a coincidence. There are no coincidences to a faithful person, a person of faith, a knight of faith.

He opened the cash box. A ring of keys, rubber bands, and two bullets of a massive caliber. Tens, twenties, singles, fives—over a hundred bucks. His note wasn't finished. But he wanted to copy it from the start on one of these good sheets of paper, using just the black pen.

I remember thinking on my last birthday: Thirty-four, and my life hasn't even started yet. I wasn't yet born, couldn't be until—until what? Until someone told me my real name, or something like that.

I'm a private detective and I'm living out a private mystery . . . Leanna, the mystery is the Mystery.

He rummaged through her drawers for an envelope and came across her .44 revolver. Altogether the weapon was well over a foot long and must have weighed, he judged by hefting it, nearly five pounds. It wasn't loaded. He added to its weight a little bit by putting the two bullets into the cylinder.

He stood in the room with the gun raised, sighting down the barrel at the water bed.

Now, what if you were home? he asked Leanna.

He'd followed everything out faithfully. He'd been true to every impulse. What was he being asked to do? Immediately he thought of taking this gun and shooting the Bishop, but that was crazy.

On the other hand—would God ask for anything sane? Did He come to Elijah and say, Go, secure a respectable position and wear out your days in the chores of it? Did His strange monstrous finger guide a person toward the round of events that wears us down and evens us out until even the meanest is presentable, if wrinkled and feeble? Or did it point straight to an earthquake and say, Don't you dare come back until you've died.

Leanna had a walk-in closet: into which English walked.

He raised a gentle clatter among the hangers by rifling through her wardrobe. It wasn't too extensive, just about right, he thought, for a mannish dyke. Dust coated the makeup items on her dresser. English laid the revolver among them next to its own reflection in the mirror. He found a blue purse and emptied his pockets into it.

How have I failed you? Always and everywhere I let you down. And you never let me down.

Give me another chance to betray you, Lord. Let me let you down again.

English took off his shirt and pants.

Nothing around here in the way of footwear would fit him. These, his own black no-nonsense Sears service shoes, marketed for the janitorial crowd, would have to do. He wished Leanna's pantsuits weren't so small—in a pantsuit and her brown fedora and this slash of lipstick and these false eyelashes, no one would know if he was a man dressed up as a woman or a woman dressed up as a man.

But it was going to have to be a skirt. This jungle cotton wraparound, with green, red, and yellow orchids flourishing on a black background, very tropical. The olive fedora set off the greens in the skirt. The black shoes were a match. The left eyelash fell off. One would do. And two bullets, he estimated, were enough to kill anybody whose time had come. He put the gun in his purse.

The important thing was to present a good front. But first you had to know how to fasten a bra behind your back. He settled for fastening it first and then pulling it over his shoulders, though this method twisted the straps. And then you had to have something in the cups.

I am going to stuff money in this bra, he announced to an audience of quivering albinos that had suddenly become his image of an all-seeing God. Back in the living room he tipped over the cash box and got on his knees and snatched at the bills on the floor. For my left breast tens and twenties, thirteen singles for my right.

None of the blouses would fit him. He had to tear the sleeves off his shirt and settle for that.

He walked downstairs and out the door and past the cabins and took several tentative steps along the sidewalk. A few people he couldn't bring himself to look at passed him as he walked toward Commercial, but nobody said anything.

On Commercial Street all the shops were open, broadcasting tears and fragrances and songs delivering their knives, the aromas of spun candy and suntan oil and incense and perfume. He immersed himself in it all for ten seconds, made an alley not half a block east, and ducked into it. Three women passed him on roller skates, wearing headphones and holding hands.

Giving up his forward progress and seeking shelter in this alley had been a mistake. For a few seconds he didn't think he was going any farther dressed like this. His imposture felt obvious. Anybody could see he was a woman who couldn't even fasten a bra. But nobody was looking at him.

He stepped onto a street filled with people in short shorts and big roller skates and earphones, a street of headgear and desperation jammed with people walking their invisible dogs, exploding with people wearing huge blue velvet novelty hats. Not even a glance from these citizens. On this avenue he was just another case of the hot-and-lonelies, another attempter working on a firestorm. There were cops on extra corners today directing traffic. They never glanced at him. Cars nudged through the throng that covered the pavement from wall to wall, cars with their tapedecks blazing stereophonically as they passed, but for the most part it seemed to be a parade consisting of children who had to go to the bathroom now, and parents who wished to go in two different directions—like life—and young, electric, vividly sexual men staring at one another through a drugged haze and couples thinking about leaving one another because the sea's erotic whisper was making them crazy. English could feel what they were thinking. And he could see plainly that this was the real and permanent Provincetown, the mad seaside hamlet that had been here since the day of his arrival, and it hadn't been disguised or overlaid by the empty winter season, it had simply drained away into the corners, and the people had turned invisible because they, like Gerald Twinbrook, were ghosts. And they, as Twinbrook had, had now turned visible and fleshly again. But only he, Leonard English, was alive. These wraiths couldn't see him.

He walked among them. He was getting used to this. Exhaust fumes on my pulse points, he thought.

The humanified forest. Nobody familiar around. Where are the people who knew me when I was knowable?

And then he encountered Berryman on the teeming street. Berryman, the drunken reporter English had shared two drinks with, and probably, when he thought about it, one of the very few people who knew him in this world. "Hey, hey, hey," Berryman said. "Uh—Leonard English?"

Fuck you, he thought. I do not know you. So please stop addressing me and touching me.

"I can give you about three minutes," he told Berryman. "I don't want to be late for Mass."

The reporter took him by the hand and pulled him close to a wall. "It's good to see a friendly face," he told English. "I've been away."

English said nothing. Somehow Berryman, by ignoring his appearance, made him feel more uncomfortable than he might have done by shouting out loud about it.

"I just got back from New Hampshire," Berryman said.

"Oh. I was there, too."

"Not where I was. I was in Edge Hill."

"Edge Hill?" English said.

"A treatment center. The paper's insurance program covered it."

"You mean—for booze?"

Berryman's look was direct—not at all sheepish. "I lost the battle and won the war."

For an awkward moment, English didn't know what to say. Berryman scratched an arm, pinched his nose vigorously.

"I see you're in costume today," Berryman said at last.

"Forget you saw me."

"I really don't think I can do that."

"Okay. I don't care. Obviously I just say, Fuck it."

Berryman seemed to be trying to glance down English's bodice. "I'm familiar with that philosophy."

English thought of reaching into his purse and taking out his .44. Giving everybody a little jolt.

"You look good," Berryman said.

"Thanks. Your three minutes is up."

"You look very, very eighties."

"Thanks."

"Take care, Lenny."

"Forget my name," English said.

To get to the church he had to double back to Bradford. He cut through the alley where the costumed roughs hung out around the A-House, a notorious leather bar, but nobody even whistled. He made himself out of breath going up the concrete flights cut into the embankment to Bradford. It was nearly ten o'clock of a Sunday morning, and that's what had him hurrying; he wanted to get to the rectory before the priest was done; he wanted to make his confession.

English heard voices in the sitting room, and so he waited by the door. He'd been in this room on his first day in Provincetown, the day he'd met Leanna. He stepped back for the person coming out, a teenage girl who couldn't have had anything very interesting to be ashamed of.

The priest, a young, angular man, was about to put on his garment for Mass. As English came in he stopped, and looked at his watch.

Dressed in these clothes and feeling beautiful, English sat down in the chair. "Bless me, Father," he said, "for I have sinned."

The priest set the garment aside and looked at English carefully, then at his watch again. "You're my last confession," he said.

He sat down next to English and put his slender fingers on the makeshift partition. "Do we need this?"

English shook his head. Father moved it aside.

"Call me," English said, "May–June."

"Ah well, I'm Father Michael." Father put his elbows on his knees and his chin in his hands, and seemed to be thinking. "May–June. You are a transvestite?"

"Yes."

"Doesn't that confuse the issue of your sexuality somewhat?"

"How can my sexuality be any more confused than it is? Give me a break."

"I speak as one who is also gay."

"I'm not gay."

"Oh." Father was surprised. "Of course, it's not always an expression of a gay attitude."

"Sometimes it's just a disguise."

Father crossed his arms before his chest and looked at English across the chasm of God's love. "Where on earth," he said, "did you shop for those shoes?"

English sighed.

Father said, "Are you serious?"

English couldn't keep back the tears. He choked on them,

sobbing. "You mean, are *you* serious. Telling me you're gay, for Christ's sake."

"A lot of people are gay. I'm sorry if I misjudged, but I thought it would help to share a truth about myself."

"I came here to confess."

"All right."

"Not to hear your confession!"

"Yes."

"I'm serious!"

"All right. Is it all right if I take your hand?"

"Oh, God," English said.

"No," Father said, a little flustered now, "only if it comforts you."

"This is getting bizarre," English said.

Openmouthed disbelief stopped the priest's face for a beat. "Oh, *is* it?"

"Bless me, Father," English begged, "for I have sinned."

"All right, then, let's do it. How long has it been since your last confession?"

"Like maybe a couple of years, at least," English said.

"And what have you done to trouble your conscience in that time?"

The room was a typically decorated vestry, or whatever the hell, English thought, you call these places. There were crucifixes all over the walls, and here and there an empty cross inviting the sinner to share in unimaginable sufferings. A long embroidered banner hung over the partition put there to hide the priest while he dressed for the service—just like the partitions they'd had in English's grade school. LOVE BEFORE ME, the banner said, LOVE BEHIND ME, LOVE ABOVE ME, LOVE BELOW ME, LOVE AROUND ME, LOVE WITHIN ME.

"Two years ago I tried to hang myself to death," English said.

"I'm listening," the priest said.

"The thing is—sometimes I think I succeeded. Sometimes I think I really died."

"Well, of course you did."

Stunned silence. The room was choked with orchids. At last somebody was telling him the truth. He was dead.

"If you tried sincerely, then you succeeded in canceling your life. It was an act of perfect faithlessness. You'd reached the absolute end," Father Michael said. "Maybe it was the only thing you could do."

"Is there absolution for such a thing?"

"Your faith is making you whole," Father said.

"But if I succeeded?"

"You did succeed. And your faith is making you whole."

They sat together in silence for a while.

"Anything more?" the priest asked.

English's sadness moved in his chest when he shrugged.

Father Michael said, "I'm going to give you my strongest absolution. The original Latin." As he stood up, he said, "Bishop's doing Mass today, I can't be late. He's in town to bless the fleet."

Father made the sign of the cross, and stooped and gave English a little kiss on the forehead. *"Te absolvo."*

English left feeling unsure—was he now cleansed, and if so, of what exactly? What crud had the winds of absolution carried off, why did he still feel such grime in the creases of him? An unspiritual explanation was that it was hot. Summer had arrived. Now it was past ten and everybody, even the most debauched, was awake and on the stroll. The crowds were of a size to menace civil authority. Was anybody left in Boston or New York? When you're this completely naked, he thought, much more naked than you'd be without clothes, when you're naked of all your signs and your moves, as naked, say, as the minute you were born, then these thousands of lives going by *will* rake you. Something like the permeable mask a fencer darkens his face with, that's what his heart needed here.

He put on a casual look: no, not at all, none of this was getting to him; but everything was getting to him—the birds of electricity beating their wings in the wires, the repertoires of ambulances, the thud of defectively muffled engines and the whacking, like rugs being wearily beaten, of stereos through the open windows of cars. The frosty pink was fading from his mouth and the sweat dripped down the inside of his thighs, although occasionally a small breeze reached under and disturbed the leaves and blossoms of his skirt's tropical motif. Above all he was embarrassed to be wearing men's Jockey shorts. It seemed an easily appreciated thing, all you had to do, for heaven's sake, was watch him walk. He had to remind himself with every breath that he was invisible to these wraiths.

At a family grocery they were putting out crates of fruit to tempt the thirsty strollers. What a miracle to see a produce truck, uncoupled, drive out from under the massive husk of its trailer. Let him treat his burdens like that!

From the end of Bradford he headed right, out toward Herring Cove. The sky was open now, he was in the National Seashore, a realm protected from civilization, and the road wasn't so crowded. Rather than walk right through the parking lot, he left the pavement a quarter mile or so below the cove and cut across the dunes that rose and fell for quite a distance before they lay down in front of the sea. A few minutes and he'd lost sight of the road, of everything but the sand and the sky; it showed him how all things could fall away in an instant; now he crested a dune and came into a crater empty of everything but sand and the intersecting footprints of other people; the notations delved here by their journeys showed him how each life was one breathtakingly extended musical phrase, and he prayed that their crossings were harmonious.

In some former existence he'd been hunted over sand like this, run down and eaten, turned to the predator's flesh and bones. He felt his life extending backward into the conflagration of all other lives. And it reached out of him like a frond of smoke, touching the tender pink future. This sand presented itself as evidence that he'd someday father children and grandchildren on the earth. He could hear their feet knocking in the rubble as they scavenged in our dregs, stumbling around after some gigantic holocaust.

As he cleared the last dune, he stood for a minute on the brink of the Atlantic and laid claim to it all. Here the Cape faced west, curving into Cape Cod Bay, and the noon sun raked the sand. English felt it piercing him as if he wasn't here. He had absolutely no protection in this guise. Everything he was —a man, an American, an image patched together out of certain assumptions and beheld mostly by itself—was burned to ash by the fire of this new thing. And something was burned away from before his vision, the veil itself that kept his eyes from the agony of brightness.

He saw a lot of people in bathing suits on the beach. Stripped down to swatches of cloth. Stripped of their disguises, stripped of any protection at all—everything about them and even about the moment itself was naked before his sight.

He walked down among them. These were not ghosts. They were looking at him, many of them, because he was fully dressed and he was moving. And he was looking back at them.

Each one was crucified and completely open, every thought, every desire floating out from their torn hearts.

A springer spaniel came rocking through the surf, tongue out, toward some toy or infant or beckoning, aged hand. And a young woman, some kind of office help or assistant floor manager, reclined toward the sun with the incense of her secrets rising from her into the clear day.

A man squatted, then knelt, before a sand castle, finally vomiting up the teeth of wolves broken off in his flesh in a previous life, and a woman who had insisted on wearing her pearls to the beach sat beneath her silver hair thinking, "I'm guilty, yes, but I deserve a trial." "Do people," a little girl ten yards away was thinking, "all see the same color when they call something green?" A white filament of tanning lotion. Her mother's hand obliterated it on her mother's skin. "No. Wait. The storm is only in my mind," a man gripping a tennis shoe was persuading himself—"Anything's possible. I could come home . . ." but a breeze woke him and crushed the sponge of grief, and he tasted another drop. A grandfather crouched behind his smile, clapping for a dog. "Others have done worse," he pleaded inside himself; "is it so bad what I've done?" Meanwhile, a young man puffed at a fly on his cheek while congratulating himself. "Just one or two minor details," he thought, "and then—" . . . and then the moment granted him a vision of his life dissolving away until there was nothing left in front of him but the sea, going on forever.

The body surfers slid along the torched and crumbling waves. "I'm only human, I've only got two hands, I can't do everything at once," their souls protested. A woman patted the sweat from under her eyes, whisked the bits of sand from her suit, and lay back trembling under the kisses of a sexual angel . . .

And the others, their chalky laughter and resonating wounds, and still others with murders swimming in their bellies, and people burned as dark and shiny as beetles, all waited at the edge of this immenseness muttering little truths. "I saw him, I sat right next to him, and you can't even tell." "It's all my fault that memory is dark." "Thank God, I'm out of that mess." "I'm fat." "I'm thirsty." "When am I going to live?" . . . As English reached the end of the beach, he found other people ripping mussels loose from the breakwater, and men and women who were going after clams with buckets and rakes and seemed to be stepping on their own faces in the mirrors of the tide pools.

This was the place where the lower Cape started to curl back around on itself in a way that got it generally compared to a scorpion's tail. The breakwater English was standing on stretched a quarter mile across the harbor, cutting the corner, as it were, between the scorpion's stinger and a point a few knuckles down the tail. A couple of boats, not much larger than rowboats, appeared to be anchored off the tip of the Cape. English crossed over on the breakwater with the idea of walking out to the very end and perhaps taking a ride in one of those boats. He had to clamber in many places across the casually piled boulders, of which the most were granite, and he got his feet wet coming off onto the beach at the other end. He saw nobody else up here. Two lighthouses warned the sailors of the Cape, one at the tip and one about a mile up, in the area of the tail's last joint. Poison ivy grew everywhere between them.

He tried walking on the beach at first, past a few car chassis beyond corrosion into decomposition, a ferric variety of putrefaction—a beach made not so much of sand as of the long seaside grass flooded by water and killed by water and heaped by the motion of water onto the shore and abandoned there, like a long, pointless rope, by water. It was slow going in this muck. Before him were the huge green flies and the stink that rose off a dead porpoise a half mile past the breakwater, and the hooting gulls that never seemed to mind the stink or eat any of the flies. Bits of light on the surge of the breakers took to the air and flew in the corners of his sight. He walked through the hordes of insects, their angry music burning in his head like something trying to wake him up. He skirted piles of garbage that hadn't quite found their way back from picnics, mostly the rottings of bait and dribbling cans of beer.

He took to the higher, sandier ground, which was covered with poison ivy. Gulls argued with him as he came too close to their nests in the sand. They rose in flocks, their shadows whirling all around him on the beach. Farther down the shore he saw them walking in little groups, ignoring each other, wise and smug, looking at nothing.

A black wasp dropped a dead spider at his feet. The gulls spoke deeply in voices he thought couldn't possibly belong to the same creatures he normally heard yodeling, and baby terns flew past above, chirping like crickets.

Seagulls reminded him of coyotes. We like them, he thought, but if we were smaller than they—say sizable as monkeys—we'd be desperate under seagulls. They'd be like land-sea-air coyotes. Gulls: Let's not forget they're carnivorous. You know what? They all look like the Pope. Power lines ran between the two lighthouses, poles spaced every twenty yards—a gull, or two or three, perched on the outflung arms of every one like vultures on desert saguaros. As he neared each pole, they jumped off. Couldn't they guess they were safe twenty feet overhead? He couldn't think when they'd started getting to him. He'd started out liking gulls like everybody else.

The gun was in his purse. It was getting heavier. He could hardly carry it. The raging molten irons at the center of the planet were dragging it toward themselves. He couldn't believe that he was actually going to do it, and he couldn't believe that he actually might not. This was the dilemma, that both ideas were absurd.

He crossed the lighthouse's fat shadow and checked on the boats. One was a wreck turned upside down, but the other had a motor and two oars and looked ready to sail just about anyplace.

English pulled on the outboard's starter rope until he was winded. He didn't know anything about these engines. He didn't know anything about boats, or the sea—I'm from Kansas, he explained to the sky, I'll have to row the thing.

Right away he could see he'd be tired by the time he reached the town pier, where Andrew, our Bishop, was blessing the vessels of Provincetown. My craft keeps tacking in a fucked-up way, he told the waters. Keeping her steady as she goes takes practice. Which I am getting.

Thank God the harbor was smooth. Beyond a little slapping to keep his boat awake, it didn't do anything but carry him. This wasn't the sea of the inexorable horizon and smashing waves, not the sea of distance and violence, but the sea of the eternally leveling patience and wetness of water. Whether it comes to you in a storm or in a cup, it owns you—we are more water than dust. It is our origin and destination. The hotels rolled out along the shore, the bed-and-breakfast places, were getting bigger. Between here and there, a few trawlers harassed by gulls.

This is sunstroke, he thought, and what a time for it, just when I'm trying to think about my strategy. I'm trying to think what I'm thinking. What am I thinking? I think this about sums it up: A 1940s-style spike-heeled shoe ripping open a child's abdomen while, in the background, Marlene Dietrich smokes a cigarette.

He waved. Avast. Ahoy. Yes, I am a sailor. One of the fleet.

There was something decimated and paltry about the Blessing of the Fleet ceremony that year. Leonard English attended, rowing a boat with a dead outboard engine, and he didn't have any fun.

It was cloudy, but the sun was still a menace. The sea was silver. English felt faint by the time he was in hailing distance of the pier. He could see somebody right at the end of the pier, higher than the rest of the crowd, the Bishop or the mayor. English's shoulders and neck were completely numb. He made for a pier fifty meters down-cape of the municipal dock, heading for the cool dark beneath it.

Two men were drinking wine under the pier. They were just laughing shadows, he couldn't make out their words. He smacked an oar against one of the piles, stood up, and grasped one of the tires nailed to the pile. "Avast!"

One of the men came a couple of steps closer and said, "Hey, that's right; that's exactly right—avast." He stepped close enough to get a look at English, said, "What! Hey!" and stepped back before he missed his turn at the jug.

"What is it?" English heard his friend ask.

"Ah, just some kind of bullshit déjà vu," the man said.

A lot of boats, dozens of them, some as small as English's and a couple of truly big—white, gleaming yachts—were circling in this part of the harbor. Their captains seemed to be trying to form the vessels into a line. There was plenty of shouting and honking of klaxons.

In order to see the town pier, English had to set himself adrift every minute or so and then row back to his hiding place.

He heard scratchy songs. Saw somebody with a monster face. George Jones was doing "One Is a Lonely Number."

And at last there he was, Andrew, our Bishop, our sad low-rent Bishop in his copper El Camino and his vending-machine sunglasses.

English, hiding under the pier, gagged on the very fertile, organic smell of the sea, overlaid with a whiff of diesel and rotting rope.

When he'd seen these things in movies, the scenes were thick with bodies and voices you couldn't see past or hear beyond. But actually attending them, a person was forced to learn how far away the sun is, how great is the sea, how diminished and insignificant our ceremonies in a swallowing silence. The mayor's thwocking pronouncements over the P.A., folded back on themselves by their echo off the harbormaster's building, blinked out over the Cape Cod Bay behind him, while the razor of Cape light served up every irrelevant word of spectators threatening their children or appreciating the boats, and the sharp clink of change at the hot-dog stand.

The Bishop had donned the great ceremonial crown of his bishopric, an ostentatious cousin to a chef's hat. His right hand, empty of anything along the lines of a scepter or wand, was raised in benediction over the fleet.

English rowed out vigorously into the harbor and set his course, thinking, Last-Card-in-the-Deck Street.

The boats were passing now alongside the pier, one at a time. Bishop Andrew leaned out and waved his hand, blessing each one.

English joined the fleet just ahead of a greasy fishing trawler and behind a smaller boat, a novelty item that was manned by a woman, as his own was womanned by a man, and peopled by papier-mâché sculptures of dwarfs and giants, one of them recognizable as Jimmy Carter, another one resembling Elvis Presley.

The crowd laughed and applauded as Bishop Andrew hailed this vessel, and they were still making so much noise, as English came beneath the Bishop, stood up, and aimed his .44 into the Bishop's face some fifteen feet above, that nobody heard the shot. English hardly heard it himself, because the pulse was roaring so loudly in his head.

Neither did he feel the gun's recoil—but he experienced the effect of it. It's not that a .44 magnum has such an awful kick, but a person should be sitting down when he or she fires one in a drifting boat, where the tiniest inertial change counts for a lot. English, however, was standing up when he pulled the trigger. Thanks to the resulting motion of his vessel, he might have plugged anyone present that day. He didn't shoot himself, which was a blessing, the only blessing his tiny boat received, because Bishop Andrew, in all the excitement, neglected his duty there.

And English certainly didn't end the Bishop's life that day. Later, he was always led into a severe temptation to claim that he'd at least shot the Bishop's hat off for him, but as far as English actually knew, the bullet plunked down, like nothing so much as a spent bullet, many leagues out in Cape Cod Bay. And down on his ass the sad assassin sat.

THE LAST DAYS

On the left side of him was a young man, very religious, who marked his Bible in several different colors and put asterisks, stars, and exclamation points in the margins. A born-again fundamentalist, he pretended not to know what English was in for; but English felt the boy's silent congratulations for shooting at the Bishop, one of the henchmen of the Vatican's Antichrist. In the right-hand cot was Jimmy, a drug runner about English's age, sucked nearly empty by amphetamines and five weeks on a trawler making between Barranquilla and Provincetown with seven tons of Colombian ganja. The Coast Guard had shredded his vessel with automatic-weapons fire, and Jimmy kept a picture of the scuttled wreck—overturned on the shore near Jeremy Point and spilling out a dozen bales on the sand, with a dead Colombian draped over the rail—under his pillow to take out and show people and say, "I landed that." It plainly wounded him to think the Coast Guard had stooped to bust English, too. Leaning over his knee with his foot up on English's bed, he pointed out that English was by no means a maritime criminal, he was just a faggot crackpot gone apeshit at a public celebration, and somebody should have just splanked him with a rock or something, and let him sleep it off.

"What'd you use?" Jimmy asked him—more than once. Many times.

"What do you mean, what'd I use?"

"What'd you use? What'd you use? Have you been butt-fucked so many million times your brain fell out your anus? What was your armament?"

"I approached from out of the West with a Reuthers .44 magnum killing machine," English said, "and I laid waste to the countryside."

"Reuthers? Reuthers?"

After checking all around the place, which was set up like an army barracks with twenty-four cots in two rows in each room, but which was, as a matter of fact, the Barnstable County Jail, Jimmy told English, "There's no such thing as a Reuthers. No such company making ordnance of any kind."

"I thought there was an R on the grip."

"Jesus, it was a Ruger. Or a Remington. Or maybe it was just a custom grip, man. Was it your gun, originally?"

"It was never my gun," English said.

"Never fired it before, right?"

"The whole thing was an impulse. Completely off-the-cuff."

"A total asshole" was Jimmy's diagnosis. He dipped his wrist. "Kind of an impromptu thing, girls. But what the fuck. That'll help you in court."

"Gene, what are you in for?" English asked the religious boy.

"Don't ask him what he's *in* for. Jesus!" Jimmy said.

"I wanted to see this girl," Gene said.

"They can't arrest you for wanting something, can they?" English said.

"She got an injunction on me. The judge said never never call her, never visit her again, but I had just one more thing to say to her."

"Ah. Right. I know," said English.

"Don't ever ask people what they're in for," Jimmy said, and then he said, "Hey—ask this guy. Ask Fred," jerking his thumb at the man on the other side of him.

"What are you in for?" English said.

"The greatest crime on earth," Fred said. "Bank robbery."

Fred was a young fellow. He looked around twenty-five, a weight lifter, perhaps, right at this moment using a sewing needle to implant shoe polish into the web between his left thumb and forefinger. He wiped the blood away under his other arm and told English, "We'll team up someday, you and me, man. I like your ideas about disguises."

"A star has five points," Jimmy said, looking at the tattoo Fred was giving himself.

"Well, this is a four-pointed star. What about you?" Fred was talking to English.

"I did a weird thing," English said.

"Everybody knows what you did," Fred said. "But what's the charge?"

"Attempted murder. Also sea piracy."

"That won't last," Jimmy told him. "You'll get off with two-to-ten, man—delay, delay, delay, and then some kind of plea bargain on a minor thing, some kind of weapons thing or reduced assault bullshit. But whatever you do, hang on to that piracy beef. That's a number that gets you in the federal pen, man, where people are civilized. Not that they'll let it stand."

"Yeah, the lawyer says they'll drop it in a while."

"Of course they will," Jimmy said. "A fucking ten-foot rowboat. You're a disgrace to the whole concept."

"Did you even nick the son-of-a-bitch?" Fred said.

"I shot his hat off," English said, "or, anyway, I think I did."

"His hat?"

"Maybe I did, I don't know." English sighed. "I don't think so."

"Man, when I make bail, I'm gonna get deeply fucked up," Jimmy said, "and I *will* make bail. I got friends. I got friends, man. Real friends. People I owe money to."

"I'm going to church the first thing when I get out," Gene said. "I'll give thanks."

"And then you'll be off to see your little Jesus-honey just one more time," Jimmy said, "and the judge'll nail you."

"I won't be getting out, I guess," English said.

"No way. Two hundred thousand bail? Not hardly," Jimmy said.

The lights went out. English put his shoes and socks under the bed and unrolled the cuffs of his jeans, which were too long, before lying down. They heard a boy sobbing in the darkness and an old man talking to himself. Jimmy whispered to English, "Do you want me to fuck you up the ass?"

"I keep telling you, I'm not gay," English said.

"A good top is hard to find," Jimmy reminded him kindly. "Don't pass it up."

Gene liked to read to his fellow prisoners from the Bible, especially passages from Revelation and so on, because he believed these parts would excite them and bring them to Jesus. "You don't go up to Heaven when you die. That's a mistake. That's like Santa Claus. What really happens is, at the end of time you get up out of your grave in the form of a spiritual body. The dead will be resurrected."

"I'll be there," Fred said.

And Jimmy said, "Fucking-A. Me, too."

Gene took that as some kind of encouragement and started reading to the three of them—English, Fred, and Jimmy—from the mistreated pages of his text: " 'It is sown in dishonor; it is raised in glory: it is sown in weakness; it is raised in power.' Wait, wait—next page, right here: 'For this corruptible must put on incorruption.' "

"That's me, boys. I'm the most corruptible fucker I know," Jimmy said.

TV hours, in the TV room, were well attended. Fred sat in the front row all by himself by virtue of his willingness, his anxiousness, to fight anybody who didn't like it. He answered everything that any woman on the television said. "We've got to get this deposition filed at once," a woman said; "I'd like to file *your* deposition," Fred said. "I'm going to have to pave this yard over with concrete," a woman said; "I'd like to pave over *your* concrete," Fred replied. "I'm feeling a change coming over me," a woman said; "I'd like you to feel *my* change," Fred said, "*I'll* come over you." All of this was easily tolerated by everyone during TV time because Fred was violent.

And English sensed, toward himself, a certain watchful hesitation on the part of the other men. There was always a vacant chair for him with a good angle on the television, and for the first time in his life he had a nickname: "Superdrag."

Jimmy said, "The bad boys, the bad boys. We're all that's happening now. The country's being melted down into baby food. There used to be demonstrations, riots, fucking *parties*, man, *orgies*, everything was"—he grabbed his crotch—"*zany* and delightful. Now they don't eat meat. Hey, I hope they put me away for twenty. Keep me away from these vegetable people. Let me out when the new millennium's here, a little chaos and shit."

Fred backed him up: "That's right. They don't even eat meat out there anymore."

"That's what I just said."

"I don't think you understand. They don't even eat meat," Fred said.

"I understand," Jimmy said. "Anyway, I thought I did."

"If you don't eat meat, you *are* meat," Fred said.

"The millennium will be here by the time *you* get out, that's for sure," Jimmy told English. "It'll probably be half over, you pitiful fuck."

"I thought you said I'd get two-to-ten."

"I was just trying to help you feel not so tortured. I'm like that," Jimmy explained. "I'm too nice."

Gene was troubled. "You don't understand, you don't, your eyes are closed, you're blind. The Last Days won't be fun for people like you, people with lost, ugly souls. There'll be cities destroyed, dragons throwing the mountains around, the earth swallowing you up, fire and chaos—and Jesus, Jesus is going to be un*pleas*ant—" He was rapidly skimming the pages of Revelation—". . . people howling, everybody getting split apart with swords—"

"Man, some of that for me!" Jimmy said.

"Goddamn right, it's worth waiting for," Fred agreed.

"Lock us up till Two Thousand!" English said.

"They're gonna resurrect me and I'm gonna have a woman hanging off my joint and my lips around the nipple of a bong," Jimmy predicted, "within fucking *minutes*. A bong full of Colombian."

"It isn't going to work that way," Gene promised him sadly.

"I'm gonna get up out of the grave and go back to the bank where they took me down," Fred said. "And I'm gonna go up to the teller's window and I'm gonna stick a gun in her cute little face and say, *Remember me?*" To English he said, "You and me will partner up when we get to the streets. We'll go marauding. We'll do drag."

Mrs. Gerald Twinbrook, Sr., gave English's court-appointed lawyer five hundred dollars to spend on whatever Leonard English wanted while he was in jail. All English wanted was cigarettes. Leanna Sousa came by one day and left several cartons on deposit with his captors.

Leanna managed to visit him by claiming to be his sister. "Well, that's what you are," he told her. They faced each other over a low partition down the middle of a long table. The visiting area was the first thing inside the electric lock. It smelled of mimeographing fluid and coffee because it was combined with the office area.

A silence. In her eyes he saw how glad she was to see him. "You're in jail."

"Am I somewhat notorious?"

"Plenty."

"Is that why you came to see me?"

"Don't be so uncertain of yourself."

"Are you kidding? I tried to kill Andrew, our Bishop."

"And you were in drag at the time."

"Who wouldn't be uncertain about themselves in a case like this?"

Leanna seemed excited and happy for him. She leaned closer to the partition and said, "I wanted to ask you why you did it."

"I'm telling you, I'm telling you, I'm telling you," he said. "God is a universe and a wall. How many false alarms? How many more? How many bum steers?"

"Was there anything behind this but a lot of paranoid mental activity?"

English shrugged with open hands. "Isn't it obvious?"

"Don't say that like that, Lenny. You're sounding crazy again. Bishop Andrew had nothing to do with anything, right?"

"Not intentionally," English said.

"And Ray Sands? Was he a great fascist leader?"

"Somebody got that wrong, I guess."

"And then somebody went a little crazy."

"Okay, all right, sure. But there *is* a pattern, a web of coincidence. God," English confided, "is the chief conspirator."

"That's what all the zealots say," she said. "And the whirling dervishes and those men who bleed every Easter."

"My conversion hasn't happened yet."

"Honey," she said, "you are the most converted person I'll ever meet."

English leaned back in his chair, an olive-drab folding chair with the number 12 written with a laundry marker on the seat of it. "What number is your chair?" he asked her, and she told him it was seventeen. He tried to think of something else. "Did they give you back your clothes?"

"They're keeping them for the trial. They're part of the evidence."

"I don't get it," English complained, "nobody else's clothes are ever used against them."

"Anyway, they're considered yours."

"Oh."

"On the day you get out, they'll give them back to you."

"That'll be awhile," he estimated.

"Will we ever meet again?"

"We'll meet again in seven million years," he said. "I'll be standing in a cemetery parking lot and I'll look up and you'll be driving a school bus past or something. And that'll be it."

"We'll fall in love again."

"I'll see you go by. You won't see me."

"Poor Lenny. They're going to put you away for a long time."

"Not so long. Less than seven million years."

* * *

Leanna's visit made English late for lunch. He didn't like that. He didn't feel he was getting enough to eat in the first place.

"So, did she ask you to marry her?" Jimmy said.

"Is she gonna break us out?" Fred said.

"God, I would love to do that!" Jimmy said. "I would love to break out. That'd rattle their little gonads, huh?"

It was overly warm in the cafeteria. Huge pipes wrapped in insulation ran through the room just under the ceiling. English kept imagining they'd burst, magnificently destroying everybody's troubles.

"I wouldn't break out," English said. "I like it here."

English felt hungry every minute. Baloney sandwiches on Wonder Bread with Campbell's soup for lunch. Cereal and re-constituted milk for breakfast, one piece of white toast. Potatoes and ground-beef gravy for supper, Wonder Bread on the side. "This is the stuff," English said, shaking his piece of bread at the man across from him. It flopped back and forth like a pancake. "I really like this stuff," he said. And he did. He liked being hungry and in prison.